ECHO
CHAMBERS

Other books by Richard Himmel:

TWENTY-THIRD WEB
LIONS AT NIGHT

ECHO
ECHO
ECHO

CHAMBERS

RICHARD HIMMEL

DELACORTE PRESS/NEW YORK

Published by
Delacorte Press
1 Dag Hammarskjold Plaza
New York, N.Y. 10017

Manufactured in the United States of America
First printing

Designed by Jo Anne Bonnell

Library of Congress Cataloging in Publication Data

Himmel, Richard.
    Echo chambers.

    I. Title.
PS3515.I7147E3   813'.54   81–15195
ISBN 0–440–02373–4   AACR2

THIS BOOK IS FOR MY CHILDREN
ELLEN MORRIS AND JOHN MAGUIRE HIMMEL.
IT IS A LEGACY LESS PRACTICAL
THAN INHERITED WEALTH BUT MORE
MEANINGFUL IN UNDERSTANDING
THE SOURCE OF INHERITED ECHOS.
ECHOS, EVEN NOW, ECHOING.

ECHO CHAMBERS

Peking Prelude: Midnight

The Chinese man, the only one wearing Western dress, was only half listening as the others argued about a name for the secret project. He had lived for so long among Americans and Europeans that the sound of his own language had become foreign to him, the cackle of excited voices grating against his sensibilities. He pushed back the chair, stood up, and walked to the window, looking out on the big square, empty in the moonlight. The huge, flag-draped portrait of Mao dominated the still plaza: a dead god reigning over a dead city. According to the timetable, when his mission was over and he was permanently assigned to Peking, the portrait would be gone, taken down quietly at night and burned while the citizens slept.

It was an end of one era, the beginning of another.

He confronted his sadness resulting from the conflict of loyalties as he remembered the years with Mao, the blind devotion to and worship of the leader who had befriended a ragged, hungry orphan and then nurtured him through the long years on the Long March, shaping a nameless boy into the man he had become.

Now, in the same chambers where Mao had reigned, he was part of the inner core plotting the systematic discrediting of the Chairman and the calculated departure from the strict Maoist doctrines.

This secret project, a consortium of world industrial and commercial giants acting as a brain trust to aid the economic development of the People's Republic, had been conceived many years before. It had even had Chairman Mao's tacit approval in the benign state it had been outlined to him. But years of struggle, world conditions, and men with personal ambition had altered the intent behind the consortium and given it sinister dimensions. As it stood now, if successful, the consortium would function as a power base for world domination—a Chinese brand of economic and philosophical imperialism diametrically opposite to Mao's teaching. Nuclear armament capabilities, aerospace technology, and laser weaponry expertise had been added to the original industrial and manufacturing aspects of the consortium. The project had *Top Priority* and *Top Secret* status. All the details, the true intent, were known only to this handful of conspirators.

Intellectually, this man in Western dress understood the need for change, the need to play, at least temporarily, the capitalist game. China must thrive. But were none of the others torn by the same conflicts that he was feeling? Maybe, he decided, the years in America had made him soft, corrupted him and infected him with sentimentality.

He was also thinking about love: the woman who was waiting for him in New York.

Looking back at the table of arguing men, he remembered how their faces looked when they were young. Did he look as old to them as they did to him? They were the survivors of the Mao nucleus. After Mao's death the hardliners, the old guard who opposed any deviation from Maoist doctrine, had been disgraced and eliminated one by one. Both legal and illegal methods had been used. There had never been any discussion of the morality of the actions.

Mao himself had taught them that. In order to accomplish an objective in a war, any war, morality had to be put aside.

Deng Xiao-ping stood up at the head of the table, walked over to the man staring blindly out the window, and put his hand on his shoulder. "Is the name agreeable to you?" he asked.

"I didn't hear."

"Chou," Deng said. "The Chou Consortium." He used the English word for consortium. "It is a good name, don't you think?" He smiled. "Even we, after all, are permitted some sentimentality." Chou-chou was the nickname Mao had given to the ragged orphan many years before. "It is fitting," the deputy premier explained. "This whole project is really your invention. You have been preparing for this for so long. You have carefully done all the groundwork, established the network for success. It is fitting that the project bears your special name. Is it agreed?"

The man said nothing.

Deng led him back to the conference table. "He has agreed," he told the others. They applauded lightly, still distrustful of the man who had lived away from China so long that he even had the odor of a Westerner.

Leaving the man standing at the opposite end of the table, Deng went back, sat down again in the American-manufactured swivel chair that squeaked as he tilted back, and ceremoniously lighted a large cigar. He motioned for the man to begin.

The man rubbed his hands against the soft cashmere of his suit lapels, stopped thinking in English, put aside his political ambivalence and erased the picture of the woman in New York from his mind.

"The plans are final now. All the preliminaries have been put into motion." He pointed to the man on Deng's right. "You will be in charge of Toshibito only. The Japanese will be the most difficult. As you know, unlike the rest of the world, we do not have a long-established underground base in Japan. In my opinion, Toshibito will be the most valuable member of the consortium. Not only is steel essential to all our other industries, the Japanese are most expert in both quality and economy of production."

His eyes shifted to the man on Deng's left. "You will handle both Salod in Baghdad and Guggenheim in Tel Aviv. They have been long established in their countries as our agents. We have funded them heavily through the years. Both men are deeply in our debt. Salod cannot resist the Arab passion for double-dealing, but I think you will find him manageable. With Guggenheim you must continue the illusion that what is good for China is good for Israel."

A very old man seated toward the center of the table said, "I don't trust Jews."

"Nor do they trust Chinese," the man answered. "Guggenheim has the genius to make weapons out of scraps. It is imperative that he be included."

Then he touched the shoulder of the man directly to his right, was aware of the rough texture of the cloth of the jacket. "You have to cover both Ugieri in Turin and Salazar in the Argentine. There should be no problem. Our underground is strong in both countries, and both men are disillusioned to the point of despair."

"It is arranged," the man said. "They will both be in Paris according to schedule."

Reluctantly, he turned to the only woman seated at the table. Her fierce face, bones structured like a Mongol warrior's, was scarred by a liver-shaped burn over one eye and extending down her cheek. The man addressing her remembered the day the incendiary bomb had exploded in her face. "Comrade Kang," he began, "you have been in constant contact with the scientists—"

She interrupted him. "Call them what they are," she said, the harshness of her scar echoed in her shrill voice. "Industrial power is useless without military strength. In five years China will overpower the world with laser and nuclear technology. We will even be well along in our aerospace program. These men are beyond scientists. They are the strength of tomorrow."

Patiently, with a smile and a gentle voice, the man said: "Of course, Comrade. We know that. We know how important these men are."

"The *most* important. *Most.*"

In many ways she reminded him of Mao's widow, Chiang Ching. It had been rumored that before the accident the two women had been lovers. It would account for many things, the man thought. "Both of these men will be at the meeting in Paris?" he asked her.

"I am personally meeting Gulbrandsen in Stockholm, bringing him to Paris myself."

"What about Andelsdorf?"

"He left East Berlin three weeks ago. There was a slight problem, but he managed to leave with all his notebooks and formulas. He has taken another identity and is waiting in Ibiza. It has been arranged for him to be escorted to Paris at the proper time."

"Good." He wiped his hand over his mouth, was aware of the pine scent of the American soap he used. "I, myself, will be in charge of de Plyssy in Paris and MacGlendon in Chicago."

The oldest-appearing man in the group, the only one still wearing the traditional Mao jacket, interrupted. "I can understand the other choices," he said. "Heavy industry is our only chance for survival. I even agree now to Comrade Kang's scientific magicians. But this MacGlendon man from Chicago . . ." His voice trailed off.

Deng said, "We have had this discussion before." He smiled across at the standing man as though they shared a secret. "I agree with Comrade Chou. The soft-goods industries are vital to our population and to sustain our economy until the heavy industries are established. At the moment it is the only area of manufacturing in which we have any experience and expertise. I agree with the choice of Mac-Glendon. Trust Tzao-tzao. He understands the Western mentality better than any of us." He winked across the table, gestured with his cigar for the instructions to continue.

But the old man pressed his grievance, talking now to Deng directly. "Even if I agreed with your point about the soft-goods industry—"

Deng cut him off. "There is no question of agreement. The condition exists. The only way we destroy Taiwan is to break down their economy. Their world export of soft goods alone is equivalent to over three billion U.S. dollars. With MacGlendon working for us, we can triple that total with our own exports. Taiwan will become nothing more than an impoverished island off the mainland again. The generalissimo's descendants will be starved into capitulation."

The old man persisted. "But this MacGlendon . . . it is my understanding that he is the only member of the consortium not philosophically committed to our doctrines." He turned to Chou. "They tell me that he is young and headstrong."

"That is true," Chou said, a ring of pride in his voice. "But, like the others, he has an insatiable hunger for money and power."

"But he is much younger than the others: he'll outlive us all," the old man said.

Deng said: "His old age will come when he has accomplished our purposes. Old age and death will come at that time no matter how young he is."

Chou swallowed the protesting words he wanted to say and looked over the table at a man bigger than the others, barrel-chested and with a flat-featured face. "Security will be the biggest problem," he said to the man. "Our enemies are many."

"The Russians," Deng interjected, but did not have to say any more.

It's always the Russians. Then Chou said the words out loud. "It is always the Russians."

The others all began talking at once, a clatter of voices recalling grievances and masquerading fears.

An American in Paris

Night was a black mirror outside the wall of windows. Rain, driven by high-velocity winds, lashed against the glass, and echoing booms of thunder were followed by crackling circuits of lightning that flashed off the wet gleaming runways of the De Gaulle airport and momentarily illuminated the prehistoric shapes of grounded jumbo jets.

The Air France Concorde Flight 002 was already thirty-five minutes late. It circled over Paris, above the storm, at subsonic speed, devouring fuel.

Inside the terminal a section of the arrival area had been fenced off with waist-high barricades strung out in an uneven line. Within the cordoned section, portable folding screens had been set up around the equipment of a television news crew. A single, empty chair was the focus of the lights and cameras.

The TV people kept to themselves, away from the other reporters and photographers sprawled on benches, drinking coffee from foam cups or sipping wine from plastic glasses. Some of the media people were at the telephones explaining the delayed flight and changing nighttime plans. All of them wore large blue-and-white identification badges.

Eight armed security guards roamed the area in a random interweaving pattern.

The press contingent was an international mixture of financial and fashion reporters. *The Wall Street Journal* had assigned one man from its Paris office, and another had flown in the day before covering for the Asian edition. *Women's Wear Daily* was represented by a tweed-suited, overweight woman covering the hard-news angle and by an effete young man who was a runner for jet-set gossip coverage.

Ben Brayden, the Midwest bureau chief for *Time,* had arrived from Chicago on an earlier flight, then gone into the city for a long, boozy lunch with a girl he knew before returning to De Gaulle. By all rights, this should have been his exclusive story. He had filed the first rumblings of it two weeks ago, based on a rumor whispered to him in bed by an unsteady blonde who was an executive secretary at Mac-Glendon Industries. But New York had rejected the lead; telexed back UNSUBSTANTIATED.

The man they were waiting for was Angus MacGlendon, the low-profile American tycoon who, three days before, had startled the fashion industry by announcing the acquisition of a chain of high-fashion women's-wear department and specialty stores in the United States as well as controlling interest in six major designer/couture houses in Paris, eight in Italy, and one in Israel, adding them to his already huge conglomerate of textile mills, manufacturing companies, and retail stores.

Overnight, MacGlendon had become the single most important factor in a multibillion-dollar industry. Since the announcement, which had been timed for late on Friday, after the closing of the New York Stock Exchange, Mac-Glendon had disappeared, making himself unavailable for comment, questions, or clarifications. This was to be his first press conference, occurring simultaneously with the Prêt-à-Porter, the international ready-to-wear women's fashion market, opening the next day at the Porte de Versailles.

Thirty-eight minutes later, after the winds had stopped and the diminished rain dribbled harmlessly onto the runways, it was announced that the Concorde would touch down in six minutes and would arrive at the gate shortly after that. The television crew woke up, tested lights and equipment. Some of the press stood at the windows, cupping their hands to shield their eyes from the inside light, watching for the plane.

The high-decibel whoosh of the aircraft rattled the glass wall. The bright lights penetrated the darkness, and finally the droop-nosed aircraft came into view, making a broad U-turn and taxiing toward the gate. The airport police formed a line containing the press corps in the restricted area and cordoning a clear exit lane for the disembarking passengers.

The engines stopped and the jetway telescoped out to engage the Concorde. Air France personnel hovered at the jetway door, and another contingent was assembled at the end of the police line. A bilingual British woman, wearing an Air France uniform and carrying a clipboard jammed with rumpled papers, stood behind the guards on one of the seats, searching the long line of faces emerging from the jetway.

She did not recognize Angus MacGlendon, one of the first passengers, and assumed that the huge, bull-necked American with the shaggy blond hair was a linebacker on a football team or an American film star. Her eyes hesitated only long enough to admire him, then continued searching the faces beyond him.

The hastily assembled information on her clipboard contained no photograph or physical description of MacGlendon. She knew that he had won the Horatio Alger Award in 1972 and was named Man of the Year by the Junior Chamber of Commerce in 1974 and had been honored by the Young Presidents Organization in 1976. The dossier included a photostated copy of an in-depth article from the March 1979 issue of *Fortune* magazine that she had not had time to read. She was looking for an older man, a face and body distorted by success.

Ben Brayden knew MacGlendon by sight. He hurdled the security fence and caught up with him just as MacGlendon was about to step on the moving runway to the main terminal. "Ben Brayden," he said. "*Time* magazine. I tried to interview you in Chicago."

MacGlendon remembered the man, remembered wondering how he had gotten his tip on the impending takeover. Brayden had known too much to be just guessing. After the aborted interview MacGlendon had summarily fired the vice-president charged with internal security, ordered polygraph tests for every person in his own executive offices as well as for the personnel in the law firm involved in handling the acquisitions. "I'll trade you an apology for a question, Brayden."

"You go first," Brayden said.

"You were right on the button with the story, but I couldn't confirm it then. I couldn't even acknowledge the possibility. The SEC regulations are tight as hell on public companies. There was no way I could have legally tipped my hand." He hesitated and then said, "I'm sorry I was rude to you."

"It was more than rude, MacGlendon. Those goons of yours dumped me on the sidewalk outside your building."

"I said I was sorry, Brayden."

The men smiled self-consciously at each other. "What's the question?" Brayden asked.

"Who told you?"

"A blonde who works in your office. I don't even know

her name. I picked her up at a singles bar. Thick legs. Big
boobs. Maybe five feet four. Drinks and fucks too much.
Both badly."

"Thanks." MacGlendon turned, started for the moving
conveyor and said, over his shoulder, "See you around."
Brayden caught the sleeve of MacGlendon's leather
jacket. "Hey, where are you going?" Brayden moved his
head, indicating the barricaded area behind them, the passengers still deplaning. "That whole whoop-de-do is set up
for you. You're having a press conference. Didn't you
know that?"

"I didn't authorize a press conference. Hell, I'm lousy at
it. Who authorized it?"

"Eberhardt and Le Croix. Local public relations outfit."
He took out the press release and held it out for MacGlendon to read. "There are forty or so people waiting back
there. I don't suggest ducking it. Your take-over isn't exactly popular in Paris. They're out there with their hatchets.
Everybody wants to know if this means the end of Paris as
the fashion center of the world. I know it's been happening
for a long time, but the fucking French never believed it
could happen until now. Your take-over could realign a big
chunk of the world economy. There are rumors that you've
got South American money funding this. Some say Chinese.
Not nickels and dimes. Big money."

MacGlendon evaluated the situation. He knew that no
one in his own organization would dare authorize a press
conference without his approval. He had never even heard
of the public relations firm that Brayden had mentioned.
He thought for a moment, decided that his press conference
was a smokescreen devised by the Chinese to disguise his
real mission in Paris, which was to attend the first meeting
of the consortium. That explanation made sense to him. The
Oriental mind worked in a convoluted way. He had had

enough business dealings with the Chinese in Hong Kong and Taiwan to know that they often used Western camouflage for Oriental purposes. The apparent accidental timing of the first meeting of the consortium with the opening in Paris of the Prêt-à-Porter was perfect Chinese-crafted design.

MacGlendon got out of the way of the traffic. Brayden stayed at his side, told MacGlendon: "You've got an all-star cast waiting out there. Besides all the financial press, you have the fashion press, and they can get bitchy. No point in pissing them off. In the end, you're going to need them."

"Who are they?"

"There's the queen herself, Bernadine Morris of *The New York Times.* And there's McEvoy of *Women's Wear.* Jim Brady is out there. They're all in a hurry because St. Laurent is having some kind of funky gala tonight. You even got Rex Reed out of his satin bedroom at the Ritz. He'll probably ask you if you sleep in the nude."

"What'll I tell him?"

"Don't tell me you wear jammies, MacGlendon?"

"Tops only."

Brayden shook his head negatively. "Even so, it's bad for the image."

"I own three fucking pajama factories."

"Even so, I suggest lying to Reed."

"What else are they going to ask me?"

"You're the new boy in town, MacGlendon. You're Mr. Glamour Puss for the moment. You're a pretty face and a big hunk of body. You're not married and you're stinking rich. They're going to ask you everything including the size of your dong. They're piranhas, MacGlendon. They're going to eat you alive, but you have to face them."

"Look," MacGlendon said, "I'll make you a deal. Stick close to me. Signal who's important and who isn't. I'm caught off guard, Ben. I didn't do any homework for this. Just give me the nod at who's important and shake me off the duds. I'll owe you one."

"You don't need me, MacGlendon. Your PR firm has two people out there. And there's an Air France press representative. They even have translators for you."

"But I need your savvy, Ben. You speak French, don't you?"

Brayden nodded. "Under duress, I can even speak Italian and bluff my way through German."

"This is duress, Ben. Be a buddy. One hometown boy helping another. Okay?"

For the first time Brayden detected something to like about MacGlendon, felt comfortable with him rather than awed by him as he had been at their first meeting. Brayden said, "It'll cost you, MacGlendon."

"Name the price."

"I ought to warn you in advance that you're going to be the cover story in next week's *Time.* Whether you like it or not, you're on the cover and I'm doing the story."

MacGlendon smiled. "Blackmail?"

"You bet. Mutual back scratching. Exclusive interview after the press conference."

MacGlendon clasped Brayden around the shoulder. "You got it. Ride to my hotel with me. We can talk then."

As they walked back toward the gate, Brayden said: "Shitty weather. Rough flight?"

"Not until now," MacGlendon said. He slowed his pace so as not to outdistance Brayden. The last passengers were off the Concorde, and the press, scanning the crowd, was irate and noisy. "I wouldn't have flown over dressed like this if I had known this press conference had been set up."

"You look fine. You look human. You're going to have to project all the humanity you can."

Brayden had already mentally noted the change in Mac-Glendon's appearance. Two weeks ago MacGlendon had been imperious, fortressed behind a massive desk and armored in a Brooks Brothers suit. He had been seated the entire time, and Brayden had not been aware of the tremendous size of the man. MacGlendon had seemed so sure of himself in Chicago—disciplined and contained, a man in complete control. His hair had been slicked down. Now he wore worn jeans and a leather jacket, cowboy boots, and an unbuttoned shirt, and his hair was long and loose.

MacGlendon swung one leg over the fence and then hesitated, waiting for Brayden to precede him. A security guard blocked MacGlendon's way, but Brayden spoke to the guard in French, identifying MacGlendon. Together they went to the screened-off area. MacGlendon sat on the stage-center chair, his head down and his hands held in a tight grasp as the grim-faced press corps converged on him. Brayden sat cross-legged on the floor under the camera like a prompter in a stage pit.

MacGlendon fielded the questions slowly at first. Then, as his confidence built, he answered easily, using the phrase "It's too soon to know" as often as a dissident pleading the Fifth Amendment. Rex Reed *did* ask if he slept in the nude. MacGlendon smiled down at Brayden, then told Reed that he did.

While the questioning continued, MacGlendon paid special attention to the Chinese man operating a television minicam and the Oriental woman who was acting as interpreter. Neither gave him any sign or signal that indicated the next link in the chain that had begun a month ago in his Chicago office by a man purporting to be a silk merchant from mainland China. MacGlendon decided it was too soon for the contact to be made, and the place was too public.

Even after the press conference concluded, MacGlendon

hung back, answering off-the-record questions as the reporters straggled away. But neither the cameraman nor the Oriental woman waited. Tomorrow, MacGlendon thought. It would happen tomorrow.

Brayden surrendered his press badge at the immigration desk, and MacGlendon flashed his U.S. passport. His two bags were the only ones remaining on the snaking belt of the baggage carrier. MacGlendon slung the larger one on his shoulder, Brayden took the smaller one, and they exited through the Rien à Déclarer door into the terminal.

Two men had been waiting for over two hours. Brayden recognized them as the goons who had ejected him from the MacGlendon Building. He also realized they had been on his same flight that morning from Chicago, vaguely familiar faces then, but identifiable now as MacGlendon strong-arms. MacGlendon waved the men away when they tried to take the garment bag from his shoulder. As they left the building, the shorter man walked a step ahead of MacGlendon and slightly to the left. The other man walked close behind him, slightly to the right.

"Good trip, Boss?"

"It was okay. What time did you guys get in Paris?"

"Eight o'clock this morning. There was some kind of religious tour on board—screaming kids. It was like a zoo."

MacGlendon asked, "Everything set up at the hotel?"

The shorter man answered: "I guess so. You're not going to like it. The rooms are so small you have to go out in the hall to change your mind."

Ben Brayden sat in front with the driver of the limousine. MacGlendon sat on the center of the back seat.

"Did you line up any action for tonight, Red?" MacGlendon asked.

"Shit, Boss, I didn't have time. I was whacked out from the trip and slept a while. It isn't easy. I have a contact, but I don't speak the goddamn language. I'm sorry."

"It's okay, Red. Something will turn up."

"You got some kind of crazy invitation for a midnight party. Dynamite chick delivered it. She was all dressed up like a man in a tuxedo, but she didn't have a shirt on."

"That's the Saint Laurent party," Brayden said. "Are you going to go?"

"Are you?"

"Let's go together. Okay?"

"You're on," MacGlendon said. "But I get the pick of the litter. I'm adding a clause to our deal."

"Every man for himself, MacGlendon." Brayden held up his hands in defeat and was wondering, if he looked like MacGlendon or had MacGlendon's money, would his wife have roamed and finally roamed far away? But Brayden remembered that MacGlendon had blown a marriage, too. A long time ago, before he was rich. "You've got a big edge. Every cunt in Paris is going to be creaming for the mystery tycoon. Maybe there will be one of them left over who turns on to making miserable guys happy."

"You're one of the good guys, Ben. White hat."

"With a little shaping up, MacGlendon, you may make it, too."

They talked casually on the way from Roissy, like seatmates on airplanes, getting to know each other; but Brayden's casual questions were pointed toward the story he was going to write, and MacGlendon's casual answers were guarded against that same story.

The man whom MacGlendon called Red kept looking out the rear window. "Somebody is following us, boss."

MacGlendon did not turn back.

"You sure?"

"Black Mercedes. Weaves in and out of traffic but always stays two or three cars behind. I wish I spoke the fucking language so I could tell the driver how to shake him."

Leaning over the front seat, MacGlendon instructed

Brayden to tell the driver to pull off the side of the express-
way at the first opportunity, let a few cars pass, and then pull
right back on again. Brayden relayed the instructions to the
chauffeur, who waited a few minutes, then turned abruptly
on to the shoulder and slammed on the brakes inches away
from an abutment.

The Mercedes sped past them, all the Chinese faces turning in their direction.

The Cadillac reentered the traffic. MacGlendon instructed Brayden: "Tell the driver to keep to the left. The
Mercedes will probably turn off right at the next exit."

Brayden gave the instructions and turned back to Mac-
Glendon. "What was that about?"

MacGlendon laughed. "Probably nothing," he said.
"Big Red here gets paranoid sometimes." He slapped the
bodyguard's knee. "But we never take any chances, do we,
Red?"

"You've had kidnap threats?" Brayden asked.

"There's always the danger of some kook or terrorist. My
corporation carries an insurance policy against kidnapping.
The insurance company insists that I keep these guys
around me, particularly when I'm out of the country. Fortu-
nately, Big Red likes jogging with me, and our new man
here," he nodded to his right, "plays a wicked game of
tennis. That makes him useful. It seems dumb," he said,
"for a guy as big as I am to need protection, but it's a clause
in the insurance policy."

MacGlendon was lying; the policy had no such clause.

A Pattern of Locusts

The Concorde had touched down in Paris at eight thirty-six in the evening. It was two thirty-six Eastern Standard Time on a sunny afternoon in New York: no clouds threatened the brightness, no undercurrent of moisture dampened the crisp autumnal air.

She was alone now, waiting for an overdue call from Paris.

The others had finally gone, leaving behind them the smell of stale smoke and rancid perspiration. There had been too many of them, cooped up in too small a space for too long a time: too much anger and anguish expended in dark, airless rooms.

The woman pulled back the draperies, letting sunlight flood the room, and opened the windows overlooking Park Avenue, knelt on the floor, crossed her arms on the sill and rested her head, inhaling deep breaths of the fresh air. She loosened the band holding her thick, red hair away from her face, ran her fingers through it and exposed it to the soft breeze. The Concorde had been scheduled to land about an hour ago. Either way—whether her son had been on the flight or not—the agent in Paris should have phoned in by now.

The others had left separately, at predetermined intervals, following a pattern set for security. Some of them had been directed to walk up or down several flights of stairs and board the passenger elevators on other floors. Two of the men had dressed as waiters, the Waldorf-Astoria crest stenciled on their short, white jackets, and wheeling room-service carts to the freight elevators, went down unnoticed, through the confusion in the hotel kitchen, put on trench coats hidden in the employees locker room, and went different directions on Forty-ninth Street. Both men made overseas credit-card calls from sidewalk telephone booths within five minutes of leaving the Waldorf.

While each had waited his turn to leave, there had been no further conversations, no attempts at small talk or polite good-byes even though they had known that this would probably be the last time they would ever meet like this. Silence was the real language of trained conspirators: everything that had to be said had already been said.

The woman walked back into the dining room where the hard core of the meeting had taken place. Dirty ashtrays, stacks of stained coffee cups, half-eaten sandwiches, and glass water pitchers sweating with melting ice were jammed together on the marble sideboard.

The telephone rang. She ran through the living room into the bedroom and was slightly out of breath when she answered the phone. "Thank God," she said when she heard the report from Paris. "Why was it late? Was there engine trouble? . . . The press conference is on now? . . . Big crowd? . . . Good. Tell Eberhardt that his check for setting up the press conference will come through usual channels. Does Angus appear suspicious? . . . Keep him under surveillance. The contact will be made tomorrow as scheduled, then the other group will take over." The agent in Paris asked a question. "Yes," she answered, "all signals are go."

After she showered, she stood for a moment in front of

the full-length mirror. The aging lines of her face stopped at the base of her neck and except for some flabbiness beginning on her upper arms, her body was still young: softer and more rounded than it had been when she was a girl.

She put on a thin, embroidered Chinese silk robe over her nakedness and walked back into the living room, stopping at the bridge table to gather up the playing cards spread out in an interrupted solitaire game, stacking the cards into a neat deck and inserting them in a small drawer under the tabletop. She moved to the backgammon table, sat down there, and rolled up the wide sleeves of her robe. Then she sorted the jumble of red and white pieces, reset the board for play, turned the doubling cube back to zero, threw one die from each cup, and began a game, playing both sides of the board.

When the house phone rang, she reached behind her, cradled the phone between her shoulder and ear, and continued the game. "Yes," she said. "It's all right to send him up. He knows which apartment." When the buzzer sounded at the front door, she smoothed her hair, rolled down the sleeves of her gown, and moistened her lips.

The man she let into the apartment was Chinese but taller than Chinese men usually are. His dark hair was streaked with a steely gray and his face was sunburned—a reddish underglow to the sallow color of his skin. He projected a vitality and physical power constrained in well-cut, conservative clothes: Savile Row, Jermyn Street, Via Condotti shoes. His fingernails were disproportionately large for his long tapering fingers, well manicured, and buffed to a low, pearly luster.

They kissed automatically, but after the first perfunctory touching of their mouths his hand pressed against her back, tried to make the kiss more forceful. She drew away, looked up at him, and placed her fingertips on his face, stroking his cheek, fondling a rare object, a priceless ivory carving. Then they kissed again with the intensity of lovers fulfilling each other's needs. She took his hand and, still without speaking, led him to the living room where they sat opposite each other at the backgammon table, reset the board, and threw the dice to begin a game.

After his opening move the Chinese man said, "They stayed longer than you thought they would." He spoke English with no accent. "Was there trouble?"

She avoided the question. "Were you waiting in the lobby?"

"Part of the time."

"Do you think any of them saw you?"

"They may have, but they wouldn't know me any more than I would know them."

"Don't bet on it," she said. "They know that someone like you exists. They know that he's Chinese. How many Chinamen sit around the lobby of the Waldorf Towers? You don't exactly look like you're making a delivery from the local chop suey parlor."

"It doesn't matter," he said.

"It *does* matter." She looked up at him. "It's not like you to be careless, take unnecessary risks. You're not taking security seriously enough."

"It's too soon to worry. There can't possibly be a leak yet."

"Don't bet on it."

"Why did the meeting take so long?"

"There were last-minute problems. Gerhardt was difficult. He has that typical German obstinacy. Words, words, words. That's all we seem to know anymore. It's been so long since we've done anything. All we know how to do is argue. Years of words." She shook her head sadly. "Now that it's time to act, I wonder if we still remember how to act." She reached across the board and touched the Chinese man's hand. Then she made her bar-point, leaving a man exposed on her ten-point.

He was remembering the green-eyed firebrand American girl, fervid with Marxist idealism, rabidly opposing the Russian form of Communism, sitting at Mao's feet and sharing Mao's dream for the Chinese people. Mao had used her idealistic compassion and enthusiasm opportunely, turning her into a spy against her own country. In many ways, he thought as he studied her across the backgammon table, she was still that same girl, dreaming the same dream. He wondered what she would do if he told her the truth about the consortium—how it had been corrupted into a malevolent power base.

The truth would destroy her, he decided. The whole purpose of her adult life would be destroyed, and it might even destroy her love for him. That he could not risk.

"It will happen now," he said. "Everything you've worked for."

"I believe that with all my heart," she said. "It's kept me going all these years."

The Chinese man smiled, hit the exposed piece of the ten-point. "You are more Oriental than the Orientals."

"I've learned from your people, darling. I've learned patience and a sense of inevitability." She shook double sixes, could not reenter the board. She repeated, "There is an inevitable pattern of justice."

Remembering the meeting in Peking, the words of Deng Xiao-ping when they named the consortium, the Chinese man said, "I was thinking before of the pattern of locusts."

Wrapped in the cocoon of her thoughts, she did not seem to hear him.

"You know about locusts?" he asked.

"Of course I do, darling." She made a fluttering gesture with her hand. "I was in China when . . ." Her voice trailed off when she understood the simile, and she locked her hands over the dice cup. "It is like that, isn't it? Every seventeen years. The pattern of locusts." Her face was furrowed in thought as she mentally calculated the years. "The first time we met was thirty-four years ago." She shook her head. "No, it wasn't quite that long ago—1947." She started counting on her fingers, then stopped.

"With the locusts," he said, "the timetable is innate. They know instinctively when the period of dormancy is over, when it is time to ravage the earth again."

She reentered the backgammon board on his three-point, moved another piece down to her own three-point, and pretended to concentrate on the game. "We don't celebrate anniversaries," she said. "We've had so many. We could have been an old, married couple by now living out the rest of our lives in Palm Beach listening to our arteries harden."

"I wanted that," he said. "I wanted that for you."

"It would never have worked. It was never meant to be." She laughed. "I don't think even now the world is ready to accept an old, red-headed Jewish broad and a Chinaman as the typical retirement couple in Palm Beach society."

She pushed all the backgammon pieces together, destroying the game, paced over to the window, looking down at the traffic, and then turned back to face the Chinese man. "The call came through," she said. "Angus is in Paris. There was a storm there. The plane was late. He's still at the airport. The press conference I arranged is taking place now. Everything is ready." She felt the chill of the air and closed the windows, tightened the robe around her, retied the sash.

The Chinese man walked over to her, held her in his arms, rubbed his cheek against her hair. "I'll always love you," he said.

For a moment she yielded to his strength, the warmth of his body, then she backed away. "That means that you have to go back to China again, doesn't it?"

He nodded. "I leave for Peking tomorrow night from Paris."

"It's permanent this time, isn't it? You'll never come back."

"*Never* is not a Chinese word," he said. "Orientals talk about *forever.*"

"What about me? What happens to me?"

"You have your destiny. I have mine."

Her green eyes sparkled with tears she was fighting back. "It ends like this? After all these years it ends with the word *destiny?*"

"We always knew that one day it would happen." He walked away from the daylight, sat in the shadows across the room. "We've both waited so long. Now it's about to happen. You belong here, doing what you have to do, and I belong in China."

"Did you try? Did you try to get permission to bring me with you?"

"It would be foolish at this point. You can't risk exposure." He went back to her, tried to take her in his arms, but she pushed him away. "I did try," he confessed. "I spoke to Deng Xiao-ping. He laughed at me, said I was corrupted by Western ways and red hair and green eyes." He laughed. "Deng sends his greetings to you and his wishes for success." This time she did not draw away from him, but submitted to his strength. "Are you afraid?"

"A little," she said. "Do I look afraid?"

"You never looked more beautiful. I have never seen you more radiant."

"I feel the way I did when I was young. I feel alive with the same kind of fervor. But then I didn't know enough to be afraid . . . and I wasn't in love with you then."

"We must continue to have the patience of locusts. Circumstances have separated us before, but we always found each other again." He put his mouth over her ear, his tongue following the snaillike contours. Her body shivered in his arms.

She leaned her head back, looked up at him, openly sensual. "I do feel young again—hungry the way I was hungry then." She stood on tiptoe, devoured his mouth, sucking in his tongue.

He stood back. "I don't leave for Paris until seven thirty." He looked at his watch. "We have an eternity until seven thirty."

"You'll see Angus in the morning?"

He nodded. "I will explain the plan, put him in touch with our people in Paris."

"Don't do anything foolish."

"Deng used those same words: *foolish and sentimental.* He thinks it's too dangerous for me to make the contact with Angus. Leave it to one of the others, he said. He called it a foolish and sentimental gesture."

"Telling Angus the truth about me would be a foolish and sentimental gesture. Destructive to everything."

"A son should love his mother . . . have respect for her wisdom."

"It's enough that *I* love him. Angus must never, never know about me. When I'm dead, he can know. But not now. Promise me," she said.

Instead of answering, he kissed her.

Muttering through the kiss, she repeated his secret name as her fingernails dug into the back of his neck. "Tzao-tzao." Tzao-tzao.

Singapore: The First Alert

Ridge Bentley had been lying awake all night in the darkness watching the red glow of the digital readout on his bedside clock, calculating the time difference between Singapore and Paris, then Singapore and New York. Singapore is in an intermediate time zone: when the rest of the world is on the hour, Singapore is on the half hour. The telephone call from Paris was overdue. The Concorde had been scheduled for a seven-thirty arrival in Paris: three o'clock the next morning Singapore time. It was now after four: still no call.

Across the room, in front of the windows, a naked Eurasian woman slept, uncovered, on a Chinese wooden bed, her body gleaming ivory against the polished dark wood. Her head rested on a Chinese porcelain pillow formed in the shape of a sleeping cat. Her long legs were crossed at the ankles, her forearms covered her breasts, and her hands were folded over the V of her shaved pubis. She slept deeply, not moving, a faint smile turning up the corners of her mouth.

The timing of the call from New York was uncertain. Bentley had instructed the double agent there to call within five minutes after the meeting in the Waldorf Towers ended. Bentley disliked doing business with Germans, and this man, Gerhardt Kline, was not only German but he was old: at an age when tending to his bodily functions superseded the obligations of his job.

The day before, when Bentley first discovered that his telephones were tapped, he had been able to use KGB channels of communication to inform Paris and New York of the danger, instructing his agents there to use a single code word for communication and then wait at a designated point for a call back. Bentley had plenipotentiary authority that superseded KGB power. His contract with the Soviet government had been skillfully negotiated to keep him independent from the spy organization yet enable him to use KGB personnel and facilities on demand.

The U.S. Securities and Exchange Commission had begun an investigation of Bentley's financial dealings in the Far East. He was the controlling stockholder and chief executive officer of two public companies listed on the American Stock Exchange; one of them was involved with Malaysian land development and the other in the leasing of freighters registered with a suspect Panamanian corporation. The CIA was backing up the SEC investigation, doing the dirty undercover work while Wall Street auditors were openly examining his books. Bentley was under twenty-four-hour surveillance. The CIA had a long dossier on him, information supplied by the FBI. Bentley had been a key figure in the dissident movements in the sixties and had been closely connected with the Chicago Seven, acting as a sub rosa legal counsel during the trial.

The telephone finally rang. He picked it up at the first sound, looked over toward the sleeping woman, cleared his throat, and waited.

The guttural voice said, "Carpathian," and the man hung up, leaving no time to trace the call.

That was Gerhardt, the Russian mole in New York who had infiltrated the Chinese spy network in the United States and, acting as a double agent, fed the Soviets the limited information available to him on the Chinese consortium. *Carpathian* meant that all systems were go and that Chou Yo-pai was leaving for Paris as scheduled to make the contact with Angus MacGlendon. So far, MacGlendon was the only name the Russians knew as being part of the projected consortium. Bentley's immediate assignment was to follow MacGlendon, break him down to reveal names of the other members of the consortium, and to use MacGlendon, however possible, as a device to break up the Chinese power play.

Bentley wondered why the Chinese were sending such an important official on this mission to Paris, risking the life of their major international banking expert on what appeared to be a routine assignment. The use of Chou to contact MacGlendon indicated that the parameters of the operation were greater than Bentley had first suspected.

A second call, this time from Paris, came through at five ten Singapore time. The woman's voice said, "Olympus," telling Bentley what he already knew: MacGlendon had arrived in Paris.

Bentley jumped out of bed, raced through the living room and out onto the penthouse terrace that overlooked the city and the crowded harbor. He felt a slight, night chill shiver through his naked body as he crouched on a straw mat and took out a telephone from a waterproof box. Earlier, knowing that his telephone calls were being monitored, he had gone on the roof of the building and jerry-rigged a connection, tying into another tenant's telephone line. While he had been working on this, he remembered all the homemade bombs he had rigged, the remote detonators he had wired and activated. It had been a long time.

There was still enough starlight in the fading night to make out the numbers on the dial. 005-1-212-555-0405. He waited through the long chain of clicking sounds until he finally heard the ringing. For a long time there was no answer, but just as Bentley was about to hang up, an out-of-breath voice said, "Carpathian."

"Where the fuck were you?"

"On the toilet," Gerhardt answered. "I didn't even have time to button my pants."

"What happened at the meeting?"

"What ever happens at those meetings? Betsy Brewster talks all the time. We were given our instructions. I'm supposed to wait in Barcelona and be contacted there. The Chinaman is going to Paris. I have surveillance teams on him. He's at the Waldorf now with that bitch."

Bentley said: "I don't want him touched. Is that clear? Let him get on the plane. My Russian friends will take over in Paris."

"It would be so easy in New York," the German said. "We could handle it easy."

"I need him alive until he contacts MacGlendon. After that, our Paris people will handle it."

"The Chinaman is scheduled to be at MacGlendon's hotel first thing in the morning. He goes right from the plane."

"I'll handle it."

"What happened in Singapore? How come I had to use code?"

"My phone is tapped. I'm having some trouble here. CIA. They may be on to my Moscow-Narodny Bank connection."

"Is it safe for you to go to Paris?"

"If I worried about being safe, Gerhardt, I wouldn't be in this business."

Bentley hung up, waited for the line to clear, and then called Paris. He relayed the information about Chou Yopai's arrival in Paris. "Let him make contact with MacGlendon and then eliminate him. After that don't let MacGlendon out of your sight."

Back in the bedroom, he stood over the Eurasian woman. Her right hand had dropped to the floor exposing a tattooed Garuda on her breast. "Wake up, baby. We're going to Paris." She uncrossed her legs, spread them apart, and stretched her arms behind her head. The tattooed mythical bird undulated in flight as she moved. From behind her head she extended her arms forward, holding them out to him.

Bentley scratched his scrotum and turned away from her. "All you ever want to do is fuck," he said.

Bal de Versailles

A different mentality possessed MacGlendon here—his daytime discipline transfixed by the amplified night music blaring at an incessant rock beat and by the sight and smell of glamorous women. Like an alcoholic watching a bartender pour the first drink, or a gambler cracking a new deck of cards, he was aware of his compulsion—helpless to stop the descending pattern.

From a vantage point at the end of one of the champagne-laden bars, he kept a vigil on the female flesh wiggling and weaving under the flashing strobe lights on the dance floor, first following the path of a lean brunette, then being diverted by the shimmer of a voluptuous blonde, and abandoning her to follow the satin, undulating ass of a tall woman with green hair and the painted face of a clown.

Ben Brayden left the arms of a bony, six-foot-tall black model long enough to gulp another glass of champagne and asked MacGlendon, "Have you ever seen so much puss in one place?" He was back on the dance floor before MacGlendon could answer.

A black-and-white-striped tent had been erected in the parkway outside the palace of Versailles. Festoons of black and white crepe-paper streamers canopied each silver-topped table, candlelight reflecting against the shiny surfaces and illuminating the centerpieces of artificial black and white calla lilies dusted with sparkles and clusters of black and white balloons.

Yves Saint Laurent sat at a table in the center of the tent, protected by the circled coterie of his followers: over-dressed women chattering incessantly and cardboard-looking men with passive expressions and restless eyes. From time to time a Seventh Avenue tycoon or a slightly drunk midwestern dress buyer would try to crack the circle but would be strong-armed away by one of Saint Laurent's American agents.

A big, gruff, bald-headed man came over and stood beside MacGlendon, shifted his cigar from one side of his mouth to the other, synchronized his eyes to the same roving pattern that MacGlendon was making. "You can get any one of them—any broad you like. You're hot stuff now, Gus. The king of the Prêt. Wiggle your little finger and they'll all roll over for you."

"That's what I had in mind," MacGlendon answered.

"People whisper a lot of things about you, Gus. You're in the limelight. People do a lot of talking."

MacGlendon did not answer. He was watching a very young girl, measuring her body with his eyes, estimating its fit against his.

"Some people," the man went on, "are saying that you like to take them on more than one at a time."

MacGlendon smiled without looking over. "I've been known to," he said.

"I can understand that," the man said, shifting his cigar again. "I was young once—played around with the models in the showroom. What the hell, you're only young once." He elbowed closer to MacGlendon. "What I don't understand is what you're up to with all these acquisitions?"

"There's no standing still in business. You know that, Al. You've got to keep moving—expanding."

"I understand your vertical expansion. You're the rag king of the Western world. More power to you. The rest of us will survive one way or another. But people are saying that you're diversifying into other industries, biting off more than you can chew. What's this hardware jazz? People are saying that you've been buying up some small midwestern companies and are now about to have a dummy corporation make a tender offer on Hard-Line Hardware. That's big potatoes, Gus. It's not like the rag business."

"No returns in the hardware business. No markdowns. No closeouts. Good cash flow. I need that maneuverability." The young girl he had been watching stood at the edge of the dance floor while her partner was threading his way toward the bar. She breathed hard and her natural color was showing through the pancake coat of her makeup. Tiny drops of perspiration glistened on her smooth forehead and in the deep crevice between her breasts. There was a sullen droop to her mouth, a pouting expression of a spoiled child. But her eyes were the eyes of a woman, wide with excitement. Without turning or speaking, grabbing a full bottle of champagne, MacGlendon left the bar making a straight line to the dance floor.

She looked up at him, then down his length and back up to his face. She threw her head back, opened her mouth. MacGlendon inserted the neck of the bottle between her lips, tilted it at an angle as she guzzled it down. Slowly, he pulled it out of her mouth. It made a sucking sound. A few drops of the wine trickled down her chin, splashed on her chest. She wiped her mouth with the back of her hand, smearing her lipstick.

"Are you old enough to be out this late?" MacGlendon asked.

She threw back her shoulders and head. Her neck was a fluid, unlined arc. "I speak English very badly," she said. Her accent was German.

"Did you understand what I asked you?"

She ran her tongue over her upper teeth and giggled. "Men," she said, "are such fools." She took his hand, led him out to the dance floor, maneuvered her body so that it contoured with his, began pelvic thrusts in rhythm to the music. "I am old enough for anything," she said. Her fingers crawled from the back of his neck and entwined his ear.

He closed his eyes and abandoned himself to the music and the female flesh counterpointing his movements. A man, breaking them apart, gave the girl a threatening look and then said to MacGlendon, "Mr. Saint Laurent would like you to join him at his table."

The German girl started to walk away. MacGlendon grabbed her arm, pulled her back against his body. "Tell Mr. Saint Laurent," he said, "that I'm busy now. I'm dancing with one of his guests."

The man spoke in French then, angry words lashing at the girl. She answered him in German, a guttural string of foul words. She stuck her tongue out at him, then buried her face in the protective hollow between MacGlendon's neck and shoulder.

When the music momentarily stopped, MacGlendon led her off the dance floor, through the maze of tables and out of the tent. He looked both ways into the night, the dark mass of the woods bordering the parkway on both sides and the towering silhouette of the palace in the distance. He lifted her up, cradled her in his arms, and carried her toward the section of the parking lot reserved for chauffered limousines. In the rear line he found an unattended, seven-passenger Mercedes 600 limousine with the key in it. He opened the rear door, laid the girl down on the length of the back seat, closed the door quietly, and got behind the wheel; then without turning on the headlights, he started the ignition, backed up, knocking over a yellow barricade, and drove forward over a lawn, then turned sharply and headed for the secluded cover of a cluster of trees. He cut the ignition, then fumbled with switches until he turned on the interior lights. He looked back through the glass divider. She was already naked, her legs spread and her eyes closed.

Before he got into the back seat, MacGlendon took off his jacket, pulled down the jump seat and placed it there, then unfastened his pants, letting them slip to his ankles. Bracing himself against the side of the Mercedes, he pulled them off, then his shorts, tossing them on top of his folded jacket. Just before he put his head inside the car, he pulled the string of his black bow tie and opened the top buttons of his shirt.

He began at her feet, tasting her, mouthing her, savoring her fleshy parts, thrusting his body forward into the car as he crept up on her. He bypassed the lips of her mouth, encompassed one eye and then the other, tracing the outlines with his tongue. He kicked off his shoes, let them fall to the ground, and brought his whole body into the car, then crouched on his knees and straddled over her. With his stockinged foot he groped behind him, locked his toes behind the door handle, and pulled the door shut.

Starting down on her, still avoiding contact with her mouth, he followed the same saliva-wet pattern in his descent, lingering longer at the bush of wiry hair, then beginning little nips at her flesh with the edges of his teeth as he went down one leg and then the other.

When he finally thrust himself into her in one riveting blow from his waist, she screamed and her hands went up behind her head, one grabbing the leather support strap and the other grasping the shirred-silk curtain on the small rear window with such force that it ripped off the fastening.

After MacGlendon exploded inside her, he momentarily let his weight go dead on top of her, crushing her against the soft upholstery; then again he started to move inside her, slowly at first, building the intensity of his humping until he ejaculated again. He pulled out of her, rolled over and lay on the floorboard of the back seat, breathing hard and hearing her gasping sounds.

As he touched her again, she shivered in a tiny, automatic orgasm. He rolled her over, facedown on the seat, and began mouthing the back side of her. He entered her from this position.

The slightly sweet taste of the champagne mixed with the lingering genital flavor still in his mouth. From the same vantage point, at the same end of the same bar, MacGlendon surveyed the dance floor again. The music was softer now, playing at a slower beat. A thin cloud cover of sweet-smelling smoke filled the tent, and the dancers moved languorously in this haze.

The party thinned out. Ben Brayden was nowhere to be seen.

Still holding his champagne glass, MacGlendon weaved through the half-empty tables, some of the candles on them burned out, some of the balloons burst. He stood at the edge of the dance floor, horse-fleshing each woman and wondering about love. Would love be the lotion that would salve his infernal itch for sex?

He chose a tall, flat-chested brunette.

He looked around for a place to put his champagne glass. The spectacled owl-eyes of Yves Saint Laurent turned up to him as MacGlendon reached over, setting the glass down on the table.

"Nice party," MacGlendon said.

Changing the Guard

The heavyset man, the man MacGlendon called Big Red, was still perspiring when he came into the hotel room; sweat penetrated the thick terry cloth of his zippered jacket and jogging pants, accentuating his muscled calves and the cheeks of his rump. He set his gun down on the night table, took the sweatband off his forehead, and reached down to shake the other man, sleeping facedown, with one arm hanging over the side of the bed and the other under the pillow cradling his head. The New Man awoke instantly and in one catlike, fluid motion, turned over, sat up, and leveled the gun he had hidden under the pillow. He smiled when he saw his partner standing over him, put down the gun, and threw his legs over the side of the bed. Covering himself with the edge of the sheet, he looked up at the man in the sweat-stained running suit. "Looks like the boss gave you quite a workout this morning."

"Christ, I thought he was going to run all the way to Germany. It's damn cold down by that river: raw as hell in the morning."

"Weather lousy?"

"Not now. It's clearing up. The sun is coming out." He lighted a cigarette, the last one in the package, crumbled the wrapper, and threw it on the floor. "Sooner or later, I've got to give them up; raise hell with my wind. I can hardly keep up with the boss anymore. He was a tiger this morning, running like the whole damn Russian army was chasing him."

"I don't know where he gets the energy. He and the *Time* magazine guy went to that party at midnight last night. For a big guy the boss moves it pretty well on the dance floor. You never saw such crazy-looking people. There was one broad there—legs that never stopped and tits to match."

"Did the boss get laid?"

"He must have. I kept losing sight of him. His tux looked like he slept in it. The little guy from *Time* got boozed up and wound up with a big, black bomber: could have been a man in drag. Jesus, what a party. We didn't get back here until four. Maybe after. What energy—stays up until four, and then he's up and running at eight. I get the tennis-court detail this afternoon. Talk about getting your ass run off. Then he'll probably want to be out on the town again all night." The New Man yawned, stretched his arms, exercising his shoulders back and forth. "What's the schedule this morning?"

"Right now he's in his suite with some Chinaman who was waiting in the lobby when we came in. The appointment wasn't on the books, but the boss said it was okay. He seemed to be expecting him. The chink looks like a banker, but he must be some kind of salesman: he has a great big sample case with him. I wanted to check it out, but the boss said it was okay. He told me to tell you to take your time, get some breakfast. He said that he would be with the Chinaman for a while and then he was going to shower and make some notes."

"What's the first appointment?"

"He's meeting the executives from one of the new companies he just bought at the Prêt. Eleven o'clock."

The New Man squinted at his watch lying on the night

table. "Why don't you go ahead and shower? You look done in. I don't have to hurry. How long does it take to get to the Prêt?"

"Maybe twenty minutes in a cab. The traffic shouldn't be too tough at that hour."

"Well, he won't need me until ten thirty. Take your time."

The heavyset man unzipped his jacket, then pulled the sweat-stained T-shirt over his head, wadded it into a ball, wiped the perspiration off his upper torso, sat on a frail French chair, and unlaced his running shoes, unpeeled his socks. The gamy smell of his body gave him reassurance. It was the locker room smell that recalled another world and a way of life he understood.

The boss called him Big Red. He had been a second-string linebacker at Nebraska and still reached his emotional peak during the football season. He remained an avid Big Red fan and got to Lincoln as often as he could to see home games.

Big Red. The boss's nickname had stuck. Everyone at the office, even the secretaries, called him Big Red. He liked that and hated the letdown of going home and being just Honey to his wife, Daddy to his children, and Albert to his parents. Big Red was who he really was.

The New Man did not have a nickname yet but probably would have before this trip was over. The boss was good at that. The new guy would say something or do something and, quick as a flash, the boss would christen him with a nickname that would stick. The boss was funny about names; he insisted that everyone call him by his first name. None of that "mister" shit. Even when you called from the outside, you asked the switchboard operator for Gus.

Big Red stood up, stripped bare, swaggered into the bathroom to take a shower. When the New Man heard the sound of water through the closed door, he got out of bed, found his robe, and put it on. He opened the door of the room, moved sideways down the narrow hall, and peered around the corner, squinting into the bright sunlight coming through the skylight to check the entrance to the boss's suite. All quiet.

The New Man wished he had thought to pee before Big Red had taken over the bathroom.

The Foolish and Sentimental Gesture

Each man knew it was a mistake: a meeting between men like this needed a more open, expansive arena. MacGlendon's hotel suite was cramped, claustrophobic. The hulk of MacGlendon alone crowded the room and made the delicate furniture seem even more fragile. The large, black sample case, which Chou Yo-pai carried as a prop to support his assumed identity of a silk merchant, was a large barrier standing upright in the center of the room.

MacGlendon was ill at ease here, out of his element. Their first meeting had been in MacGlendon's Chicago office. The vastness of his corporate headquarters, the uncluttered expanse of his own private office were unspoken credentials establishing who he was, the extent of his wealth, and a reflection of his power. But now, this hotel room—overwrought with froufrou and fake-antique charm —put MacGlendon off base. Compounding the problem was his awareness of the strong smell of his own body. After the long run along the Seine, the odor of sweat contaminated the room and made him vulnerable vis-a-vis the pine-scented elegance of the Chinese man. MacGlendon needed time to regain composure and self-confidence before he played the intricate Chinese game.

"Look," he said, "I wasn't expecting you this early. Give me a couple of minutes to run into the shower."

"Unfortunately, Mr. MacGlendon, there is no time. Not even minutes. My hours in Paris are limited." He bent over, unfastened the hardware on the sample case and began to take out carefully folded pieces of fabric, placing them on backs of chairs and spreading them out on the floor.

MacGlendon stood with his arms folded across his chest, trying to contain the odor emanating from his armpits. "Showing me those samples doesn't mean anything. It's a waste of time. I don't know anything about the fashion business. It's just another commodity to me, another way to make money."

"I know that," Chou said, "but it is important to keep up the pretense. I warned you in Chicago about secrecy and security. There are many factions, including your own government, who would be desperate to abort the establishment of this consortium."

"You keep talking about a consortium. What consortium? What kind of consortium? Who else is in it? Give me some names. I like to know the people I'm doing business with."

"In time," Chou said. "Everything will be explained in time."

"You just told me that there wasn't any time."

Chou, still spreading out samples, smiled. "The Chinese clock works on a different mechanism from the Western world, yet the hours are the same."

"Is that one of those Confucius-says anomalies?"

"I believe Confucius talked about the sands of time." He flattened the last silk sample, sat on a straight chair. "Please sit down, Mr. MacGlendon. Be more at ease."

MacGlendon turned a chair around, straddled it. "I'll

level with you, Mr. Chou. I'm not at ease. I'm as nervous as hell about this. I've just borrowed two hundred million dollars to make these acquisitions. Unless I can get manufacturing facilities in your country to produce the volume of merchandise I need, that two hundred million is down the tube."

"The bank loan," Chou said, "is not to worry."

"That's easy for you to say. So far all that you and your people have put up is a lot of talk and veiled assurances. There's not one piece of concrete evidence that you're committed to this project."

"Not true," Chou said. "We have indicated the possibility that you, personally, can control the soft-goods market of the world."

"*Indicated.*" MacGlendon echoed the Chinese man's word. "*Possibilities. Maybes.* In the United States we have a question we ask in our business dealings. We ask it often. *What have you done for me lately?*"

Chou picked up a silk sample beside him and ran his fingers over the slick, sensual surface. He looked over at Betsy Brewster's son, trying to detect evidence of the mother in the son. It seemed impossible that this mountainous man could have emerged from that delicate, sensitive body. "When your usual banking sources reneged," Chou said, "using the excuse that the loan for the acquisitions was unwise in the current economy, it was suggested that you contact a certain bank in Toronto." Chou looked directly at MacGlendon. "That's correct, isn't it?"

"Tomlinson at Citicorp. It was his idea."

"The Toronto bank, which gave you the loan, is owned by Chinese interests," Chou explained. "The Hong Kong and Shanghai Banking Corporation and private Chinese interests have guaranteed the loan to the Toronto bank. That indicates something more than veiled assurances.

There is no *maybe* about the bank commitment." He waited. MacGlendon said nothing. Chou asked, "Why don't you ask me your question now?"

"What question?"

"What have you done for me lately?"

"It's not a one-way street, Mr. Chou."

"Of course it isn't. In the long run China stands to gain greatly from its investment. Chinese are great gamblers, Mr. MacGlendon, but they compute their odds carefully."

He searched MacGlendon's face for a reflection of Betsy's capacity for tenderness or the light in her green eyes that illuminated the quickness of her mind.

"The consortium . . ." MacGlendon began, his voice trailing off in an unfinished question.

"The consortium will be made up of men like yourself, but representing other industries. Men from around the world. Men as yet unknown to each other, as you are unknown to them. China needs the expertise to drill oil, manufacture aircraft and sophisticated weapons. We need to manufacture our own automobiles. We need steel. We need farm machinery. We need the arithmetic of gross national products, the balance of trade." Chou stood up, paced to the door of the suite, cracked it open silently, peered out through the slit opening. The circular corridor was empty. He wheeled back to MacGlendon. "There are conflicting factions in China. The so-called Cultural Revolution was actually anticultural. We need five years to industrialize China, become a major world power."

"Five years is too little time," MacGlendon said. "Your public commitment is to industrialize by the year 2000. How do you expect to speed it up to five years?"

"The consortium," Chou answered. "The men you will meet with—there will be eight of you—represent the most sophisticated minds in each of their fields. All of you are the dominant factor in your own country in your own industry. But each of you is plagued by diminishing returns on investments and by rising costs of labor, runaway costs of energy and raw materials. Each of you is thwarted by the changing tide of political factions. You, in your country, are being made helpless by conservationists and the restrictive laws against pollution. You will find that none of these hindrances exist in China."

The heat of the room was too intense for MacGlendon. He drew the sweat shirt over his head, threw it on the floor among the silk samples. He peeled off his T-shirt, wadded it, and patted the perspiration from his bare chest. "What's the catch?"

"We are not innocents, Mr. MacGlendon. Nor are you."

"What is that supposed to mean?"

"It will all become clear in time." Chou looked at his watch. "There will be time to examine mutual motives during the first meeting of the consortium."

"When is the meeting?"

"You will be informed. In good time. You will be contacted."

"Will it be in Paris?"

"You will be informed," Chou said. He reached into his pocket, took out a tiny tissue-wrapped package.

"Why all the mumbo jumbo? Why all the secrecy?"

"There are enemies, Mr. MacGlendon. China, when it comes to exist as a major world power—not alone by the size of the country or the numbers of its people, but by the volume of its industrial output—will realign the balance of geopolitical power of the world as we know it today. All of this within five years." Chou continued: "Russia is the enemy; China is the sleeping, shackled giant on its borders. In five years China will awaken, reenergized, and break the chains of underdevelopment. And Taiwan is another enemy. In five years we will outproduce them at lower prices. They'll be strangled into submission, become a part of the People's Republic. The giant will be whole again. Even your own country, Mr. MacGlendon, is an enemy. In five years your own country's productivity will have withered away in face of low-priced competition, competition unhampered by laws of the so-called democracy. It is a pattern that began many years ago. Even now you cannot compete with the Japanese automotive industry or the steel production in Japan. In five years China will even be able to outproduce Middle East oil."

Chou stood up, unwrapping the little packet in his hand, pouring out a snaking chain of shimmering gold with a carved jade medallion suspended from it. "Even at this minute our enemies are trying to stop us, break the back of the consortium before it begins. Russian agents have followed me here. They have you under constant surveillance. Trust no one," he said. "I warn you. Trust no one. Everyone will try to stop the consortium." He stooped to the floor, picked up a bright red silk sample covered with white Chinese calligraphy, perfect brush work forming vertical lines. Cupping the chain and medallion in a clenched fist, he held the outstretched silk sample in front of MacGlendon. "Do you recognize any of these words?"

"I don't know any Chinese."

"Think back," Chou instructed him. "Think back many years." MacGlendon's memory was blank. "When we first met in Chicago," Chou continued, "there was a letter opener on your desk. It is shaped like a Chinese dagger. The ivory handle is inlaid with jade characters." He lowered his chin to hold the silk sample in place and with his free hand, pointed out a vertical series of brushwork calligraphy.

MacGlendon said, "A friend is nearby." He thought for

a moment. "My mother gave me that dagger many years ago. She lived in China for a long time right before and right after World War Two. She was married to an American diplomat stationed with Chiang Kai-shek in Peking—Blair Brewster."

Chou raised his chin, released his hold on the silk sample: it slithered to the floor. He walked behind MacGlendon, fastened the gold chain around MacGlendon's neck, came around in front of him, and centered the jade medallion at the base of MacGlendon's throat. The disc was tiny against the breadth of his chest. "The same words are carved on this piece of jade: 'A friend is nearby.' Only eight of these medallions exist: one for each member of the consortium."

"You knew Blair Brewster?"

"Those were tumultuous years for China. We had at last driven the Japanese back into the sea, then we turned on each other: the Maoist forces from the north against Chiang Kai-shek and the Imperialists in the south. Blair Brewster and I crossed paths during those times."

"You knew my mother?"

Chou nodded, held back any expression of his feelings.

"I know about my mother," MacGlendon said. "I know what she was like then. When I was in college, I studied the transcripts of the McCarthy trials, read the coverage in old newspaper files. I know what McCarthy tried to do to my mother, what kind of a woman they tried to make her out to be."

"Your mother was very beautiful," Chou said. "I remember that."

"The publicity finally drove Brewster to suicide. McCarthy killed him. Did you know *that?*"

"Those were confused, unhappy years," Chou said, then added, "for all of us." He looked at his watch again. "Time runs out for me, and it just begins for you. It begins this morning. The first contact is at eleven o'clock. You must be at the appointed place." He handed MacGlendon a slip of paper. "The address is written there. Memorize it and then destroy the paper before you leave this room. Go alone. Our people will protect you; there will be no need for your own bodyguards."

"Who do I meet?"

"You will meet a young woman. The address that I have given you is an art gallery. The young woman is an artist. Her paintings are on exhibition there. She will be expecting you. You will talk to her of making special designs to be printed on silk fabric to be manufactured in China. Have patience, Mr. MacGlendon. Trust the girl and the people she leads you to."

"Will you be at the meeting?"

"I return to China today. Perhaps when you come to China," he began, then thought about the enemy agents who had dogged him from the Waldorf to Kennedy Airport and who had been secreted as fellow passengers on the transatlantic flight and were waiting for him now in the lobby of the hotel. "When you're in China . . ." But again, he did not finish the sentence.

"The meeting will be in China?" MacGlendon asked.

"Patience, Mr. MacGlendon. You must learn to be patient."

"I didn't get where I am by being patient. I'm the ugly American and I'm proud of it." He unfastened the chain from the back of his neck and threw it on the floor. "The ugly American may be ugly, but he's straightforward. A deal is a deal. A handshake is a contract. There's no mumbo jumbo of jade medallions or ivory-handled daggers."

"Your mother," Chou said, "as I remember her, was a

woman of great grace and delicacy, yet none of that hampered the brilliance of her mind or dulled her perceptive capabilities."

"I'm on the hook for two hundred million bucks, Mr. Chou. Talk to me about money. Talk to me about the details of the consortium. I already know what kind of woman my mother was."

Death of a Salesman

A California-based dress designer, arriving in Paris from a vacation in the south of France to attend the Prêt-à-Porter, had just registered at the reception desk of the Hôtel Guy-Louis Duboucheron on the Rue des Beaux-Arts and was threading his way through the elegant lobby. The designer was sun-tanned and was accompanied by a black-leather-clad tough he had picked up in a bar in Nice. He considered the hotel to be his spiritual second home and stayed there whenever he came to Paris. He liked the opulence of the tiny rooms padded in velvet or satin and cluttered with antique furniture and chic bric-a-brac. "I'd kill for the *boiserie* in the elevator," he had confided to the black-leathered tough.

As he always did when he first checked into the hotel, the designer stopped in the center of the eight-story rotunda, enjoyed the spotlight of the sun coming through the clear glass dome, and put a loving arm around the hard, leathered shoulder of his friend, pointing up to the circular core of ornate French architecture, the endless ring of Louis Quinze ironwork balustrades and balconies on the circular stairs.

A hurling body appeared silhouetted against the ceiling,

plummeting, and squashed, facedown, on the intricately patterned marble floor, narrowly missing the two men but spattering them with blood.

The dress designer screamed.

For a moment this first scream hung in mid-air in the hollow void of the rotunda. Then the sound ascended, increasing in volume as it ricocheted against the glass dome and bounced back again to the marble floor. The designer's scream started a chain reaction of screams as hotel guests burst out of their rooms, looking down at the horror below.

The designer fainted. The black-leather-clad tough touched his finger to a spot of blood that had splattered his face, put his finger on the tip of his tongue, tasted the blood, and then licked it clean.

When the first scream sounded, MacGlendon was just out of the shower, toweling himself dry with the thick, luxurious bath sheet. The first scream from the lobby barely penetrated his preoccupied consciousness. But when other screams followed, he wrapped the towel around his waist, bolted through the bedroom and living room, saw that the Chinese man and the sample case were gone; then he ran into the hotel corridor.

Before reaching the railing, his bare feet slammed into a hard object. He stumbled, was thrown off balance, but braced himself against the iron rail. He looked down and saw the heavy, black sample case. At the base of the vertical shaft of the rotunda he saw a battered corpse lying facedown, arms extended—a flowing pool of blood beginning to encircle the body.

The immediate problem was to hide the sample case before it could be connected to the Chinese man and then linked to MacGlendon. Except for the fat *femme de chambre* bent over the balcony, there was no one in the corridor.

MacGlendon lifted the case, wondering how the wiry Chinese man had had the strength to carry it, then backed up and placed it inside his suite.

He stopped to rub the pain from his foot, then went back and stood next to the *femme de chambre* who rattled off a string of French words he didn't understand. Across the circle of the rotunda, directly opposite MacGlendon, a German rock star— MacGlendon had seen his photograph on the cover of a recent issue of *Der Spiegel*— sauntered out of his suite in neon-green French briefs. He glanced down at the confusion, across to MacGlendon to momentarily appraise him, then down to the spattered body without registering any emotion on his chiseled Germanic face. Two girls followed the rock star out of his suite; both had long, stringy blond hair and both had arms crossed over their bare breasts. Their flimsy cotton bikini underpants only thinly veiled full bushes of black pubic hair. A third, almost identical girl hovered in the open door. MacGlendon closed his eyes, shutting out the view of the near-naked girls in the corridor. But he could see cunt with his eyes shut, taste it in his dry, closed-lipped mouth; and even though his hands were clenched, he could feel his fingers fingering it.

He shook his head to clear it of distracting thoughts. The death of the Chinese silk merchant dispelled his last doubts of the imminence of danger and increased the dimensions of the importance of the Chinese project.

Down below, the police were arriving and adding to the frenetic activity around the flattened corpse. Loud, insistent wails of sirens became deafening as other police cars tried to penetrate the narrow, traffic-jammed Rue des Beaux-Arts. MacGlendon heard heavy breathing beside him. It was the New Man. He had run up the eight flights of circular stairs.

"You okay, Gus?"

MacGlendon nodded.

"The Chinaman? Big Red said that you had a Chinaman in your suite."

Again MacGlendon nodded.

"What happened?"

"I don't know."

"An accident? Are you sure that everything is all right?"

"It's fine. Go back and finish your breakfast."

"I was almost done eating. I'd just as soon stick around here. The joint is crawling with cops and kooks."

Other hotel guests had come out of rooms, ringing the railing, asking each other questions.

"Maybe you'd better get back in your suite," the New Man said, but MacGlendon did not move. The New Man crossed his arms over his chest, keeping one hand inside his jacket on the cold steel of his gun in the shoulder holster. He shouldered MacGlendon away from the railing, following him closely as MacGlendon went back into his suite. The New Man saw the sample case and began to reach for it.

"Don't touch it." MacGlendon did not explain.

"The cops will ask questions." The New Man waited for clarification.

"I'll handle it. Go back and finish your breakfast."

The New Man shrugged, hesitated, then began to walk out but stopped and said: "I'll be back at ten thirty. You have to be at the Prêt by eleven."

"Change of plans. Something has come up. You go ahead to the Prêt. I'll catch up."

"I don't like leaving you alone, particularly with what's going on here. Maybe I ought to wake up Big Red."

"Let him sleep. I wore him out this morning." He touched the New Man's shoulder. "Are you going to be in shape for tennis at four?"

"You bet."

"No going easy on the boss. You know the rules. Play as hard as you can. Sooner or later I'm going to beat your ass."

The New Man smiled as he left the suite.

As soon as he was alone, MacGlendon's body broke out in a cold sweat, a delayed reaction to fear. Death, which had been an abstract part of his life, was suddenly very real. In retrospect, reliving the exact details of this final meeting with Chou, recalling each word spoken and each gesture made, MacGlendon saw Chou in the new light of a man condemned to death and during his last hours adjusting the priorities of his life.

MacGlendon wiped the wetness from his chest. It reappeared like moisture in a soaked sponge.

Fear.

He went back into the bathroom, showered, and washed his hair again. After fumbling with the electrical converter, he got his dryer to work, styled his hair carefully, raised one arm at a time, enjoying the hot air against his armpits, lowered the dryer and moved it in a circular motion around his genitals, cupped his scrotum, and spread his legs slightly, tilting the nozzle upright so that the hot blast blew directly between his legs.

While he dressed, MacGlendon reconstructed his first contact that morning with the Chinese silk merchant. When he and Big Red had come in from jogging, there had been two men sitting in the shadows of the lobby. At first glance they were indistinguishable from each other: both Chinese and about the same build. But the man he knew as Mr. Chou stepped forward, held out his hand. The other man carried the sample case to the elevator and then disappeared.

Only one man had been on duty behind the reception desk, and there had been a hotel porter lethargically dusting furniture. No other personnel or guests had been around at that hour.

Knowing from previous meetings the Chinese man's predilection for covering his tracks, MacGlendon guessed that the two men had come into the hotel unnoticed and probably had not made any inquiries at the reception or concierge desk. MacGlendon decided that the Chinese man could not be linked to him without exhaustive investigation. He wondered about the other Chinese man, what his function had been. If he was a bodyguard, he had done a lousy job.

MacGlendon remembered that the calligraphed silk sample had been left neatly folded on the desk in the parlor. He went out, got it, and picked up the gold chain with the jade medallion and took the objects back to the bathroom where he unfolded the sample and hung it over the heated towel bar. Then he studied the characters incised in the jade, trying to match them to the calligraphy on the silk sample. He found the section of the design where the inscription matched exactly the intricate design of the jade.

A friend is nearby.

Fumbling first, he finally refastened the chain around his neck; then he took the silk sample, went into the closet, and stuffed it into the toe of one of the cowboy boots he had had custom-made at Cutter Bill's in Dallas. Except for the crumbled piece of paper with the address of the art gallery, these items were his only link to the factories in mainland China.

He would have to elude his own security staff, make sure that neither Big Red nor the New Man kept track of his movements.

The Flower Child

When the sun became momentarily obscured by a passing cloud or by a tall truck lumbering down the narrow Rue St.-Denis, Paula de Plyssy felt the cold air penetrate her wool-lined trench coat. Her reaction was botanic as she recoiled against the elemental change. She lowered her head, huddled her shoulders, crossed her arms, and tightened her legs together until the sun reappeared, and then she unfolded again, open to the warmth of it.

The Chinese silk merchant was five minutes late. He had explained that there was a possibility that he would be delayed, but his instructions to her had been explicit: wait ten minutes for him. Wait ten minutes exactly. No more. She looked at her watch again and sipped from the small cup of syrupy, sweet coffee.

The row of tiny café tables was blocked off from the busy foot traffic on the Rue St.-Denis by a barrier of wooden flower boxes, freshly painted green and orange, planted with late-blooming lavender chrysanthemums. Unconsciously, she touched one of the tight-petaled blossoms, her middle finger grazing the cluster of stamens at the center of the flower, disturbing the dry, dusty pollen. Her fingertip penetrated the stamen and pistil, plunged into the warm moisture deep inside the vulva of the flower. She closed her eyes, was aware of her own moisture, became absorbed in these sensual stimuli.

In five minutes she would begin walking toward the high-tech clutter of the Pompidou museum, following her usual route at her normal pace but not window shopping or stopping to talk to the few old shopkeepers who still survived from the days when this area had surrounded Les Halles. The Chinese man had repeated three times the importance of not stopping en route to the gallery.

At first, the silk merchant's contact had seemed a natural enough occurrence. When they had meet three weeks before, he had explained that he was in Paris in advance of the Prêt-à-Porter to work with dress manufacturers on fabrics for the next autumn collections. He explained that one of his friends had taken him to see the showing of de Plyssy paintings at the small gallery on an *allée* just behind the museum, confided that seeing her superrealist, macro-size flowers had been an emotional experience for him. "Particularly poignant," he had said, "after seeing the slapdashes of American abstract expressionist paintings in the group show at the main gallery of the Beaubourg. Most distracting, most disturbing to the eye. But with your flowers, one sees and feels the sensuous serenity of nature."

She had fondled the words in her mind: *the sensuous serenity of nature.*

"To the Oriental eye," he continued, "the flower is the most perfect creation of nature, the most exquisite delight to the eye. The Japanese, in their frenzy to Westernize, have lost their traditional reverence for the flower. But we Chinese revere our cultural heritage. The delicate flower is a symbol of that."

The American woman who owned and ran the little art gallery had spontaneously interjected an idea directed to the Chinese man. "Why don't you commission Paula to design fabrics for you? Wouldn't it be wonderful to see those exquisite flowers printed on silk?'' She was a brassy blonde, overweight and heavily made up, smears of colors ineptly applied over her eyes and blazoned across her mouth and cheeks. Her voice was midwestern flat, harsh sounding. "I'd love a long, flowing gown for myself. I can see it now: pale pink with the vine starting at my neck, snaking through my boobs, and a big passion flower right over my snatch."

The Chinese man seemed embarrassed by the bawdy language but intrigued with the concept. "An artist is an artist," he said. "I think that commercial application of their art is often offensive to them."

"A buck is a buck," the art dealer said. "Paula can use the money. What's so terrible about living with art? Or wearing it? Art shouldn't be an esoteric acquisition of the rich. I remember the thirties when art belonged to the proletariat. As in your People's Republic, Mr. Chou: art should belong to the people. That stuff about commercialism being offensive to the artist is bullshit." She touched the artist's arm, and the arm automatically recoiled from contact. "You think it's an exciting concept, don't you, Paula love?"

"It could be," she said.

"If it is not offensive," the Chinese man was smiling, communicating his understanding and sensitivity to Paula de Plyssy, "I would like the opportunity to explore the idea further. There are many manufacturers who would jump at the idea."

"Stay away from that couture shit," the art dealer said. "They make three gowns and that's it. Get into the mass market, get into the youth market."

It had started that way, apparently unpremeditated: an accidental meeting at the gallery, an off-the-cuff idea tossed out by the art dealer.

At the urging of the art dealer, she had even discussed

the business potentials with her stepfather, the Count de Plyssy. Since she had moved out of his house and into her own apartment, she rarely saw either her mother or the Count. But when she sought him out, to tell him she had been approached about the possibility of designing fabrics in China, he had been very encouraging about the project, had told her to keep him informed about the progress of the negotiations.

Early that morning the silk merchant had telephoned her from the airport to explain that he had made contact with a young American who headed a large conglomerate of retail stores, fabric mills, and manufacturing facilities. "As a matter of fact, he's in Paris now. He's on his way to China to explore the possibilities of opening manufacturing plants in Peking and Shanghai. I have been acting as liaison between him and the authorities in the People's Republic. This man has reacted most favorably to the idea of reproducing your flowers on silk for the garment industry. If it is agreeable, I have arranged for a meeting at the gallery this morning at eleven." The Chinese man insisted that she keep the details of the meeting secret but did not explain why. His instructions were mysterious but explicit: he went over them twice in great detail before he hung up.

Excited voices on the Rue St.-Denis brought her back to the imminence of the timetable. An overwrought motorist was out of his car, shouting and waving his hands at a truck driver who countered curse with curse without expending any energy. Paula de Plyssy looked at her watch. Another two minutes. Although the silk merchant had warned her that another appointment might delay him, she decided that she would wait another five minutes. A few minutes could not mean disaster, and she needed the strength of the Chinese man's understanding as a buffer against the American tycoon. To her, all Americans were like the art dealer: brash and abrasive. She had long ago stopped thinking of herself as an American, so completely had she assumed the mentality of the Parisian.

Three minutes after the prescribed time, suddenly hurried, she left a twenty-franc note on the table, the flimsy paper secured from the wind under the Bol ashtray, overtipping because she had stayed so long and spent so little. Huddled in her coat, she started walking down the Rue St.-Denis, reminding herself to walk at her normal pace.

Even at this time of the morning prostitutes were in the doorways, blocking the narrow sidewalk, some of them clustered in groups around the shops signed in neon with the simple explicative *Sexy.* From the Rue St.-Denis she walked across the Fontaine des Innocents, seeing peripherally the usual clusters of pigeons feeding in the square. She continued down the narrow Rue Berger and waited for the light at the Boulevard Sebastopol, then crossed at a slight diagonal, passing the Café Jardin de Beaubourg on the Rue Quincampoix where she often had a second cup of coffee. Before turning off on the Rue Aubry le Boucher, she stopped one store before the gallery to look into the window of an *antiquaire* and arrange her hair in the reflected image. She glanced at her watch once more and then went on, turned, and opened the door to the art gallery.

The sheer size of the American, standing with his back to her, frightened her. Yet against the sixty-square-meter painting of a rubrum lily blossom, he seemed in proportion —the oversize man and the oversize flower. Her silent entrance had been unnoticed. The American was absorbed in the painting; the gallery owner was harassing an employee in her high school French, speaking each word slowly and disdainfully as though only the mentally retarded could not speak or understand English.

When she saw Paula de Plyssy, she stopped in the middle of a sentence and walked quickly over to her. "Paula, love, you look delicious. This crappy French weather has put roses in your cheeks." She grabbed her hand and led her toward the American who was turning around, the expression on his face reflecting his uncertainty. "This is Angus MacGlendon, love . . . the man Mr. Chou spoke to you about."

Paula nodded, was warmed by the slight smile beginning on the American's face that gradually broadened into a boyish grin. Despite his bulk, Paula de Plyssy could see that this was a gentle man capable of handling fragile objects. He held out his hand, and she put hers into it and let it linger there, absorbing some of the heat of the man's body. "Gus was a little early. He loves the paintings, Paula. Loves them. I can tell." The art dealer grabbed his elbow, turning his body so that he had to look back toward the painting. "I've been watching you study that painting," she said. "There are two things I know in this world: one of them is great art and the other is men. Christ, I've devoted my life to both of them." Coyly, she inserted herself between MacGlendon and the painting. "I was reading your mind. You were thinking it's the first time in your life you ever wanted to fuck a petunia, isn't it?"

MacGlendon laughed. "I think it's a lily."

She looked back at the flower. "I'm blind as a bat without my contact lenses, and I flunked biology. But what's the difference . . . petunia or lily? The important thing is that you want to fuck a flower. Not since Georgia O'Keeffe has anyone made a flower look like that, breathed that kind of sex into it. That's what art is all about in my opinion: the totality of the emotional and intellectual experience."

He turned back to Paula de Plyssy. "It's remarkable work. You must be a remarkable lady." He smiled again to smokescreen his feelings. "I have to confess that Miss Goldberg is—"

"Phyllis, Gus. Call me Phyllis."

He repeated, "Phyllis read me correctly. I reacted instantly to the sensual qualities of your paintings." He looked at a canvas on an adjacent wall. "You have a remarkable talent."

The art dealer said: "You ought to hang it over your bed. Every bachelor should have one over his head . . . puts him in the mood." She slapped his arm. "But if I know my men, you're always in the mood. How about it, Gus? Am I right?"

MacGlendon smiled and said nothing.

Embarrassed by the hard sell of the art dealer, Paula de Plyssy sat on the center banquette, unbuttoned her coat, and opened the belt. "Are we going to wait for Mr. Chou?"

The art dealer and MacGlendon exchanged glances. The woman came over and sat beside Paula de Plyssy. "There's been an accident, love."

"What kind of accident? What happened?"

MacGlendon said: "No one knows, exactly. He was up in my suite showing me samples, speaking about the possibility of you doing some designing of fabrics, and then he seemed to become impatient, said we'd meet here later. I went in to take a shower and left him folding samples. When I came out, he was gone. I heard some noise in the hall, went outside, and there he was: he had fallen over the railing, down eight stories."

She shivered as she felt the cold that had been outside penetrate the heat of the gallery, and she hunched cocoon-like in her coat. Tears appeared in her eyes. *The sensuous serenity of nature.* "I hardly knew him," she whispered, "yet I feel the loss. It was as though he expected something like this to happen. He was so insistent that I keep this rendezvous and that I be exactly on time whether he came or not. He seemed to know that he was doomed."

"Well, look," the art dealer said, trying to break the gloom, "it's a terrible tragedy; but hell, accidents happen.

They happen all the time. The rest of us have to go on living. Right?" She put her arm around Paula de Plyssy, pressing her against her own body, and looked up at Mac-Glendon. "Mr. Chou was negotiating a deal for you in China. Is that right?" MacGlendon moved his head in a noncommittal gesture. "You're still going to Hong Kong, aren't you, and on to Peking?" This time the affirmation was clear. "Well then, hell, there's no reason not to pursue the idea, is there? A good idea is a good idea, right? Paula could do a dynamite fabric line." She looked to MacGlendon. He nodded, walked from painting to painting, studying each one intensely.

Huddled in her coat, Paula de Plyssy felt naked, as if her most private self were being exposed to the American stranger as he examined her paintings. No longer cold, she stood up to remove her coat and went to stand beside him to see what his eyes were seeing. He turned and studied the long, lean line of her body and the wide, heavily lashed gray eyes. "You're like your flowers," he said.

"Ils sont moi—je les suis."

"I don't understand French."

"They are me. I am them."

"You speak English without an accent." MacGlendon's statement was a question, an invitation to intimacy. "Are you interested in pursuing Mr. Chou's idea?" he asked.

"You think it's a good one?"

MacGlendon shrugged. "I can see men being turned on, but will women relate to it?"

"It is their essence: a thing of beauty by itself, not an object to be violated. It has its own existence, independent of men."

"Interesting theory. I'm no botanist, but it seems I've read somewhere that it takes a drone to spread the pollen around."

"Not always," she said. "Not every flower."

"Now I know what kind of flower you are."

"Yes. I am like that."

"Interesting" was all he said.

Their tentative communication was interrupted by the brassy voice of the art dealer. "Geoffrey, you old fart!" They turned and saw the woman embrace a rather short man who had just come into the gallery. She stood back to examine him. "What have you done to yourself? You look gorgeous. Fame and money certainly agree with you. If I had known you were going to turn out like this, my whole life could have been different." She kissed him on the mouth and tried to overpower him with the full mantle of her body. When he did not respond, she pulled back, reaching to straighten her hair. "I'm too late, huh? Well, I don't blame you. Who wants to fuck around with an old broad when you can have the pick of the Hollywood litter?" She took his hand and led him toward the back of the gallery. "Come on, I want to introduce you to two friends of mine. This lovely young girl is Paula de Plyssy. She did all these marvelous, marvelous paintings. She's a real talent, Geoffrey, not a late bloomer like you." They shook hands. "And this is an American compatriot of yours—Gus MacGlendon." As the two men shook hands, she said, "This is Geoffrey Plantagenet. None other. I knew him when . . . when he wasn't famous and wasn't such a handsome dog."

MacGlendon recognized the name.

The man said, "Is Gus short for Angus?"

"Yes."

"I knew an Angus MacGlendon once. Many years ago. When I was in college. The University of Chicago. Angus Andrew MacGlendon."

MacGlendon understood the intricacy of the Chinese design, none of it as happenstance as it appeared but planned with precision and Oriental patience. First the Chinese man who had known his mother in China. Now the celebrated novelist who had known his father in college.

"That was my father," he said and waited for the next move on the Chinese checkerboard.

The First Encounter

MacGlendon sat fully clothed on a chair placed at an oblique angle opposite the bed, watching her. There was an Oriental quality to the image of her naked body, erotic lines reminiscent of antique Japanese pornographic drawings elongated to Modigliani proportions in Paula de Plyssy's tall, angular body. The ivory-white flesh was opalescent against the deep rose-colored satin sheets, her body shaved hairless so that the mouthy slit at the base of the V was as bare and as innocent as that of a prepubescent child.

The hothouse heat of the bedroom was intensely humid and made more sultry by MacGlendon's own heat. Without diverting his eyes, he slipped out of his jacket, removed his tie, unbuttoned his shirt to the waist, rolled up his sleeves, reached down and took off each shoe, pulled off each sock. For a moment the hard marble floor was cool against his bare feet, but as he continued to watch her, his heat overcame the chilly floor.

From this angle he could see her directly and also see her image reflected in the full-length mirror that stood at the foot of the bed. The top of the mirror was tilted forward and a circle of magnifying mirror superimposed in the center of the tall glass enlarged her reflected genitalia into a macroimage when she spread her legs in near-orgiastic rhythm.

Her hand appeared as a giant insect hovering over the source of nectar, the long center finger extending to penetrate the blossom as the surrounding fingers fluttered like wings. Then the insect fluttered away, out of the circle of mirrored enlargement and again became an artist's hand: her hand.

MacGlendon unfastened his belt, released the exterior and interior buttons of his pants and carefully drew down the zipper over the bulge of his erection. By pressing his elbows against the arms of the chair, he raised his body, fumbled and forced his pants down and kicked the pants aside, momentarily feeling the cool of chintz upholstery on his bare skin before being overcome by the heat again.

Her fingers returned to the source, working to unfold the petals, the lips within lips, orange-pink gashed with red and shimmering with slow-secreting viscous moisture.

MacGlendon gripped the arms of the chair, fought back the magnetic forces of his own sensual needs and the lure of the naked woman writhing on the bed, undulating in a dual-directional rhythm. He tore at the constraint of his shorts. His penis sprung free, purple with the force of burgeoning blood. The sound of his own internal voice, warning him against the dangers, receded into silence. He was the suicidal man standing on the edge of a precipice hopelessly drawn to the chasm below.

He stood in front of the full-length mirror at the foot of the bed, blocking out the reflected image of her genitals with the fleshy reality of his body. Her eyes widened: horror replaced pleasure. Her body froze motionless. Her self-stimulating hands went up to cover her eyes, blocking out the sight of him.

MacGlendon dived forward, lessening the impact of his

weight against her by flattening his hands against the soft mattress to absorb the shock.

She screamed in terror, took her hands away from her eyes and clawed at his face with long fingernails—a cornered, desperate animal fighting an oversize predator. The wordless horror in her eyes stabbed his body with a shattering chill. He backed off, stood again at the foot of the bed, and felt the pleasure-pain of the claw marks on his face, touching his cheeks.

MacGlendon retreated to the lair of the chintz chair, his erected heat still unexpended, and watched transfixed as the other animal on the bed slowly recovered from the trauma of attack, flesh gradually melting from the rigidity of self-defense to the soft, undulating rhythm of pleasure.

Their orgasms were simultaneous. With their bodies three yards apart, their orgasms were explosively alike in sound and depth, their movements contrapuntal. The spasms subsided slowly.

For Paula de Plyssy there was a depth of sensation and release she had never felt before. It was the first time she had permitted an observer to this masturbatory ritual. The fact that the American had begun an attack, but had sensed her fear of penetration and then retreated, reaffirmed the affinity she had felt in the art gallery.

She slipped out of the smooth, satin sheets and stood tall, proud of her nakedness. She walked over to MacGlendon, dropped to her knees in front of him.

MacGlendon was slouched in the chair, his head back and eyes closed, his outstretched legs ramrod straight. His penis was still hard. Paula de Plyssy, coiled on the floor, deep in the protective fence of his legs, put her head in his lap, her cheek making contact with the sticky seminal fluid in the bristly hairs. She tasted it with the tip of her tongue, tasted a greater quantity, then mouthed it hungrily.

His hand touched the back of her bobbing head gently, then dropped limply as he let himself be sucked deeper into the whirling vortex that had begun with a Chinese silk merchant.

After he had ejaculated into her mouth, he kept his eyes closed longer than the aftermath of the orgasmic sensation lasted, deliberately keeping them shut against the reality of the sexual experience. He heard the padding of her bare feet against the cold, marble floor, the opening and closing of the bathroom door, and finally the sound of water running behind the closed door.

Weird, he thought. *Fucking weird.*

His hand was glazed with his own semen, beginning to dry and making his skin taut. He opened his eyes and looked at this hand. He remembered the forty-three nights of his marriage, then shook his head to clear it of those memories. He stood up and walked to the window in the half darkness, then opened the curtains to the afternoon sun and looked around the room in full light. None of her paintings were hung on the walls, which were bare white, unornamented.

Fucking weird. Yet why, he wondered, did he feel fulfilled, sexually sated? Last night, at the Saint Laurent party, it was a dry, hollow experience compared to this.

There was a wicker bookcase painted white and stacked with neatly arranged books, all of them in French, most of them cookbooks. Staggered randomly between clusters of books was a collection of porcelain flowers of varying sizes and small bowls of dried flower petals. He held one of the bowls to his nose. There was no smell.

And why did he feel comfortable, not like an intruder in this intimate place, as though it were permissible for him to enter this cloister and fondle the frail objects? *Fucking weird.*

On the lace-covered top of the light wood dresser was a

collection of framed photographs. He recognized the face of the largest photograph—an international film star—but he did not remember her name. He picked it up to look for an autograph. There was none. There were three little snapshots individually framed. All of them had been taken on the same day—the same little girl with the same man in a bathing suit holding her hand. The eyes of the little girl were unmistakable.

He lay on her bed and felt the cool caress of her satin sheets, aware of the vague scent of her flowery perfume. From this angle all he could see reflected in the mirror was the bottoms of his feet. He leaned forward, tilted the mirror to a higher angle, and lay back again. He made one more adjustment before the magnifying disk on the mirror reflected his own genitals. He spread his legs, studied himself. *Fucking weird.* He clenched his soft penis in his fist, felt an ooze of hot semen, and took his hand away.

There was a serenity of satisfaction lying in her bed in her nunlike cloister: no obsessive, continuing need to fuck himself raw and into the oblivion of an exhausted stupor as there had been the night before.

She came out of the bathroom, her nakedness natural to her, and lay beside him in the narrow bed. Words formed in MacGlendon's mind, but he could not say them. Instead, he said, "That picture on the dresser, it's a famous movie star, isn't it?"

"Yes. Andrea Standish. Isn't she beautiful?"

MacGlendon nodded.

"She's my mother."

"That's why you talk English without an accent. Is your father French?"

"No. He was American, too. My stepfather is French. My mother remarried when I was very young. I was brought up in Paris, went to French schools; but my mother and I always speak English to each other. My stepfather hates it, insists that we talk French in front of him. He understands and speaks English very well, but he says that we are French now and we ought to talk French." She laughed a little. "He's silly about it, but I can understand why. He's a very important man in France. He controls the manufacture of military aircraft. It's a most sensitive position. I think he's embarrassed to be married to an American: he isn't pro-American at all. But then, he's pro-nothing but France. He's descended from the old nobility. You know how those people are." She raised up on one elbow, looked down into MacGlendon's face. "Why aren't we talking about us?"

He laughed. "I never discuss business in bed with a naked woman."

"I don't mean business. I don't mean talking about designing my flowers on the silk." She sat up straight and crossed her hands over her breasts, rubbing her arms. "Mr. Chou," she said, "was a lovely man. I only met him twice, but I feel as though I've lost a friend. It's like that sometimes. You don't have to know a person very well to feel an affinity. Sometimes it happens instantly." She bent forward, stroked his moustache with the tip of her finger, then lowered her head and kissed him. "It was like that with us," she whispered. "Didn't you feel it?"

He looked over at the tiny clock on the nightstand. He didn't have to meet the New Man for tennis until four o'clock. "Yes," he said, "I felt it, too."

Her hands started their butterfly fluttering over his body. He closed his eyes to the sensation of her touch, remembering from time to time that this strange, beautiful woman was the link to his future, and behind the soft gray eyes, the Mona Lisa half-smile, was a fragile thread to a secret consortium and billions of dollars.

Le Sporting Club de France

The New Man was late. MacGlendon was suited-up, ready
to play, clutching his tennis racket by the handle, seated in
one of the French chairs along the sidelines, looking beyond the empty court that had been reserved for him to a
hard-hitting game in the next court. He tried to convince
himself that the New Man was late because he was unfamiliar with Paris streets and Paris traffic and could not speak
French. MacGlendon had had the club locker room attend-
ant phone the hotel to check for messages. There were
none, and neither the New Man nor Big Red answered the
room phone. The concierge did not remember seeing either of them come in or go out, but explained that the hotel
was very busy: the Prêt had started and a Chinese man had
been killed in an accident that morning.

While he waited, MacGlendon had time to sort out and
examine his feelings, ask himself questions, and trace the
Chinese puzzle that had started with the silk merchant and
his unfinished words of warning. Paula de Plyssy was somehow a vital part of it. The man he had met in the art gallery,
the novelist Geoffrey Plantagenet, was another piece of the
puzzle. So was the brash, blond American art dealer. *And
what about the New Man?* While he waited for him, Mac-

Glendon wondered if he was another player, one more person who was not what he appeared to be. He should have checked the man's personnel records himself. In a case like this what was unsaid in an employment application was more important than what was stated. *Is that why he's not showing up?* "I think we both have the same problem." The voice was low-pitched, the accent Italian, the English learned in the British public school system. "My game has also not come. Everyone in Paris is late. It is perhaps the impossible French traffic." The man himself was short and wiry; he appeared unmuscled until he moved, and then the musculature defined itself under his sun-tanned skin. "If you wish, we could warm up until our games appear." He nodded his head toward the empty court. "It is reserved for you?"

MacGlendon nodded, sized up the small man, guessed he was a powerhouse player. "Good idea." He held out his hand. "Gus MacGlendon," he said.

"Renzo Crespi." The handshake was firm, brief, businesslike.

Both men started slowly, noting each other's strengths, probing for weaknesses—like first-time lovers tentatively embracing. The strokes of the racket became stronger and more furious as the men became surer. Then gradually the Italian began placing his shots, making MacGlendon run from side to side, race toward the net to return a short shot and then deep to return an overhead power drive. Mac-Glendon sweated profusely, breathing heavily from the exertion. The Italian stayed dry, immaculate, seemingly expending no energy in the intense volleys.

Distracted by a figure standing at the side of the court, MacGlendon missed an easy shot and stopped mid-court, then recognized Big Red standing near the net. MacGlendon held up his hand to call time out as he walked up to the net, took his towel from the post, then wiped his face and arms, stepping toward the bodyguard as he was doing it. Big Red started talking immediately. MacGlendon touched his shoulder and frowned to stop the words. He led him off to the side of the court where they sat together in the spectators' chairs. MacGlendon's face showed no emotion as the rush of words came out of Big Red in a hoarse, emotional whisper.

The Italian had turned to watch the doubles game in the adjacent court and seemed to pay no attention to MacGlendon and Big Red. But even while he listened, MacGlendon's eyes stayed on the Italian. MacGlendon asked Big Red three questions. Big Red nodded affirmatively to each one. MacGlendon put a consoling hand on the bodyguard's arm and told him to go back to the hotel. Big Red argued. MacGlendon insisted. Reluctantly, he left the court and MacGlendon walked to the net and draped the towel back over the post. The Italian came forward. "My game is not coming. He's been delayed at Porte de Versailles," Mac-Glendon said. "If you like, we could play a few sets."

"I am sorry, but I am also glad. I think we will make an interesting match." The Italian smiled. "We are warmed up enough, yes?"

MacGlendon nodded and picked up three tennis balls. He put one in his pocket, held one in his hand, and with his racket bounced the other ball against the court as he walked back behind the line.

The Italian beat him three sets: six–four, six–two, and six–love.

When they were out of the shower, drying themselves in the narrow aisle between two rows of old wooden lockers, MacGlendon said, "It's time you told me what this is all about." He wrapped the towel around his waist and sat down on the bench.

The Italian did not feign surprise. He moved the towel off his body, using it to rub his wet head vigorously. Throwing the wet towel on the floor, he padded barefoot to the end of the bench, took a dry towel, put it around his waist, came back and sat next to MacGlendon. "It was meant to be a warning," he said.

"An innocent man is dead. My own man has a bullet through his shoulder. I'd call that more than warning."

"The stakes are very high in this game you play. You knew that when you began."

MacGlendon reached into the locker for his shorts, stood up and put them on, then sat down again. "The man who was killed was mistaken for me. My schedule called for me to be at the Prêt from eleven to two. I was scheduled to be in *that* place at *that* time."

The Italian shrugged. "I have many friends in Taiwan. They asked me to wait here for you and to warn you."

"If I had been on schedule, gone to the Prêt as I was supposed to, you would have been waiting for a dead man."

He thought for a moment. "My friends in Taiwan did not mean to kill you. If they wanted to kill you they would have. They only meant to warn you."

MacGlendon stood up, put on his shirt, threaded his tie through the collar, buttoned each cuff, started buttoning up the center. "You are a specialist in warnings?"

"I do as I am told. Except that I do not kill unless my own life is in danger."

"It's in danger," MacGlendon said.

The Italian smiled. "I think not. You have no weapon."

"Bare hands."

"It would be ungentlemanly: two foreign guests in a very proper French gentlemen's club. It is not your style, Mr. MacGlendon. Nor is it mine."

MacGlendon slipped on his pants, then took his shoes from the floor of the locker and sat down again to put them on. "If your specialty is warning," he said, "suppose you begin warning me."

"It has been accomplished. My mission is done."

"Be more explicit. Tell me what you are warning me against. Tell me *who* is warning me."

"The suggestion is that you cut short your stay in Paris: cancel the remainder of your trip." He was dressing now and seemed bored by his own words. "Forget your business proposition with the People's Republic. Those kind of Chinese are always the same: not to be trusted. In the end you will thank us for keeping you from this involvement. It is like the mouth of a crocodile. The power is not felt until the jaws snap closed, then it is too late to escape."

"You're an economic philosopher as well as a professional warner." He put on his suit jacket, then took a comb from the inside pocket and squatted down so that his face was level with the small mirror on the back of the locker door. "I have a warning for your friends from Taiwan: I'm quite capable of running my own business. I always have and I always will. If *they* interfere, remind them that bullets fire in both directions."

MacGlendon put his trench coat over his shoulders. The Chinese silk merchant had warned him that Taiwan was an enemy. MacGlendon knew he was as outclassed here in the locker room as he had been on the tennis court. The Italian was too disciplined to reveal any information inadvertently. He turned his back on the man and walked down the long, narrow aisle of the empty locker room, aware of how good a target he made.

Just before he turned off into the center corridor, the Italian called his name, and it echoed in the empty space. He slowly turned and was surprised when there was no gun leveled at him. The half-dressed Italian was walking toward him slowly.

"Two things," the Italian said. "First, the new friends

you are making are not your friends. They will end up as the Chinese silk merchant ended. If you persist, you will also end that way."

"And the second thing?"

The Italian smiled, reached out, and put his hand on MacGlendon's arm. "Work on your backhand," he said.

Notre-Dame

A vintage Cadillac limousine was parked at the curb when MacGlendon came out of the Sporting Club. The uniformed chauffeur sat at attention behind the wheel, and a large man with a prizefighter's nose lounged on the sidewalk leaning against the door to the back seat, his bulk enclosed in a belted trench coat. MacGlendon looked both ways for a taxi, but there was almost no traffic on the remote street.

His hand thrust into the slash pocket of the trench coat, the man leaning against the Cadillac straightened up, walked slowly toward MacGlendon. MacGlendon's first instinct was to run, but he stood firm, measuring the hulk of the man approaching him. In less than twenty-four hours he had for the first time in his life begun to be concerned about physical threats. Before, his adversaries had been men of equal capital, matching maneuverable assets of public companies. Now, he was looking at the physical size of his adversaries and estimating the caliber of their weapons.

The man took an opened identification case from his pocket, held it in front of MacGlendon's face, and then quickly withdrew it. It was a U.S. State Department document issued to Francis James O'Connor and was accompanied by an official seal over the unmistakable photographic reproduction of his pushed-in face. "I'll give you a ride back to your hotel," he said. The grip on MacGlendon's arm was a steel vise. "You've had a hell of a busy day, haven't you?" He opened the door, pushed MacGlendon forward, then climbed in next to him, activating the automatic door locks. "You've worn out two of my surveillance teams. I had to send for replacements from my Stockholm staff. But don't feel bad about it. Nothing really ever happens in Stockholm anyway."

"What's this about?" MacGlendon asked as O'Connor was instructing the driver to go to the *quai* opposite Notre-Dame cathedral. MacGlendon repeated the question. "What's this about?"

O'Connor thought for a minute then said: "Treason. I guess that that's the bottom line. Treason." He smiled at MacGlendon. "You ever play football?" MacGlendon shook his head. "You're big enough so that you could have. I played for Notre Dame. Then I played second-string pro ball for a while. Was never really good enough. Had the size but never the killer instinct."

"One of the men with me used to play for Nebraska, but it must have been after your time."

"You and I are the same age," O'Connor said. "You're older by about two weeks: not enough to treat you reverently."

"What's all this shit about treason?"

O'Connor pressed the button to raise the glass baffle between the front seat and back. "That's what I want to know. What is all this shit about treason?"

"I don't know what the fuck you're talking about."

"Aid and comfort to the enemy," O'Connor said. "That's a quote from Article Fourteen, Section Three, of the Constitution."

"What enemy?"

"That's the damn problem, isn't it? When you've got a

fucked-up foreign policy, it's hard to tell from day to day who your enemy is. To a guy like me, trying to substitute chicken chow mein for Mom's apple pie is a form of treason."

"I'm doing legitimate business with the Chinese."

"It's a family tradition, isn't it?" O'Connor waited for a reaction. MacGlendon's face was impassive. He said nothing. "I've done my homework, Gus. I know a lot about you. Not only do I know the date of your birth, I know your blood type, your mother's maiden name, and your grandmother's maiden name. I know the date of your bar mitzvah. I mean that really knocked me out: here's a guy named Angus Andrew MacGlendon—you can hardly get more Scotch than that, can you?—and here he is getting bar mitzvahed in Skokie, Illinois. It's like me bowing to the queen of England."

"I was brought up by my grandparents as an Orthodox Jew."

"I mean it really knocked me out," O'Connor said.

"Okay, so you know everything about me. So what? What does that have to do with all this shit about treason?"

After his first meeting with Chou, working through a dummy corporation in Portland, Oregon, and using a major Washington, D.C., legal firm, MacGlendon had had the legal aspects of international cartels and consortiums researched. The information he had received was inconclusive, filled with shadowy, uninterpreted cases untested in federal courts. He had come to the conclusion that his position was tenuous and decided to play a wait-and-see game until the details of the consortium were made explicit.

"No guy who has made as much money on his own, as you have, can be that naïve, MacGlendon." The limousine had stopped across the river from Notre-Dame. The setting sun was reflecting on the rose window, making it colorless, without dimension in this light. "When I was playing ball at South Bend, going to school there, I always considered this cathedral as the home office: the place where it all started. I went in there for early mass this morning. The joint is sure run down." He turned his head away, looked directly at MacGlendon. "I'll level with you, Gus. It's all right to call you Gus, isn't it?" MacGlendon nodded. "Everyone except my sainted mother has always called me Pug. Even when I was a kid—like they knew I was going to keep getting my face bashed in all my life—everyone called me Pug."

MacGlendon said, "You were going to level with me."

"We know something is going on but we don't have any explicit details. We've got lousy intelligence in China. They've got it closed tighter than a can of beer. We do know that there was a lot of internal fighting for a long time after Mao died, a seesaw battle for power. That little guy, Deng Xiao-ping, seems to have won out. They really did a number on Mao's widow and her Gang of Four. The internationalists took control of China—their policy is play ball with the world. It's a very complicated geopolitical game plan. I, for one, don't trust their motives. Some of my high-up bosses feel the same way. We watch them as close as we can. Particularly this little Deng guy." O'Connor took a deep breath, slouched deeper in the cushioned seat. "Did you know that he was a crackerjack bridge player? Deng Xiao-ping, I mean? He was originally one of Mao's boys, but even Mao got pissed off when Deng was more interested in playing bridge than worrying about the people. Damnedest thing: In the old days he and your mother used to play in the same bridge tournaments in Hong Kong. I came across that information accidentally while I was checking something else."

"I have the feeling that not much you do is accidental," MacGlendon said.

"I do my job," O'Connor answered. "I'm good at it."

"You were leveling with me," MacGlendon reminded him.

"Well, we know something is going on and that you're part of it. There's a lot more. We've got Interpol feeding us information. The Chinese guy who got pushed over the railing this morning has been traveling around the world a lot, talking to some very big people. We don't have dates and all the names yet, but there's enough evidence to convince us that something big is about to happen." He crossed his legs, reached behind him on the bulkhead, and took a can of American beer from a paper bag, offered it to Mac-Glendon, who refused it, then tore off the tab and drank. "I thought maybe you could fill in some of the details; like names of the other members."

"I don't even know as much as you do."

O'Connor wiped foam from his mouth. "This light-beer stuff you see all those jocks advertising on TV is a lot of shit. You drink twice as much beer this way."

"We were talking about treason," MacGlendon said.

"I'm no fucking lawyer. I had a crack at law school once and blew it. But I was brought up a religious man, and I have a feeling for the spirit of the law. Morality, maybe. I'm a moral man. It has nothing to do with fucking or fooling around. I do my share of that. Maybe I confuse morality with decency. I'm a decent man. I believe in innocence . . . until proven guilty. Do you know what I mean?"

"No offense, O'Connor, but I'm not interested in your autobiography."

"You ought to be, Gus. Just a little." He held up a small space between his thumb and index finger. "You ought to be interested enough to know that I'm prepared to believe a man can become innocently involved with something illegal or immoral, but when he discovers that, he has choices. I'll cite you an example. Say that this Chinese deal appears on the up-and-up. You got into it with good faith.

Okay? Then somewhere along the line you realize that it's counterproductive to your own country's interests." He looked over at MacGlendon. MacGlendon was looking in the other direction. "When something like this happens to an innocent man, he has choices. He can withdraw, or he can play along and cross the line from legal to illegal. He's no longer an innocent man. Those are two of the choices. Right?" He waited for an answer, but MacGlendon remained silent. "The really brave man, the guy with balls, has a third choice: he can hang in there, destroy the problem at the source, destroy it before it can become dangerous to his own country. Get the picture? See what I mean?"

"I've got to get back to my hotel. I have a dinner date, and I need shut-eye."

"Frankly, Gus, I'm stalling. I'm giving my boys from Sweden time to get into position. In case you're having any delusions of getting cute, I'm warning you that you're being double-teamed. The Russians also are watching you, in case you didn't know." He leaned forward, tapped on the glass compartment with his beer can, motioned the driver to proceed. He bent his head and looked out at Notre-Dame again before settling back in the seat.

"You're way off base, O'Connor."

"I don't think so. It's a feeling I have. Like my sainted mother." The beer sloshed in the can as he made the sign of the cross. "She could always tell the day before when it was going to rain."

Respite

Patience, like a pinstripe, vested suit, was an acquired characteristic in MacGlendon, a financial establishment technique that went against the grain of his own innate aggressiveness. Patience was a device he was forced to use to accomplish certain business deals. Based on previous experiences, he had known from the beginning that negotiating with the Chinese would be a long and complex procedure: teacup after teacup of small talk diverting the main thrust of action into a tortuous, circuitous route and consuming precious dollar-producing hours. It took patience.

MacGlendon's natural instinct was to throttle information out of the players in this Chinese game. The Italian in the locker room: MacGlendon's initial instinct had been to beat him bloody and pound answers out of him! *Who had fired the shots at the Prêt and wounded the New Man and killed a bystander mistaken for MacGlendon?* But the rules said that MacGlendon had to cool his fury, have patience and settle for vague, thirdhand threats relayed from Taiwan by this slick Italian knitwear manufacturer.

And who ramrodded the Chinese silk merchant over the iron railing and spiraled him to an instant death? Russians? Chou had said that the Russians were the enemies. *Where the fuck are the Russians? Which ones are they?* And the brassy, big-boobed blonde at the art gallery knew some of the answers. Twisting her fat arm, slapping her around would get the truth out of her. *Easy.* And that effete, foppish novelist . . . that was no chance encounter, no accident that he happened to come into that particular gallery at that particular time. Geoffrey Plantagenet had been there by design—*Chinese design.* And that shit about having known MacGlendon's father in college. Plantagenet was the first man MacGlendon had ever met who had known his father. *Coincidence: my ass.*

Even the beautiful Paula de Plyssy . . . he could have fucked the truth out of her. *Why didn't he? Why did he feel different with her, transfixed into another level of consciousness?* MacGlendon blocked the resurging image of her out of his mind. *Love,* he reminded himself, like *fuck,* is a four-letter word.

Back in his hotel room, leaving a weary Big Red standing guard in the circular corridor, MacGlendon stripped off his clothes, felt the heat and tasted the bile of frustration. He reminded himself that these were the highest stakes he had ever played for, but he was bound by the house rules, and the house rules were Chinese.

What about the big jock flashing State Department credentials—Pug O'Connor? He was obviously CIA. And even O'Connor—a man molded, mind and body, by football and the all-American way—was playing a Chinese game: talking in circles, playing a soft offense when every indicator signaled a blitz.

MacGlendon stood under a cold shower using the practiced regimen of his adolescence to chill his body heat, regain the dominance of reason over emotion. Dripping wet, his teeth chattering from the cold, he went back into the living room and flipped through the stack of elaborate invitations from fashion designers and glanced through piles of telephone messages: mostly urgent calls from his Chicago office.

When the telephone rang, the overcultured voice said: "This is Geoffrey Plantagenet. We met this morning in Phyllis Goldberg's art gallery in Les Halles. Do you remember?"

"Sure."

"You have to forgive an aging man his indulgences in memories. It's been a day of . . ." He hesitated, laughing as he stumbled for words. "I was going to say déjà vu, but it isn't déjà vu precisely. You look so much like your father, it was shocking to me. It was as though time had taken a giant step backward and everything was the way it was then. You *are* aware of the amazing resemblance to your father, aren't you?"

"My mother has mentioned it."

"Tell me about your mother. I haven't seen her in years. That's part of the déjà vu. I've been thinking about her a lot: thinking about those terrible, wonderful days when we were young. I've been considering writing a novel about those years: the way it was in the late thirties and early forties. If I do write it, your mother will be the heroine. She's the perfect heroine. Physically perfect and perfect intellectually and spiritually." He laughed again. "I think you can tell by the tone of my voice that I was more than a little in love with your mother in those days. I think your father knew it and was amused by it. I wish that he'd have been wildly jealous. It was degrading to be amusing rather than threatening. But the reality was that I was a fat, acne-pocked kid . . . horrendously ugly. No one took me seriously as either a political entity or as a lover." Plantagenet was silent for a moment as he thought about himself. "What is your mother doing now?"

"She lives in New York, still at the Waldorf Towers.

Busy lady. Nothing changes with her. She's still beautiful. She looks ten years younger than she is."

"What does she do with herself?"

"Bridge and backgammon, mostly. She plays in a lot of tournaments all over the world."

"No more causes to fight for?"

"She has quite a bit of money now; has had since Blair Brewster died. Her crusades are limited to stray and mistreated animals. Nothing political."

"Money," Plantagenet philosophized, "makes Republicans of us all." He sighed as though he was indenting a paragraph. "I always meant to get in touch with her after that McCarthy mess and Brewster killed himself, but there was always one thing or another that came up."

"Most of her old friends kept their distance during that period. She understood. But she's perfectly safe now. She no longer has a political thought in her head."

"Pity," Plantagenet said. "The heroine in my novel won't end like that."

"I'll be anxious to read it."

Plantagenet cleared his throat. "I'm forgetting why I called you. Age takes its toll on all of us. With tennis players the legs go first. With writers it's the reality of the moment that eludes them. Are you free for dinner tonight?"

"I guess I can shake loose."

"And that young lady . . . the artist who paints those outrageously gynecological flowers . . . do you suppose you could bring her with you?" He laughed again. "I must sound like a dirty old man, but I want to look into her eyes and find words to describe them."

"I was planning to be with her anyway," MacGlendon said. "I'll bring her along."

"My suite at the Ritz. Eight o'clock. I'm on the Vendôme side."

MacGlendon hung up. The Chinese game continued. He

wondered what words Plantagenet would find to describe Paula de Plyssy's eyes: there weren't adequate words in MacGlendon's vocabulary.

MacGlendon computed the time difference between Paris and Florida, took out his black book, checked a number and then direct-dialed Miami. The phone rang seven times before a sleepy, gruff voice answered it.

"Tony?"

There was a grunt.

"This is Gus. I'm in Paris. Stop fucking whatever you're fucking and get a pencil. I need some information and I need it fast."

"You know what time it is?" the angry voice asked.

"You get double time for nightwork, Tony. Get a pencil."

In a moment the voice was back on the line. "This is going to cost you, Gus. I got something in bed with me that you wouldn't believe."

"With you, Tony, I believe anything. Now, listen carefully, I need a rundown on a man named Geoffrey Plantagenet." He repeated the name, spelled it out. "That's not his real name. He's a novelist. If you weren't illiterate, you'd know who he is. He went to the University of Chicago in the late thirties or early forties. He may have some Communist affiliations from those days. Check his publisher and his agent. Get as much poop on him as you can. Got it?"

"Got it," the man said. "Who else?"

"Andrea Standish. Used to be a movie star. She's married now to a French count named de Plyssy." He spelled out both names. "You can even check out the count but I doubt if you'll find out anything through your connections. Get back to me with a rundown as soon as you can." He gave him his telephone number in Paris.

Requiem for Dead Lovers

It was over now: the cathartic of tears had washed away the first impact of self-pity, the few hours of Nembutal sleep had dulled her grief, and Betsy Brewster was able to see beyond the reality of Chou's death and consider alternate plans of action.

The telephone call from Paris had come through at five thirty in the morning New York time. The harsh, nasal voice of Phyllis Goldberg, the Paris art dealer, reported Chou's death in a matter-of-fact flatness, repeating what she had learned from Angus MacGlendon and filled in with information from a connection at the French Sûreté. "Somebody must have pushed him over the railing. Eight floors." Betsy Brewster began sobbing uncontrollably. "Gee, honey, I didn't know you were going to take it this hard." Her voice softened. "I mean I know that you and the chink had a thing going, but I didn't think it was all that serious." While Betsy continued to sob, the art dealer put a cigarette into her mouth, patted the piles of catalogs and papers on her desk, trying to feel through the debris for a buried matchbook. Spotting a French assistant across the gallery, she pointed frantically to the unlighted cigarette, put her hand over the mouthpiece, "Get me an *alumette,* you asshole." With the cigarette finally lighted, she talked back into the phone. "For Christ's sakes, pull yourself together, Betsy. Decisions have to be made. Geoffrey Plantagenet is waiting. He wants to know if we proceed as scheduled."

In heavy breathing, the words separated by sobs, Betsy Brewster asked, "Who did it?"

"I'm not sure. Angus told me the hotel is swarming with police, but they won't find anything. It was probably the Russians. It's always the fucking Russians. You should know better than anyone. It's always the fucking Russians."

Betsy Brewster bit back the tears, fought off the fury. When she spoke, her voice quavered. "Tell Plantagenet to go ahead. The signal is still *go.*"

"Honey, you'd better think about this before you make any decisions. I mean, we've been waiting for so many years, another couple of hours isn't going to make that much difference now."

"The signal is *go.*"

"But we don't even know how much Chou told your son. Gus showed up here: that's all we know."

"Plantagenet is the next contact. Let him take over. Tell Plantagenet to go ahead."

"Look, Betsy, you're all shook up. People make the damnedest mistakes when they're in an emotional state. I should know all about that: I keep fucking up my life by making emotional decisions. Don't you think you ought to talk to someone in China or something?

"Anyway, I don't understand why you insisted on using Plantagenet for this. Today was the first time that I've seen him in years. With the hair transplant and the nose job, he does look like a new man, but I talked to him for twenty minutes and decided that he's still the same old schmuck he always was. Can you trust his judgment? I mean with Chou dead, it puts Plantagenet in a much more important position. Do you think he can handle it?"

In spite of Chinese objections she had insisted that Plantagenet be used as a contact with her son. Secretly, she had instructed Plantagenet to get her son interested in his dead father, romanticize the father to the son. When it was time for Angus to make a decision, she wanted him to have the idealized picture of his father clearly in his mind, be able to identify with him.

"Geoffrey," she told the art dealer, "has always been a little in love with me. Faithful as a puppy dog. He used to baby-sit when Angus was an infant. He cares about Angus. He cares what happens to him."

"I don't think that old fart cares about anything but himself. If I were you, honey, I'd play it safe and not depend on Plantagenet. You'd better call China and get somebody to replace Chou."

"Tell Plantagenet to go ahead with the plans we made." Then she added, "That's a direct order."

"Okay. But stay in touch in case you change your mind or anything." The ashes fell from her cigarette. "Girl talk, Betsy," she said, her voice softer, less brash. "I'm sorry about Mr. Chou. I didn't know you were going to take it this hard. Pull yourself together. You've been through this before. You, of all people, should know that life goes on."

The line to Paris went dead. Phyllis Goldberg had hung up. Betsy Brewster continued holding the phone, clutching it ferociously, letting the instrument absorb some of the shock of death. Then she began to cry again for Chou, and she cried for the other men she had lost by violence in the inevitable progression of history.

Time should have hardened her by now, conditioned her to tragedy; and in a way, she thought, it had. This was not nearly as devastating as the first time. Or was it a difference in depths of love? Had she loved the radical young MacGlendon so totally that no other love would ever be the same? It was forty-one years since he had been murdered, one of the young Americans killed in a Stalinist-plotted assassination attempt on Leon Trotsky. The young Americans had been bodyguard-secretaries to the exiled Trotsky in Mexico, working with him on the establishment of the Communist Fourth International. Trotsky had survived the first assassination attempt, but four Americans had died protecting him. Her husband died not knowing she was pregnant.

And while she cried for Chou, she also cried for Blair Brewster, reliving that nightmare when Blair Brewster killed himself, no longer capable of living with the mistakes of his own political naïveté or the constant pressure of McCarthy and the congressional investigations. But most of all, Brewster could no longer go on living with the truth of who his wife really was.

All the griefs were over now, cried out. Betsy Brewster was left with a hollow of loneliness. She dialed a number in Montreal. When a voice answered, she repeated a series of identification numbers and waited through a long series of clicking sounds as her call was routed through a serpentine network to the other side of the world. When the voice there answered, Betsy Brewster spoke in fluent Chinese.

The Vendôme Side

MacGlendon and Paula de Plyssy met again, by prearrangement, at the lobby bar on the Vendôme side of the Ritz Hotel. They met as strangers without any easy words to say to each other. In the interval since he had left her bedroom, the transforming magic of being near her had had time to dissipate. In that interval the recalled images of their encounter seemed less real, more of a dream. There had been time enough for MacGlendon to rationalize the impact she had made on him, to reduce it to a minor experience . . . *fucking weird.* A cold shower and a process of self-analysis had turned him back into a hardened man emotionally incapable of loving.

But now, being with her again, it was all back: the dizzying, irrational sensations, her scent, almost hallucinogenic.

They clutched each other instead of speaking and sat side by side in the deserted bar, the brushing contact of their bodies reestablishing the physical intimacy that had begun earlier in the afternoon. MacGlendon abandoned himself to the inexplicable force of being with her.

Big Red, exhausted and unshaved, stood an uneasy guard outside the bar, squinting into the wall-mounted glass cases of diamond jewelry dazzling under high-intensity lightbulbs. Then he sat tentatively on an ornate chair, testing its strength, finally letting his body relax and sighing with the weariness he felt. The woman with the boss meant the beginning of trouble.

MacGlendon was thinking about love, marveling at Paula's free-flowing, dark hair underlit with hints of fiery red, and realizing that no other eyes like hers existed anywhere in the world: transparent violet-and-gray irises veiling the light of another world beyond them.

She said: "I thought I would be embarrassed when I saw you again. There was time to think, and I thought what a fool I had made out of myself. There was time to think it all through, and I realized that I was being silly, that what happened to us was a spur-of-the-moment thing that didn't mean anything." She lowered her head, held his hand tighter. "But it isn't like that. It isn't like that at all." She raised her head, faced him directly. Her eyes questioned him.

"No," he reassured her, "it isn't like that." Aware that this woman was a baited trap, MacGlendon said: "It was a beginning. *Our* beginning." He heard his own words and wondered what complex series of mechanisms, hidden inside him, had motivated and verbalized them. "It was something that belongs only to us."

"You seemed to understand," she said. "I mean, without saying anything, you seemed to have understood the way I am."

MacGlendon could not think of what to say, decided not to say anything. He continued to think about love, remembering earlier conflicts. Suddenly, without knowing he was going to say it, he said, "My mother and father made love for the first time while he was handcuffed to a radiator." Surprised that he wasn't embarrassed by this revelation, MacGlendon laughed. "It was the first night they met. What I'm trying to say is that things begin like that sometimes—with no warning and no reason."

"You're a romantic, aren't you?"

"No one ever accused me of that before."

"Mr. Chou warned me that you would appear gruff and cold-blooded and that I wasn't to be put off by it. He said that you were really a very gentle man."

It was too soon, the thread between them still too tenuous to ask direct questions and probe her relationship to the Chou group. "I wonder, sometimes, what kind of man I really am."

"You're a very gentle man."

"That's not a very universal concept of me." He drew his hand away from her, picked up the iced glass of wine, and sipped it. "I was married once." He waited. "Briefly. Only three months. It didn't work out." He took her hand again. "Don't you want to ask why it didn't work?"

Paula de Plyssy shook her head, her hair flying in the violence of her reaction. "Questions spoil things."

"You don't want me to ask questions about you?"

"It's enough to be the way we are now."

"Sooner or later—"

She put her fingertips over his lips. "Later. Not now." She felt his tongue wet against her fingers, drew her hand away and closed her arms around her own body, shivering with an internal chill.

MacGlendon put his arm around her, rubbed his cheek against the silk of her hair, and whispered into it. "I've been lonely for so damn long. It takes time and I never give anything time enough. I'm always in such a goddamn hurry."

A trench-coated man, carrying an attaché case, hurried past MacGlendon, went directly to the bar. Big Red had followed him, taken one step into the area, hovered at the door. A Eurasian woman, huddled in a full-length sable coat, slinked past Big Red, joined the man at the bar, holding the fur coat closed at her neck. The bartender knew the man, had begun pouring a brandy as the man was striding through the room. "Welcome back to Paris, M. Bentley. Will you be staying long this time?"

The Eurasian woman reached over the bar, took an olive and placed it between her lips, and then sucked it in.

"Not long, Emile," Bentley said, wiping his mouth. "It's never long enough." He stalked back out toward the lobby, looking directly ahead, not appearing to notice Paula and MacGlendon huddled in the circular banquette. The Eurasian woman took another olive, performed the same ritual with it, then followed Bentley, walking slowly, putting one foot in front of the other like a showgirl on a runway. Even holding Paula protectively, his face against her hair, MacGlendon's eyes followed the Eurasian woman, his senses distracted by the lingering scent of her musk.

Big Red returned to his vigil on the ornate French chair.

"Only one question," Paula said. "Why was your father chained to a radiator?"

MacGlendon laughed. "I guess my father was a hothead. This all happened in the late thirties. They were all involved in some kind of radical movement. I guess it was a lot like college campuses in the sixties. Demonstrations. Sit-ins. All that stuff. They were keeping my father chained up because his life was in danger. He wanted to lead a demonstration. His friends had to restrain him. My mother makes the story sound very romantic."

"Is your father dead?"

"He died before I was born."

"The man at Phyllis Goldberg's gallery . . . the novelist . . . didn't he say he knew your father in college?"

"We're going to have dinner with him," MacGlendon said. "He called when I got back to my hotel. He invited both of us for dinner. That's why I arranged to meet you here. Plantagenet is staying here at the Ritz." He looked at his watch. "We're going to meet upstairs for a drink, but there's plenty of time." He signaled for the bartender. "We're going to have more wine."

Burrowing deeper into the curved hollow of MacGlendon's body, Paula said: "My real father is dead, too. He committed suicide. I was eleven years old." Her voice lowered. "He raped me and then killed himself."

Dinner at La Serre

"I first met your father in New York," she was saying, "and I ran into him again, quite by accident, in Spain. It must have been in 1938. Perhaps '37. It doesn't really matter anymore, does it? It was important at the time whether it was '37 or '38, but history capsules decades, dismissing years of anguish and rapture in one compound sentence." She reached into the wine bucket beside the table, took an ice cube, and dropped it into her wine. "In those days one ran into simply everyone *quite by accident* in Madrid. The Spanish civil war was rather like a gruesome cocktail party that one is forced to attend because it is *the* place to be. One was conspicuous by one's absence if one didn't show up in Spain during the war: that is, of course, if one was involved politically. God knows that your father was involved politically. He loved, ate, and breathed his political beliefs. So impetuous." She smiled at a memory. "And tempestuous."

The woman talking to MacGlendon was Angelica Boren, a sparse, bony, leathery-faced woman with close-cropped gray hair and gnarled, bony hands freckled with brown splotches of age. She touched MacGlendon's face, turned it toward her. "Are you like that?" she asked. "Are you as unrestrained and passionate as he was?" She hesitated a moment. "Do you fuck with that kind of ardor?"

MacGlendon felt the blood rush to his head. He said nothing.

"I don't suppose you do," she said. "You're from the generation which my generation is accused of inflicting hang-ups on." She touched his face again. "Don't fret. I understand that you're wildly successful financially. Acquiring money is a second-best gratification but better than no gratification at all. Pity. Your father's passion would have been such a lovely thing to inherit."

After drinks in Geoffrey Plantagenet's suite, they had moved on to have dinner at La Serre. The whole sound of the restaurant was New York: New York voices, garment industry talk. Plantagenet and Paula de Plyssy sat side by side on the banquette against the wall. MacGlendon and Angelica Boren sat facing them, seeing their own images and the crowded restaurant reflected in a mirror.

"As I said, I first met your father in New York. I was working for the Hearst syndicate at the time and getting ready to go on assignment to Spain. It was late April. I remember that vividly. I went to say good-bye to Siqueiros at his studio on Fourteenth Street. They were all painting banners and floats, getting ready for the May Day parade. Your father was helping Jackson Pollock paint something riotous on a streamer of brown wrapping paper. When your father understood who I was and that I was going to Madrid, he wouldn't leave me alone. He was so young and eager: not much more than a boy. His head was bandaged. I remember that. He had some kind of frightful experience in a dock strike. It got quite a bit of publicity at the time. Capitalist's son sides with striking workers. That kind of thing. Marvelous copy in those days. Your father was beaten up by his father's strikebreaker goons. Communist son versus capitalist father. The story was a sob sister's delight. It all happened, didn't it, in Scranton?"

"Erie," MacGlendon said. "My grandfather owned a fleet of freighters operating out of the Great Lakes."

"Then you know the story."

"I went to Erie once, looked at old issues of the newspapers in the library. I don't think that my mother even knew about it. He never told her."

"As I understand it, they were married a very short time, weren't they?"

"Less than a year," MacGlendon said. "I was born after my father died."

"Such a pity that you never knew him. What a divine man. He died so bravely." Then she added: "And in the end, uselessly. I always thought that Leon Trotsky was a buffoon: not really worth defending. Certainly not sacrificing one's life for. Don't you agree?"

"As far as I'm concerned they were all just a bunch of Communists. My father included."

She smiled at him, put her gnarled fingers over his lips to stop the flow of words. "Curious pattern," she said. "Your father defied *his* capitalist father by being a Communist. You defy *your* Communist father by being a capitalist. I wonder sometimes if it isn't all emotional rather than political. Perhaps you're more like your father than I first thought. It would be so lovely for you—being more like your father," she said.

There was movement behind them. MacGlendon turned his head. The headwaiter was easing the next table away from the banquette, allowing room for the Eurasian woman he had seen in the Ritz bar to squeeze through. She was still wearing the long sable coat, clutching it closed at the collar. Her face was like the mask of a Balinese dancer, frozen and unmoving in an expression of sensuality. The same man, looking directly ahead, sat opposite her, his narrow shoulders not more than a foot away from MacGlendon.

The woman released her hold on the coat, and the fur slithered away from her body, sliding down her bare shoulders and off her arms.

"Your father wanted, more than anything, to be able to fight in Spain." The journalist's voice droned on, but MacGlendon wasn't listening anymore.

The Eurasian woman's breasts were only partially concealed by a low-cut, loose-fitting, thin black dress and almost completely exposed when she leaned forward to reach for a carrot stick arranged like part of a bouquet in a carved ice bowl. A colorful Garuda was tattooed on her left breast, the claws of the mythical Indonesian bird encircling a bright pink nipple.

"Your father had this bandage on his head and it made him seem so vulnerable. Because of what had happened in Pennsylvania, he was a cause célèbre with the New York Communists. He finally did get to Spain, but when I ran into him again in Madrid, he seemed so shattered, so disillusioned by that Mickey Mouse war." She touched MacGlendon's arm to distract him from the Eurasian woman. "That's the difference between you and your father, isn't it? You're never shattered, are you? You seem so self-assured. Were you always?"

MacGlendon turned his head back toward the Eurasian woman, glancing at the Garuda clawing the pink nipple, then looked at the journalist. "So far," he said, "my track record is pretty good."

"I've decided that you're not like your father at all. With you I feel afraid—threatened, somehow. Your father, on the other hand, triggered instant compassion. He made a woman aware of her potential, both as a lover and a mother. I made rather a fool of myself over him. I was much older than he, but age is unimportant in a war: human needs are in such sharp focus. Bombs were dropping on Madrid, and we drank the raw gin that Hemingway kept in his hotel room. And the world was falling apart around us. I'm not making excuses; I'm trying to explain the way things were. Your father was so vulnerable. I tried to limit my instincts to maternal ones, but in the end, as it always did in those days, my cunt had its own mentality." She broke a piece of bread, tore away the soft doughy center, and gnawed at the crust. "Your father, as it happened, was an indefatigable lover."

MacGlendon reached under the table, removed Paula's hand from his knee, smiled across to her and backed up his chair, excused himself, and keeping one hand in his pocket to disguise his erection, threaded his way through the tables of the crowded restaurant, nodding to familiar faces, and bulldozed through the traffic of busy waiters to the men's room. Rather than standing exposed at the urinal, he locked himself in the toilet compartment, unzipped his pants, urinated and thought about corporate organizational problems until his penis became limp and retracted to almost normal size.

When he came out, Ben Brayden, the *Time* bureau chief, was splashing cold water on his face. "You still owe me, MacGlendon. I need that interview. I tried to reach you all day."

"Sorry, Ben. Today was a wild one. How about breakfast in the morning?"

Brayden was examining the condition of his eyes in the mirror above the sink. "What time?"

"I start jogging at seven. How about eight o'clock at my hotel?"

"You're imposing wartime conditions on me, MacGlendon." He smiled. "But eight o'clock it is." He dried his hands, fumbled for change, and dropped some coins in the plate on the counter. "Who's the chick with Ridge Bentley?"

"Who's Ridge Bentley?"

"The guy sitting at your table. The one with the Eurasian doll."

"He's not with us. They're at the next table."

"Hot-looking lady," Brayden said. "I almost didn't recognize Bentley since he cleaned up his act."

"I don't know who Bentley is. Should I?"

"Where were you in the late sixties, MacGlendon, shooting pool?"

"I was figuring ways to make it big."

"Ridge Bentley was making it big . . . even then. He was the silent brains of the Chicago conspiracy trials. He was the Yippie Bernard Baruch; sat on a bench outside the Federal Building and masterminded the action. Hoffman and Rubin and Tom Hayden were the wild-eyed fanatics. Dave Dellinger was the intellectual dreamer. But Ridge Bentley made everything work. He was the real brainpower of the dissidents. He looked like the rest of them, then—wild and wooly hair . . . a big beard. Dirty feet in sandals. The whole bit."

"Why the transformation?"

Brayden knocked his knuckle against his forehead. "Smart," he said. "Smart as hell: so smart he's scary. He saw the handwriting on the wall after Kent State and got rich in the seventies and cleaned up his act. Or maybe it was the other way around. Maybe he started looking like a men's cologne ad and then got rich. He's the American success story." Brayden looked up at MacGlendon. "Kind of like you, Gus, only the other end of the stick. Bentley is not going to win any Horatio Alger Award. He didn't go from ragged jeans to riches in the old-fashioned way. Bentley is more a man of his time than you are." Brayden thought for a moment, forming his words, testing a journalistic concept. "You're really an anachronism in your time. You came up the old-fashioned, straight-as-an-arrow way. Bentley is more relevant to the times. He has a terrorist mentality.

He's a skilled terrorist technician. It's an interesting comparison of dynamos."

"Are you going to use that angle in your story?"

Brayden laughed. "In the evening," he began, then looked at his watch, "usually about this time, the world becomes very clear to me. I have the clarity of vision which gives a man brilliance. Unfortunately, the booze that creates the clarity reverses the action at some point and dulls all the senses." He touched MacGlendon's arm. "The chances are better than ever that when I wake up in the morning and tough my way through a hangover, I won't be able to remember how brilliant I was at this moment."

"I'll remind you," MacGlendon said. "Breakfast at eight. Be on time. I have a full day."

When MacGlendon came back to the table, Ridge Bentley had moved over, to occupy the vacated chair next to Angelica Boren and was talking to Plantagenet. They were all so engrossed in listening to Bentley that not even Paula looked up while MacGlendon stood awkwardly in the aisle. To get out of the way of an elaborate dessert cart being wheeled through the narrow aisle, MacGlendon sat down in Bentley's empty chair and faced the Eurasian woman who was crumbling a piece of bread and nibbling at the crumbs from her long, talon-nailed fingers. Her expression did not change as she looked at MacGlendon. He smiled, shrugged his shoulders, cocked his head toward Bentley to indicate his dilemma. She leaned forward, speared a rosette of butter, making no effort to conceal her exposed breasts. MacGlendon was transfixed with the undulating flight of the Garuda as the Eurasian woman moved. His penis was erect again.

Finally, Bentley finished his story and stood up. He shook hands with Plantagenet, bent down and kissed Angelica Boren's leathery cheek and took Paula de Plyssy's hand and locked his hand with it in a comradelike vise. MacGlendon stood up, and the two men were body to body in the narrow space between tables, close enough so that Bentley was aware of MacGlendon's erection. They sidestepped into the aisle, changed places without speaking to each other.

Plantagenet had begun a reminiscence of an experience in Hollywood. The women were so enraptured that neither looked over to acknowledge MacGlendon's return.

Maybe, he thought, the Italian tennis player's advice was good. Improve his backhand and get out while there was still time. The Chinese silk merchant had ensnared him in a tangled web of uncoincidental coincidences. He had lived his whole life without ever meeting anyone who had known his father. Now there was Plantagenet and Angelica Boren who had both known him well. No coincidence. And Paula, like a Venus's-flytrap, exuding a drugging aura, ensnaring him into an experience in which he could not separate the emotional and sensual into distinct entities—entities to be dealt with one at a time. His instinctive reaction to Bentley was as an opponent. MacGlendon's Wall Street smarts had equipped him to smell out an adversary even during a casual introduction.

And the Eurasian woman was no accident, either. He glanced over at her. She had been custom-designed to slip over his cock. She was the only element of the fragmented puzzle about which MacGlendon had any certainty. He was going to fuck her until the expressionless mask of her face cracked in pain or pleasure.

MacGlendon reminded himself of the billion-dollar stake of the factories in China. He turned to listen to the end of Plantagenet's story: was ready to continue playing the game and to watch the actors act out their parts.

A Long Night: Beginning

Paula de Plyssy would not let MacGlendon come up to her apartment. While the taxi waited at the curb, they sat on a bench in a sheltered section of the courtyard of the apartment building, near the concierge's door. "I need time to think," she explained. "My whole life has been structured one way, and now in one day all that structuring has fallen apart. I need time to think about everything." She looked up into the clear night, laughed a little. "This should all have happened to me when I was eighteen years old and I could run to my mother's room and cry in her arms and listen to her advice." She huddled deeper in the warm hollow of MacGlendon's body. "But things were never like that between my mother and me."

"It has to be tough having a movie star mother," MacGlendon said. "Half the men in the world were madly in love with her—jerking off to pictures of her in magazines. It has to have been a tough thing to grow up with."

"But it wasn't like that. She kept me sheltered from most of that. I didn't know until I was quite grown up how famous she was—or had been. My real father was a film writer—he was blacklisted for being a Communist sympathizer, could never get a job after that. I used to blame my mother for walking out on him. You've read about Lillian

Hellman, about how she stuck to Dashiell Hammett through all those black years—supported him emotionally and financially. My mother should have been like that. My own life would have been so different. My father wouldn't have gone raving mad."

"None of us can change who his parents are—or the way they are—or what they did," MacGlendon said. "It's like a geometric theorem: there are certain given, irrefutable factors. The problem has to be solved on the basis of those given factors."

"I never wanted a man to be a given factor in my life. I thought I had solved all my problems by being self-contained, self-sufficient. I've trained myself to be everything I need." She kissed him suddenly, open-mouthed and hungrily. When she pulled away, she said, "You've spoiled all that for me." She shook her head violently. "I don't want to be like my mother. I don't want to be a sexual commodity on the marketplace, incomplete unless a man wants me."

"I used to think that no one is complete unless someone wants him. I was married once," MacGlendon began, and then he didn't say any more.

"You told me that earlier."

"Did I? I forgot."

"It must have been very shattering for you," she said, and when MacGlendon began to answer, she put her hand over his mouth. "I don't want to know anything. It's all too much, too quickly." She stood up, ran across the brick paving, her spike heels clattering as she ran, and stood in front of the door to her building, blowing a kiss into the soft wind.

MacGlendon waited on the bench until he saw the light go on in her apartment, then watched as she opened the tall windows and stepped out on the balcony. When she saw that MacGlendon was still there, she stepped back inside for a moment, then came out with a single flower and flung it over the railing. Then she backed up inside, drew the heavy draperies closed. MacGlendon picked up the flower, put it to his nose, smelled the waning fragrance of it, and told himself, *You're acting like a fucking adolescent.* But in spite of his own warning, with the flower held high in his outstretched arm, he leaped straight into the air and laughed at himself when he thudded flat-footed against the pavers. *Fucking adolescent.*

The taxi had disappeared from the curb. The familiar hulk of Big Red appeared from the shadows across the street. "You're losing your touch, Boss. I figured you'd be shacked up there for a couple of hours. I let the taxi go."

"It's a beautiful night," MacGlendon said, putting his arm around Big Red's shoulders. "Let's walk a while."

"The New Man was released from the hospital. He's got his arm in a sling, but otherwise he's taking it pretty well. All in a day's work, I guess."

While they walked down the narrow Left Bank street, a car started up behind them, creeped along without turning on its headlights. In the shadow of a doorway at the end of the block, unseen by either Big Red or MacGlendon, a nondescript man whispered into a high-powered walkie-talkie.

A Long Night: The Analytical Hour

The Chinese merchant's silk sample was spread on the floor of his hotel suite. The delicacy of the Chinese calligraphy was serene and mystical. MacGlendon studied the mysterious words woven into the fabric, thought about cunt, and saw an image of it replacing the vertical calligraphy. Remembering the conversation with Angelica Boren, he wondered about his father's sexuality, blamed heredity as the source of his own satyriasis.

Looking at the time on the electrified antique clock hung on the upholstered wall, he checked for accuracy against the Seiko world-timer on his wrist, then pushed the button on his watch that flipped the hours back to Chicago time. Picking up the phone, he direct-dialed his private line that had network extensions to his key personnel.

His secretary said, "Are you all right?"

"I'm in good shape."

"We've all been worried sick. What happened at the Prêt? We heard that there was shooting."

"Somebody went berserk. I wasn't even there. The New Man got winged in the shoulder, but he's all right. His arm is in a sling, but he's back on the job."

"We heard a rumor that somebody was killed."

"An innocent bystander," he said, assessing his own responsibility for that death. "It was a buyer from North Africa. It could be one of those PLO things. The police are investigating."

"I'm so relieved."

"What's happening there?"

"It's been a madhouse since the rumors started. But no urgent messages. We had a lot of rain, and your caretaker called and said there's a leak in the roof of your house in Barrington and what should he do."

"Call a damned roofer."

"I told him, but he likes to hear it from you."

"What else?"

"Nothing that I can't handle. Sid Wolf is desperate to talk to you. Ditto Wally Armstrong and Craig Andrews."

"Usual or special urgency?"

"Somehow they all get frantic when you're gone on one of these extended trips. Every message I get from them has a death-knell immediacy."

"Put me through to Sid Wolf," he said. "Talk to you tomorrow night."

"You're sure that you're all right?"

"Perfect," he said. "Put me through to Sid. Have the others stand by." He waited through the mechanical clickings of the relay for his financial vice-president.

"Are you all right, Boss?"

"Fine."

"What happened?"

"An accident. June will fill you in on the details. What's going on with you?"

The man hesitated. "Funny damn thing," he said. "That Hard-Line Hardware acquisition was going like gangbusters. It was a piece of cake all the way. All of a sudden somebody is taking potshots at us. I had the financing all set at the Bank of Omaha. Duck soup. All of a sudden they want more financial information, some kind of crazy details

that seem irrelevant to the deal. It's a stall, a very definite
stall. It's the kind of jazz we used to get from banks before
we went big time. It's a lousy fifteen million. Petty cash
compared to the bucks involved in the deal. I don't understand it."

"What else?"

"The tender offer we had on the Broadway chain . . ."

"What about it?"

"Out of left field, Federated stepped in with a higher
offer. What the fuck do they want with the Broadway chain?
They've got enough of their own problems."

"What does Salomon Brothers say?"

"They're as baffled as I am. Where do they suddenly get
that kind of dough?"

"Back off," MacGlendon said. "The Federated offer is a
bluff to get more money from us. Call Sol and say you talked
to me and I said that we're pulling out and that if the
Federated deal blows and they come back to us, our offer
is lowered by three bucks a share."

For a moment the man did not respond. "Are you sure
you know what you're doing, Boss? We need Broadway.
It's the pivotal point in our expansion program. We need
that leverage. They know that."

"Back off."

"You're the boss," he answered. "What about the bank
in Omaha?"

"Play the same shtik. Tell them you spoke to me in Paris
and that I said we won't make the deal unless we get another quarter point."

"They're going to tell us to fuck off. I don't want to blow
that Hard-Line Hardware deal."

"Play it my way."

"What if they get scared and say okay at the original
terms?"

"No deal. I want the quarter point."

"Something funny is going on, Boss. I can't quite put my finger on it yet, but somebody is taking some high-caliber potshots at us. The Omaha and Broadway deals are the only two real pieces of evidence, but I've been getting funny calls from New York, veiled questions asking me to substantiate rumors that we're shaky—bit off more than we can chew. There's rumors about a billion-dollar deal that backfired on us. Do you have any thoughts about what could be starting this scare campaign?"

"Maybe you're just imagining it."

"I don't think so. My antenna is usually pretty good."

"Anything else?"

"Isn't that enough for one day?"

"Tell Wally and Craig to hold whatever they have. I'll talk to them tomorrow at the same time."

"Jesus, Boss, they've been on the horn every ten minutes to see if I've heard from you yet. They'll shit in their pants if they don't talk to you."

MacGlendon hung up, checked his watch again, searched through his pocket-size telephone book, then dialed another overseas number, studying the upside-down calligraphy of the silk fabric lying on the floor as the call relayed through the computer and rang in Chicago.

A gruff voice answered. "Dr. Goodman."

"How are you, Bernie? It's Gus MacGlendon."

"Gus? You sound funny."

"I'm in Paris."

"Anything wrong?"

"Not a thing, Bernie. Not a thing. Is your family fine?"

"You didn't call from Paris to see how my family is, did you? As a matter of fact, you're lucky to catch me. I'm between patients."

"I'm not a patient, Bernie." He laughed. "At least not yet. But this *is* a business call. I need some information. I'll pay you for your time."

"Go ahead. I'll start my meter running."

"In the back of my mind I seem to remember that you had something to do with conspiracy trials in Chicago. That Grant Park thing. Didn't you tell me about that once?"

"There was a team of three psychiatrists. I was one of them. I doubt if I would have discussed it with you. Ethics, you know. You probably remember it from the newspapers. I got a lot of press at the time. All three of us did."

"No, you must have told me on the golf course. I didn't follow the damn thing at the time. When did it happen? 1968?"

"The Grant Park riot was in '68 during the Democratic Convention. I wasn't called in until 1969—toward the end of the trial."

"In 1969," MacGlendon said, "I was more interested in investment bankers than Yippies. That was the year I was putting my shit together to go public. The whole thing is fuzzy in my mind. They were called the Chicago Eight, weren't they?"

"Seven."

"I thought it was Eight."

"It started that way. But they had tagged on the name of Bobby Seale to get a black man on the indictment. I don't remember the details, but early in the trial his name was taken off to be tried separately. Actually, his part during the convention week was limited to one speech made in Lincoln Park."

"Who did you testify for, the government or the defense?"

"Weinglass called us in as alienists for the defense. I didn't realize it at the time, but it was a calculated trick. All three of us, at one time or another, had been involved in some psychiatric therapy involving some member of Judge Hoffman's family. Somebody on the defense staff thought they could use that as a blackmail device. But as it happened, none of us ever testified. We gave newspaper and television interviews, but never got to the witness stand. You remember how Judge Hoffman ran that show? In my opinion he's the one who needed the psychological evaluation." Again the analyst cleared his throat. "Why is all of this suddenly important to you?"

"During that time did you ever run into a guy named Ridge Bentley?"

There was a pause before the psychiatrist answered. "Yes. Why do you ask?"

"Give me a one-word reading on him."

"Brilliant."

"Another word," MacGlendon demanded.

"Weirdo."

"What the hell kind of psychiatric evaluation is that?" MacGlendon repeated the word. "Weirdo." He let out a deep breath. "That's the kind of judgment a layman makes —a damn bigoted layman at that."

The doctor answered: "I could give you all kinds of medical terms, but you asked for one word. If you want, I'll go through all the professional mumbo jumbo, but it would still come out the same. Weirdo."

"Bright?" MacGlendon asked.

"Frighteningly so."

"Meaning?"

"In many ways Bentley ran the show. In spite of the armies of legal teams, strategy and tactics seemed to be directly under his jurisdiction. He combined the brilliant, conceptual legal mind with terroristic know-how. Deadly combination. He had a thing about being enclosed in a room. He sat on a bench outside the Federal Building during the trial. Rain or shine. Runners kept going back and forth from the courtroom with messages and questions for him. During the breaks the big guns would come outside and confer with him. He listened to the paranoia on both sides and had the genius of cutting through obfuscating emotional shit and putting his finger on real issues, distilling them into simple terms and making simple solutions obvious. And he also had that marvelous military capacity of turning defeats into victories." MacGlendon interrupted. "It's called making lemonade out of a lemon."

"The rumor was that he was the terrorist specialist, knew how to direct it and how to provoke it in adversaries. That's what I know about Ridge Bentley." He waited for the next question. After a long silence he raised the volume of his voice. "Are you still there, Gus?"

"I'm here. I'm thinking."

"About what?"

"About Bentley. I met him tonight. He sure doesn't look like a hippie or Yippie now."

"In a way, he didn't then. He had all the symbols—the beard, the long hair, the frayed clothes. But it was almost like a Yale man going to a costume party in Palm Beach. The basic elegance of the man surfaced through it all."

"Why a weirdo?"

"Just a feeling. Like you feel a cold chill in the summer —for no reason but real nonetheless." He waited, and when MacGlendon didn't answer, he said, "I assume you got the same reaction?"

"Is there a medical term for the way he is? Schizoid? Paranoid?"

"Maybe."

"I wasn't with him long enough to get a good reaction . . ." MacGlendon trailed off and in the lengthening silence the hum of the long distance wires grew louder.

"Well," Goodman broke the silence, "you called me from Paris to satisfy your curiosity about an old hippie you met at some cocktail party?"

"More or less," MacGlendon said. "I'm involved in a business deal with him. I just wanted a reading before I get in too deep."

"My professional opinion, for what it's worth, is that you may have at last met your match."

"Say hello to Betty and the kids for me," MacGlendon said. "Send the bill to the office. Mark it to my personal attention." Then he hung up.

A Long Night:
The Third Person

A crumbled brown paper carry-out bag, two empty Big Mac containers, ripped foil catsup packets, used plastic salt sacks and grease-spotted french fry cartons littered the marble-topped cocktail table in the parlor of the suite on the Rue Cambon side of the Ritz Hotel. Ridge Bentley poured the last of the white wine into the thin crystal glass and inserted the emptied bottle, neck down, into the melting ice of the silver wine bucket. He leaned back against the stiff sofa, studied the cuticle on the nail of his left thumb, pressed it back with the nail of his right thumb, bit at a hangnail on his index finger, and wondered about this man MacGlendon. Seeing him face to face was unnerving. The dossier and documents had not prepared him for the man himself.

Framed in the doorway, with the dark bedroom behind her as a black background for her luminous naked body, the Eurasian woman watched him. When he leaned forward to reach for the wineglass, she asked: "Aren't you coming to bed? I've been waiting."

He sipped the wine. "No," he said, "not tonight."

"Why not?"

"Because I don't feel like it."

"What are you going to do?"

He put the wineglass back on the cocktail table, did not answer.

"Are you going out?"

Bentley looked at his watch. "Yes."

"To one of those places?"

"Business," he said.

"You're lying. You're going to one of those places."

Bentley did not answer. The woman stroked the mystical bird tattooed on her breast; the nipple on that breast tautened. Backing up, she retreated into the darkness of the bedroom.

Bentley finished the delicate wine, turned the fine crystal glass upside down, and placed it beside the bottle in the silver wine bucket. Looking at his watch again, Bentley began to undress, loosened the laces of his shoes, and kicked them off, then stripped completely. His clothes lay where they fell.

In the bedroom he manipulated the complex switch for the lights, turning the ornate gold handle until the center light as well as the side lights on either side of the wardrobe were illuminated. The Eurasian woman turned in the brass bed, but did not awaken. Bentley took out a black-leather sling pouch, threaded his legs through the elasticized strings, and adjusting it up around his hips, inserted his penis through the opening; then he stepped sideways to look at himself in the mirror. The pouch, cupping his testicles, thrust his entire genital formation up and forward. He put on a pair of worn jeans, sucked in his already lean and hard gut to close them, then looked in the mirror again. A worn, lighter blue spot accentuated the outlines of his penis. He slipped on a black fisherman's-net T-shirt and over that a black, diagonal-front leather jacket studded with silver discs. He took a mass of keys on an oversize brass ring and put them into his back, right-hand pocket so that the bulge was visible through the pocket, then inserted a bright pink handkerchief behind them. He took a pair of black cowboy boots from the closet and tugged them on over his bare feet. The Eurasian woman sat up in the soft bed, the pink linen casting a rosy glow on her ivory nakedness. "Don't go," she asked. "You don't have to go out. Do it to me. You can do it to me. This time I'll let you. I promise. I'll even do it to you. Anything you want. I'll do it to you."

Bentley ignored her. He took a sparkling silver crash helmet from the shelf, roughed his hair, put on the helmet, then lowered the attached black rubber-framed goggles over his eyes and left the room without saying good-bye or turning off the lights.

Below, on the narrow Rue Cambon, diagonally across the street from the Chanel showroom, a large Harley-Davidson hugged the curb, engine running in a staccato, jerky idle, the high chrome handlebars gleaming in the reflecting street lights. The helmeted driver steadied the vehicle with one booted leg on the curb, the other outstretched, slung over the support of the handlebars. When the driver saw his twin figure emerge through the revolving doors of the Ritz Hotel, he took a last drag of his joint, then discarded it on the brick street and swung his legs into position, his black-leather-gloved hands poised on the handlebar controls. When he felt the weight on the seat behind him and the arms go around his waist, he activated the engine. A *vroom* of acceleration shattered the night as the motorcycle leaped up and forward, a futuristic monster attacking the night, leaving an afterglow of ricocheting sparks, noises of backfire trailing in its wake.

Ridge Bentley shouldered his way through the wall of black-leathered men, hearing familiar words spoken now in a foreign language. The odors of Montmartre were coated with a thin layer of perfume and scented pomade as well as the jock smell of sweat and leather. Most of the men were drinking beer from bottles, gesturing with the bottles as they mumbled to each other. American music, at full volume, blasted from the jukebox, but was muffled by the mass of the crowd and was almost inaudible except directly in front of the speakers. Bentley pushed his way until he was level with the sound; then the sound diminished again as he went toward a door at the very back of the bar, beyond the toilet.

The door to the back room was made of thick oak, faked to look ancient and studded with iron bars in a regular pattern. The door hung from two sets of massive black hinges, locked with an elaborate system of heavy iron rings, the chains coming together in the nape of a fifty-pound padlock. Bentley hammered the heavy door-knocker, one short, two long, and then two short blows. A mechanism opened to allow one-way vision. Then he remembered and moved the goggles from his eyes, snapped them back into place on the top of his helmet. The door opened. Bentley went inside.

All the sadomasochist machinery had been moved aside, and a long table set up in the center of the room under the single exposed light bulb that glared but spread little light on the faces in place around the table.

Bentley took off his helmet and smoothed down his hair. Except for the man at the far end of the table, the others stood up for Bentley, sat down only after he sat at the near end of the table.

Although he knew no names other than some code names, Bentley knew all the KGB faces except three. He assumed that these three were the contingent in from Moscow on this special assignment. The project had been coded Xiao Ching. Moscow had given superplenipotentiary powers, highest priorities to the project. The consortium must be destroyed before it was established. MacGlendon was the only name they knew. But MacGlendon would lead them to the others.

Reaching under the table, Bentley removed his boots, feeling relief from the hot abrasiveness of the suede lining against his bare skin. He took off his leather jacket and tossed it on the wood floor, then adjusted the leather pouch that had slipped and was binding him.

The man at the other end of the table waited until Bentley had settled down. He nodded his head in the direction of one of the men from Moscow. *"Commencez,"* he instructed.

Bentley yawned, slid his hand down under the table, and scratched the instep of his bare foot, barely listening to the droning Russian voice giving him information he already knew, repeating warnings Bentley had already heeded.

By the simple device of clearing his throat, Bentley stopped the report of the special agent. All the faces around the table turned toward him. When Bentley spoke, his voice was low, his manner offhand. "MacGlendon," he said, "is the only known factor we have. MacGlendon must *not* be killed yet. I forbid it under any circumstances." He looked directly at the special agent still standing. "I will decide *when* MacGlendon can be eliminated. Is that clear?"

The Russian agent reluctantly nodded.

"Then sit down and listen. Get the blood out of your eye." Bentley waited while the humbled official sat down. "It is my opinion that MacGlendon can be terrorized into submission, will turncoat and work for our side. He is vulnerable on two levels: emotional and financial. The financial terrorization has already begun. We have the power to weaken his empire, bring him close to financial ruin. He will do anything, including becoming a Russian friend, before he would let his conglomerate be destroyed. The emotional harassment begins tonight." He checked the dial of his watch. "In thirty-two minutes, to be exact. Give me three days and MacGlendon will be as obedient as the special agents from Moscow. He will supply us with all the information we need to destroy the consortium before it begins." Bentley looked back at the disgruntled Russian agent. "When MacGlendon has done his job for us, then the KGB can go in for the kill and get all the glory."

The Frenchman, the man at the opposite end of the table from Bentley, asked, "How can you be so certain that Mac-Glendon will turn and work for us?"

"I've studied the man," Bentley answered. "I know his history and I know how he thinks. I know what turns him on and what turns him off. If we had programmed and nurtured a candidate from childhood, we couldn't have created a more perfect set of environmental circumstances. I know how to motivate MacGlendon for our own purposes." Then he turned back to the special agent from Moscow. "Did you bring the money?"

The Russian stood up, carried a large canvas duffel bag, and set it in front of Bentley. Bentley squeezed the soft case, felt and heard the crisp crunch of American dollars.

A Long Night:
67 rue des Cinq Fleurs

The unfamiliar, high-pitched, repetitive sounds at first seemed to be part of his dreaming, but the persistent ringing penetrated the dream and awakened him. MacGlendon's hand groped toward the telephone, knocking over a glass of water on the nightstand beside the bed before he got the instrument off the cradle and answered with a gruff grunt.

"Soixante-sept rue des Cinq Fleurs." A woman's voice gasped, the words tight with terror, a small, deep-breathed shriek separating the *"Cinq"* and the *"Fleurs."*

"What?"

"You must come. Please. You must come."

"Who is this?"

The voice became quieter, more controlled. "Angus?"

"Yes. Who is it?"

"Soixante-sept rue des Cinq Fleurs. You must help me."

"Who is this? Paula?"

"They say they will rape me. Both of us. You must come." Terror was twisting her voice unrecognizable. "Help me, help me," the voice pleaded. There was a split second of silence, then a siren of a shriek. "Don't! Don't! Oh God, save me. God save me." There were other words but indistinguishable through the tears of fear. MacGlendon heard the telephone drop, a dull thud on a carpeted floor and then a single, piercing scream.

MacGlendon held the phone away from his ear, turned on the light in the room, tried to separate the panic of his dream from the panic of reality. Another woman's voice spoke. She was more controlled, but there was the same underlying tremor of terror. "You must do as they say. You must."

"Who is this?"

A hand went over the mouthpiece, blocking out all sound.

"Who is this?"

A man's voice answered this time, his words barely understandable through a muffler of cloth over the telephone. "You have thirty minutes, MacGlendon. Thirty minutes or they get it, both of them. *Soixante-sept rue des Cinq Fleurs.* Calling the police won't help. Then they're killed for sure. Thirty minutes, MacGlendon."

The phone went dead. The threatening voice had been American.

MacGlendon's immediate reaction was to dial the hotel operator and have her call the police. He dialed O but hung up before the switchboard answered. Instead, he direct-dialed the room of his security staff. A sleepy-voiced Big Red finally answered it. "Pack your artillery. Get dressed. Get a taxi. Meet you downstairs in four minutes." He hung up before the bodyguard could answer and began to get dressed. Knocking over a chair as he kicked apart a pile of shoes on the floor of the closet, he cursed the clutter of the rooms at the hotel, impeding his movement. He found one of the shoes, not the other, and tried to remember when he had taken them off. *Twenty-four hours of insanity. Not even twenty-four hours. Twenty-four hours of life happening to someone else.* Remembering, he stretched flat on the floor, knocking over a fragile standing lamp, groped under the bed until he found the other shoe, and put it on. *Thirty minutes. Shit, he hadn't looked at his watch.* He checked the time and tried to estimate how long it had been since the muffled voice had given him the final warning. *Two? Maybe three.* He put on his trench coat and started through the living room before he remembered he hadn't taken any money, and went back and grabbed a wad of fragile French money and stuffed it into his coat pocket. Another two minutes had gone by. Twenty-six minutes left.

Sixty-seven rue des Cinq Fleurs.

Big Red was waiting at the elevator. There was a placard looped over the call button with a silk rope: Pas de Service. Without breaking stride, MacGlendon signaled to Big Red and started down the wide circumference of the circular staircase. He felt a vertigo begin on the third flight down, hesitated, steadying himself against the railing. Big Red stopped. Breathing heavily, MacGlendon motioned for Big Red to keep moving and hollered after him, "Get a taxi."

Downstairs, he went outside and found Big Red waving frantically to the nothingness of the Paris night. There were no cars, no pedestrians. Dim lights reflected on the empty streets. MacGlendon looked at his watch. It was 4:59 on the digital dial. Eleven minutes since he had last looked at his watch, the telephone call four or five minutes before that. Fourteen minutes left. Fourteen minutes to get to 67 Rue des Cinq Fleurs. Or was it 76? What had she said? *Soixante-sept* or *soixante-seize?*

MacGlendon remembered a taxi stand three blocks from the hotel, up the Rue du Bac and left on Boulevard St.-Germain. He touched Big Red's shoulder, started running faster and stayed far ahead of Big Red; he ran in the center of the tiny streets, feeling the impact of the cobblestones under his feet.

The taxi stand was not on the block he had remembered. He stood in the middle of St.-Germain, looking in

both directions, trying to see some traffic movement anywhere. Big Red caught up to him. He, too, was breathing
heavily, already soaked with sweat. "Fucking town," he
said. "Cleveland ain't this dead in the middle of the
night."

Abreast of each other, they ran another block, then saw
the yellow sign that indicated Tête-de-Station. A single taxi
was parked there, the driver asleep over the wheel. Even
the sound of the rear door closing did not awaken the
driver. MacGlendon reached over the seat, roughly shook
the shoulder sagged in sleep. The driver jolted awake,
looked from side to side, then straight ahead. His head
dropped back into a sleeping position. MacGlendon
grabbed his shoulder, shook him awake. Automatically this
time, the driver turned on the ignition, started the engine.

"*Rue des Cinq Fleurs,*" MacGlendon shouted. "*Dépêchez!
Dépêchez!*"

In a hoarse, sleepy voice, the driver mumbled words at
a fast pace. MacGlendon could understand nothing.

"*Rue des Cinq Fleurs.*" He was shouting as though the
volume of his voice would make the driver understand.
"*Dépêchez,* you bastard. *Dépêchez!*"

From the glove compartment the taxi driver took out a
worn street guide, turned on the little map light and patted
his chest pockets to find his eyeglasses. They were not in his
shirt or leather jacket. MacGlendon grabbed the directory,
and leaned toward the street light, fingering the book, but
he could not understand the organization of the fine print.
By now the driver had found his glasses in his side pocket
and turned around to reach for the guide. MacGlendon
thrust it at him. "*Dépêchez!*"

"*Quelle rue?*"

"*Rue des Cinq Fleurs!*"

The driver wet the end of his index finger, began turning
the corners of the tissue-thin pages. "*Quelle arrondissement?*"

MacGlendon said, "I don't know what fucking *arrondisse-ment.*"

"*Hein?*"

"*Je ne sais pas,*" MacGlendon answered.

Hunched forward, holding the street guide under the map light, the driver ran his finger down the lines of closely printed street names. "*Ce n'est pas la rue de Fleurus.*" "*Rue des Cinq Fleurs. Cinq Fleurs.*"

The indexing finger of the driver stopped. "*Voilà!*" He turned the guide sideways, thumbed through the series of street maps, found the proper one. With his stubby finger, he traced the route until he found the tiny, twisting line of the Rue des Cinq Fleurs. "*C'est ça.*" He put the guide book back into the compartment, took off his glasses, placed them in the breast pocket of his jacket, straightened up in the seat, and at last gunned the engine.

"*Est-ce qu'il est loin?*" MacGlendon asked.

The driver did not answer.

"*Est-il loin?*"

In English, the driver said, "No English."

The taxi pulled into the Boulevard St.-Germain. The driver looked both ways down the wide, empty street, made a U-turn, started speeding.

Helpless at the moment, cramped in the taxi and at the mercy of the obstinate driver, MacGlendon leaned back in the seat and tried to stretch his legs.

He looked at his watch. The thirty minutes were almost gone. He would be too late. Too late for what, he wondered? Rape? Murder? A hoax? A threat?

Big Red finally broke the silence of MacGlendon's thoughts. "You going to tell me what's happening?"

"I wish I knew."

"What's this about?"

"A girl I met. She called and said someone was going to rape her."

"Why you? I mean, why did she call you? I mean if it was a girl you just met?"

"I don't know."

"It's been a hell of a day," Big Red said. "Don't you think you ought to let me in on it? My official corporate title is chief of security. I can't protect anything if I don't know what the fuck I'm up against."

"I wish I knew."

They drove at high speed for twenty minutes through the empty streets, from one broad boulevard to another, through the connecting mazes of tiny, twisting streets. Finally, the driver slowed down, rolled down his window, and began driving with his head out the window, looking at the street signs. He found Concours d'Anjou, sped down the street for four long blocks, slowed down, and began reading street signs again. The underglow of daylight was becoming brighter under the cover of the night. The driver made a hairpin turn to the right and then a sharp left. He peered at the street sign. *Rue des Cinq Fleurs.* He held up his hands in despair, slapped them down in anger against his legs. *"C'est interdit. Sens unique."*

MacGlendon pushed the driver's shoulder, shoved him forward. *"Allons."*

"C'est interdit. Sens unique." He pointed an angry arm out the window, shaking it at the red symbol with the white X forbidding entrance.

MacGlendon pushed his shoulder again, but the driver remained intractable, folding his arms, determined not to touch the steering wheel. MacGlendon reached in his pocket, pulled out two fifty-franc notes, and held the crumbled bills in front of the driver's face. Angrily, the driver snatched the bills, started the car up the sharply inclined street, driving slowly, looking for numbers on the row of elegant nineteenth-century town houses. *"Quel numéro?"*

"Soixante-sept."

He sped up a little, then slowed down. *"Voilà,"* he said, pointing at a darkened house behind a high iron fence. *"C'est ça."*

MacGlendon opened the door on his side to look at the house. There was no sign of any activity. The mansion looked serene and secure in the light. He wondered again about the street number. Had she said 76 or 67?

There was a sound from the top of the hill. A speeding dark car without headlights seemed to come from nowhere, lunging at high speed down the hill. MacGlendon pulled in his head, slammed the door shut just in time. The whoosh of night air was cold against his face as the car passed. He looked up ahead, started to prod the driver when a screech of brakes pierced the quiet. The car below had stopped, reversed gears, at first labored slowly uphill and then accelerated faster and faster. Big Red pulled MacGlendon down, covered him with his own body, the two bulky forms crammed into the narrow floor space of the taxi. The other car backed up past them, stopped, changed gears again, then gunned forward again down the hill. As the car sped past, a riddle of bullets penetrated the taxi, shattering glass, ripping the night with explosive sounds. After the roar of the escaping car faded, everything was deathly quiet again.

MacGlendon was unhurt. There was a jagged piece of glass lodged like a dagger between Big Red's shoulder blades. The taxi driver's body was slumped over the wheel, most of his head blown away by the blasts.

Big Red's body was twisted in pain, his sweat shirt stained with a thin line of blood. He managed to open the car door and crawl backward into the street, where he fell and lay facedown on the cobblestones. The edges of the jagged piece of glass, which was rammed into his back, refracted the light from the streetlamps into a rainbow of color.

MacGlendon crawled out the other side of the taxi. Staying on his hands and knees, he looked up and down the street, but saw no sign of any movement or activity, no lights being turned on inside houses. He stood up and walked past the driver's side, retching at the bloody mass that had been the driver's head, then ran around to the other side, where he saw Big Red flat on the street, and knelt beside him, touching his neck to feel a pulse.

At the contact of the hand against his neck, Big Red turned around, staring at the face hovering over him until he could focus through the pain and identify MacGlendon. His body relaxed and his face fell back against the brick-paved street. "Did you get hit, too?"

"No. I'm all right."

Held-back tears broke through the football-tough barricade. Big Red cried like a hurt little boy. MacGlendon patted the rump of the prostrated player, soft-punched his arm. "You're all right," he said. "You're tough, Red. You always have been."

Big Red braced himself up on his elbows, used one hand to wipe the tears, smear them into the cold sweat on his face. "Where did they get me? All I feel is pain. All over." Then he reached behind his back, touched the dagger of jagged glass pierced between his shoulders, drew blood on his own hand, saw the blood, and collapsed again against the street. "Jesus, Jesus," he cried.

"Hold on," MacGlendon said. "You're scared more than you're hurt." He took his jacket and, using it as a protective glove, gently put his hand over the jagged piece of glass. "It's only glass," he said. "I don't think it's in very deep. Grit your teeth. I'm going to pull it out." He tightened his grasp and then pulled up with all his strength. The arrow-head of glass came out clean. Big Red shrieked once and then was silent. MacGlendon pulled up the sweat shirt and the layers of a sweater, shirt and T-shirt underneath. The wound was superficial, penetrating only the outer layers of thick flesh on Big Red's back. "You're okay," he said and stood up, reaching over to support Big Red's arm and shoulder. "Try standing up."

Timidly at first, Big Red raised himself up, then smiled when he felt no pain. "I'm okay." Leaning on the support of MacGlendon's brace, he got to his feet but was still crouched over. Gradually he straightened up and grinned when he realized that he was all right. "Son of a bitch," he said. "I'm all right."

"You saved my life," MacGlendon said and touched Big Red's arm. "I guess there's only one way to say thank you. Thank you."

There was the great run he made in the stadium in Lincoln. It was like that now. He returned the touch of Mac-Glendon's hand with an open-handed whack across Mac-Glendon's rump as they had done to him the day he made the big run, one by one, every player on the team. "Doing my job," he said. "All in a day's work." He looked up at the sky. "Night's work."

"Are you okay to go on?"

"Up and at 'em." He started to trot up the hill. MacGlendon held him back.

"Easy," MacGlendon said. "No use killing yourself." He turned back toward the bullet-ridden taxi and dead driver, discarded on the Rue des Cinq Fleurs. "We're too late anyway." He took Big Red's elbow and side by side they walked up the steep hill.

Number 67 was a house larger than the others surrounding it. It was protected from the street by a stone wall, penetrated by high, arched iron gates at either end of the circular driveway. There was no light from this house, either, but the iron gates were open, one of them hanging at an oblique angle, partially torn from the hinges. "Give me your gun," MacGlendon said.

"But, Boss . . ."

MacGlendon grabbed it away, crouched down, hugged the arc of thick shrubs lining the driveway approach to the house. Big Red dogged his steps, imitated his crouched position.

The front door was half open, a faint light visible at the end of the depths of darkness inside. Both men darted across the drive, flanked the entrance, staying out of range of a clear shot from inside. MacGlendon kicked the door all the way open and cautiously moved his head around the corner to peer inside. He kept his body flattened, protected by the brick wall. There was no sound, no movement inside. He signaled Big Red, and together they went into the house. There was enough reflected light from the streetlamps to make out the confines of the vestibule and see through the glass partition to the entrance hall and the wide staircase leading to the second floor. There was light at the top of the stairs, dim, but enough to guide them.

They followed the curve of the staircase, MacGlendon leading, the gun steady, his finger ready to react to any movement.

The light was coming from the far end of the upstairs hall where double doors were flung open. Careful to stay on the narrow carpet runner so that the sounds of their steps would be silenced, they moved toward the doors and waited outside, listening for sounds.

The sudden blast of a radio at high volume startled both of them. MacGlendon's hand started to squeeze the trigger, but he caught himself in time. The volume lowered and music played very softly. He motioned for Big Red to stay in position, shook off the grimace of protest, then turned away and walked on tiptoe into the bedroom.

The woman he recognized as Andrea de Plyssy was sitting in front of a dressing table, her face close to the mirror, applying makeup to disguise a large, fresh bruise on her high cheekbones. Her hair was disheveled, but otherwise she seemed unruffled, calm.

Without turning around, she said, "You must be Mr. MacGlendon." She swiveled on the stool and faced him. "You've come too late," she said.

"What the hell is going on?"

Her bruised face was impassive, but her famous eyes were wide open, frozen in a shocked stare, still glistening with the reflection of unrelieved horror. Her voice was consciously controlled. "Suppose *you* explain what is going on."

"Where's Paula?"

"She's in her room." MacGlendon turned and started back toward the hall. "I wouldn't go in there." MacGlendon stopped. "She's not pretty to look at just now."

"I don't give a shit what she looks like. Is she hurt?"

The actress turned back to the mirror, smoothing the makeup over the first trace of the blood-red bruise; then she picked up the brush and started stroking the tangle of her hair.

Some instinct made MacGlendon stop before he grabbed her. He wanted to shake the truth out of her, but he held himself back. "Damn it, don't play movie star with me! Is she hurt?"

The woman tightened her mouth, fought back tears. "Yes. Badly."

"Was she raped?"

She shook her head, brushed her hair harder. When she answered, her silver-screen voice was low, the same volume as the soft music from the radio. MacGlendon had to strain to hear the words. "It's worse than rape," she said. "She was sexually brutalized—terrorized." The actress swung around, the hairbrush aimed at MacGlendon, outrage and anger contorting her face. Her eyes narrowed with hate. "We both were," she said, then screamed the words, "We both were!"

The combination of bewildered anguish and physical exhaustion disintegrated MacGlendon's strength. He collapsed on the large bed, let the gun fall to the floor, rubbed his face and then his eyes as though there were tears in them. His shoulders slumped as he sat there, his forearms against his legs supporting the weary weight of his head. "I'm sorry," he said, his voice hardly audible. "I'm sorry."

Andrea de Plyssy walked across the room, sat beside him on the bed and touched his shoulder. "What has happened," she said, "is irrevocable, can never be undone. The depravity. The torture. Even revenge won't reverse it. Nothing will ever be the same again for either of us."

They both looked up as Big Red burst into the room. Big Red's forward motion was stopped by the tender position of MacGlendon and Andrea de Plyssy on the bed. Instinctive fear at seeing Big Red made the woman's body stiffen; her nails dug into MacGlendon's arms as she grasped him for protection. "It's all right," he assured her, as he waved Big Red back into the hall.

"Who was it?" MacGlendon asked. "Who did it?"

She shook her head. "There were two of them. One held the gun. He was masked. A ski mask, all black, pulled down over his face. The other man . . . the one who did the torture and the beating . . . was black. Native African, I think. He was big . . . so terribly big and so powerful. He never said a word, not even grunted. He was like an animal, a chained, starving animal. The masked man directed him, told him what to do, cheered him on. He spoke to him in a language I didn't even recognize. I suppose it was one of the African languages. I don't know, really." She closed her eyes against the image recalled in her mind. "It was like a savage orgy."

"The other man, the masked man, was he black?"

"I couldn't tell at first. He was dressed all in black leather and wore black leather gloves. The face mask only had slits for his eyes and mouth, and he wore a helmet over his head that covered his ears." Andrea de Plyssy's face dropped. She shook her head in disbelief.

MacGlendon restrained himself from holding the woman again to comfort her. "The man in the mask . . . you said that you couldn't tell at first whether he was black or white."

She stroked her hair again, the tangle being brushed smooth into a silky texture. "While the black man was . . ." She started again. "While the black man was . . . slashing Paula, the man in the mask took out his penis." She lowered her head. "His penis was very white."

"He's the one who talked to me on the phone?"

She nodded.

"He sounded American," MacGlendon said, "but I couldn't be sure. His voice was muffled over the phone."

"No question about it," she said. "He was American. There was a faintly southern sound to his voice. Actresses are aware of those kinds of things."

In the distance, becoming louder, the wail of police sirens violated the stillness of the early morning. MacGlendon went out into the hall. Gray daylight was coming through the stained-glass ceiling over the staircase. "Go down," he said to Big Red, "and close the front door. The police are coming. Somebody has reported the taxi. If the bell rings, don't answer it."

"They'll see the gate. They'll see that it's knocked off the hinges."

"Maybe. But we'll have to chance it. Get going." He pushed Big Red's shoulder. "Move."

In the half-light of the upstairs hall, muted hues reflecting from the colored glass, MacGlendon looked down the long corridor of closed doors. He opened the first door on the right and then on the left. Both bedrooms were empty. The third door on the left had an oval plaque hung on the outside, a faded and peeling design of painted cherubs, flowers, and ribbons entwined in a border. The worn, cursive lettering in the center of the medallion read, "Paula's Room."

MacGlendon opened the door softly and looked in. At first the fluffy room appeared to be empty; the bed, turned back with fresh linen embroidered with borders of violets and roses, had not been slept in. As he started back, he saw her huddled in a corner, a naked body sitting on the floor, her arms and legs coiled around her as a shield for her nakedness. Her wide gray eyes were wide open, staring in a blank fix on nothing.

Tentatively, softly, he called her name. There was no reaction, not even a flicker of her eyelids. He went to her, knelt in front of her, and moved his hand up and down in front of her eyes. Again there was no reaction. Tenderly, he touched the artery in her neck, felt the slow beat of the pulse there. Her body was cold to the touch, rigid from shock. He kissed her forehead, stroked her hair, and looking down through the locked arms, saw a series of small burns on her breasts, each scarred circle coated with ointment.

MacGlendon took a flowered, crocheted blanket from the foot of the bed, covered her body with it and went back to Andrea de Plyssy's bedroom.

"I saw Paula," he said. "Did you call a doctor?"

She shook her head. "I gave her some of my pills and put a salve on the burns. The wounds will heal . . . those wounds, anyway. Not the others. Paula is a strange girl. She always has been. She's always been on that thin edge between reality and another world."

"You ought to call your doctor."

"I can't. You don't understand. There can't be any publicity. And my husband must never know. He would be horrified. My husband is an important man in France. He is deeply involved in air defense and missile projects, and the de Plyssy name carries much prestige in Paris. Even marrying an actress was a risk for him. He must never know what's happened here tonight." Her voice softened. "He would never forgive me."

"Christ, I would think he would want to bust this thing wide open. You're not going to call the police, either?"

"Never."

"They're down the street now investigating a taxi full of bullet holes and a dead driver. They're going to ring every doorbell on this street."

"I will tell them nothing."

"You're one tough lady, aren't you?"

She hesitated, mulled the words she wanted to say. "I've sacrificed too much to give up the security I now have. What would I do if my husband divorced me? Go back to films? What parts would I get? Old hags in horror films? Dragon ladies in outer space?" She looked at him straight in the face. "You bet that I'm one tough lady. Tough ladies survive."

"What about Paula?"

"Paula is a grown woman."

"She'll need help."

"Are you going to give it to her, Mr. MacGlendon? I should think that you would. You appear to be that kind of man and, after all, this is your fault, isn't it? Everything that has happened to Paula and me is your fault. We were victims. Doesn't your world have compassion for victims? Isn't that the American ethic, the American tradition? You have such compassion for your enemies that after you devastate them with bombs, you build them up again to become your enemies once more."

"Fair play," MacGlendon said.

"Bullshit. Guilt. The great American guilt."

"How can you abandon your own daughter?"

"Until tonight, Mr. MacGlendon, I had not seen my daughter for almost eight months. Not even a phone call. Not even an invitation to her art exhibition in Beaubourg. I keep her bedroom here as kind of a shrine. I haven't changed a thing in it, hoping that there would be a time like tonight when she would come home because she needed me, needed my love."

"Why *did* she come here tonight?"

"Because of you. She fell in love with an American, she told me. Love at first sight. She told me that you were a big, powerful man, but that you were gentle. She thought she'd found a kindred spirit. Paula herself is very gentle. Tough ladies sometimes have very gentle daughters." She smiled to herself at a secret memory. "She wanted to know about love, Mr. MacGlendon. She wanted to know how I felt when I fell in love with her father."

MacGlendon lowered his head, weighted down by accumulated guilt and the exhaustion of confusion.

"I thought you had made love yesterday," she said. "I was pleased, delighted that Paula had at last found a kind of happiness. Frankly, Mr. MacGlendon, I thought my daughter was a lesbian. Part of it was my own guilt in not succeeding in establishing love between us. She's always had kind of an immaculate, unravaged sensuality about her. I watched that being destroyed tonight, right over there." She pointed to the spot of blood on the floor. "Why, Mr. MacGlendon? Why have they violated us to get to you? Why?"

He shook his head, did not answer.

"What have you done, or what are you about to do, that would make these people use such violence to stop you?"

"I don't know those answers," MacGlendon said. "None of it makes any sense. You have to believe me. I don't

understand who and I don't understand why. It's a nightmare."

"You're not an innocent, Mr. MacGlendon. Why did
they use *us* to threaten *you?*"

He shook his head again.

"They must think that you love Paula and would risk
your life to save her."

MacGlendon said nothing.

"Did you fall in love with her? Was it like she told me?
Did you both find love?"

"We both felt an understanding of each other. We
seemed to feel each other's souls. There was a communication between us that didn't need words."

"But not love . . ."

He thought about it, not certain of his own feelings.

"I wonder if you're capable of love," she said.

MacGlendon stood up, straightening his clothes. "What
kind of a drug did you give Paula?"

"I don't know the name. My doctor prescribed it. When
I can't stand the torment anymore, I take one. It knocks me
out, saves my sanity."

"How many did you give Paula?"

"Two."

MacGlendon took the gun from the bed. "You could
have killed her with that dose."

"I saved her, Mr. MacGlendon. Saved her."

In the corridor he handed the gun back to Big Red. "I'll
be awhile. Stand guard." He patted the security guard's
shoulder. "You feel all right?"

"My back and arms are beginning to stiffen up."

"Turn around. Let me have a look." He pulled up Big
Red's clothing to examine the wound. There was an inflam-
ation and swelling around the penetration. "Look," he said,
"you ought to get a doctor to look at that. There may be
fragments of glass in it. Find a hospital. Have the wound

RICHARD HIMMEL / 141

checked out in the emergency room. Tell them that you fell through a glass door. Make up any story that will keep you from being identified with the taxi. Okay?"

Big Red nodded. "I don't think I ought to leave you, Boss."

"It'll be all right, Red. Nothing more is going to happen." He touched the man to reassure him, reached into his pocket and handed a wad of French money to Big Red. "Sneak out the back. The police may be combing this area. Don't get caught. You'll find a taxi somewhere."

Paula de Plyssy had not moved from the corner of the room. Her eyes had closed and her head had dropped, but her body was still rigidly coiled. MacGlendon disentangled her arms, winced at the pattern of burns on her breasts, straightened out her legs and saw a trickle of dried blood and an ugly welt on the sensitive, clean-shaven skin at the V-base of her torso. He picked up the cold body, carried it to the narrow bed, pulled back the bed covers, and placed her on the clean, crisp sheets. He went into the adjoining bathroom, wet a washcloth with warm water, brought it back to the bed, spread her legs apart, patted off the dried blood.

Then he undressed, lay beside her, pulled the blankets over them, turned her inert body so that he could encompass it and warm it with the heat emanating from his own body.

In spite of his determined will, his eyes closed and yielded to exhaustion. He succumbed to the unconsciousness of sleep while he was establishing priorities of action in his mind.

A Long Night: Ending

Daylight was beginning, a brightness penetrating the fading night. MacGlendon still held the tortured body of Paula de Plyssy. Slowly, her body was beginning to generate its own warmth, the death chill thawing as her metabolic rate increased and the protective shield of shock cracked, exposing her to physical pain. She convulsed violently, screamed, shattering the stillness. MacGlendon clutched her tighter, used his body as a tourniquet against her, covered her mouth with his mouth, absorbing the terrifying sounds into the depths of his own body, making her pain part of him.

Then, as the spasm of violence subsided, he carefully unwound his legs, gradually released the pressure of his arms clutching her. There were sucking sounds as he broke the seal of sweat binding their bodies together. He backed off toward the edge of the bed, waited to see if she would reach out for him, and then turned and stood up. He gently covered her nakedness with the flowered sheet, leaned over, and brushed her forehead with his lips.

In the bathroom he splashed his face with handfuls of cold water, studied his haggard image in the mirror. His face was still the same: no reflection of the torments consuming him. Where were the festers of wounds? Where were the bloody, broken vessels of anguish? He was miraculously unscathed: the innocents carried the scars of guilt—the squashed body of a Chinese silk merchant, the blown-off head of a taxi driver, the quivering dagger of glass in Big Red's back, the gunshot through the New Man and the burned, abraded, and abused body of Paula de Plyssy.

He dressed quickly, stood over her for a moment, and then walked through the quiet house, down the stairs, and out the front door.

As MacGlendon walked up the crest of the Rue des Cinq Fleurs toward the intersection, a dark green car sped past him, braked to a screeching stop, backed up, and the rear door opened. "MacGlendon," Pug O'Connor hollered out, "you're going to make an old man out of me."

There was relief and protection in the armor of the green American car and clumsy warmth of the big Irishman smelling faintly of stale beer. "You've been a busy boy," O'Connor said. "You've torn up the town pretty good and you're not even warmed up yet. People are getting killed and maimed, and you just walk around with those wide-open big blues of yours. Suppose you start at the beginning, MacGlendon. I need answers. Names. Give me a clean-cut narrative."

MacGlendon didn't say anything.

"Think of it this way," O'Connor said. "You're one of those guys in the top tax bracket, right? You pay a wad to the government and bitch that the government spends it on indolent vagrants and dollar-consuming bureaucracy. Right now you have a chance to get some service from your tax dollars. I'm in your employ, MacGlendon. Think of me as one of your flunkies. You pay my salary. Get your money's worth, MacGlendon. You understand that kind of logic, don't you?"

"This is strictly a business deal, O'Connor. Like all business deals, the information is privileged to the principals."

O'Connor applauded, his ham hands clapping together in a loud sound. "Bravo, bravo. Spoken like the voice of capitalism. The fact that innocent people are getting chopped up doesn't mitigate any of the circumstances, does it?" He waited. "Of course not. Unfortunate. Send a check to take care of the widows and orphans and wipe it off your conscience."

"You should have been a priest, O'Connor."

"My sainted mother wanted that, but I couldn't handle the poverty and chastity bit. Otherwise, I have a godliness about me."

"There are a lot of strange people playing God these days." They drove in silence for a few minutes; then Mac-Glendon said, "I want to go to my hotel."

"Exactly where you're going, and then you know what's going to happen? You're going to get locked in your room like a bad boy, and you're going to stay there until you decide to be a good boy and tell Father here what this is all about."

"You have no authority to detain me."

"I have a very strong right hook and a very deadly gun, MacGlendon. The easiest thing would be to shoot you accidentally. It's like preventive medicine. I'd probably be saving a dozen lives if I did."

"What do you know about Paula de Plyssy?"

"You're the one who has been fucking her, MacGlendon, not me."

"What do you know about her?"

"Clean, as far as our records show. Fucked up, but clean. She keeps some suspect company, but I read her as an innocent."

"Who's the suspect company she keeps?"

"You."

"Besides me?"

"An old broad named Phyllis Goldberg. The art dealer.

She's a holdover commie from the old days—the first wave of radical chic. She gets funded from somewhere. That art gallery of hers is a blind. She advances certain artists big hunks of dough and never sells any paintings. Your friend Paula has been paid twelve thousand bucks and nary a flower has left the gallery."

"Then how come you think Paula is innocent?"

"She's flaky. No offense, MacGlendon, but that's one flaky tomato. As far as I can tell, she lives in kind of a dream world. Frankly, I don't think that she's got enough marbles to be dangerous."

"You're reading her wrong, O'Connor. You don't understand her kind of intelligence—too ethereal for you."

"You're probably right about me. I don't turn on to that ethereal shit. Last night I fucked a woman who kept her boots on, and I think I fell in love. Gross, huh? But that's me, MacGlendon. Gross. Honest and straight from the shoulder, but gross." He wiggled in his seat, rubbed his hand over his face. "I ought to warn you that Paula has a long history of psychiatric treatment. Shock treatment once. Not exactly a stable broad."

"I know about that," MacGlendon said, "and I know why."

"Bully for you, MacGlendon. But she's a kook all the same."

They were driving down the Boulevard St.-Germain now, nearing the hotel. "I'd like to get out here," MacGlendon said.

"Would you now? And why is that?"

"I usually jog every morning for an hour. I have an appointment with a guy from *Time* magazine. For a lot of reasons, I'd like to adhere to my schedule, make everything look normal."

O'Connor reached forward, touched the driver's shoulder: the car stopped. "I need promises and assurances from

you, MacGlendon. I need a scout's honor. I'm sure you
were a Boy Scout."

"Eagle."

"It figures."

"What do you want me to promise?"

O'Connor scribbled on a piece of paper. "That's a telephone number. Before you leave your hotel again, call me
and tell me where you're going. And why. Promise?"

MacGlendon took the slip of paper, folded it, and put it
in his pocket. "I can take care of myself."

"Look, MacGlendon, if you get killed, my life is easy. I
can file you away and forget this whole thing. But you're
not going to get killed. For some reason everyone seems to
want to keep you alive. At least for a while. But other
people are getting killed because of you. That complicates
my life. Now be a good boy, and call me up and tell me
where you're going and why, and who you're going to
see." He held out his hand. "Deal?" MacGlendon nodded.
"Scout's honor?" MacGlendon raised his hand.

"While you have nothing to do, O'Connor, check out a
name for me, will you?"

"Give."

"Ridge Bentley."

"Ridge Bentley?"

"You know him?"

The CIA agent shook his head sadly, said nothing.

As MacGlendon jogged around the corner from the Rue
Bonaparte into the Rue des Beaux-Arts, a man from New
York who controlled the Courreges franchises in the
United States caught hold of MacGlendon's arm. "I have to
talk to you, Gus." MacGlendon pulled free, made a vague
gesture that broke the pumping rhythm of his arms, but did
not break the pace of his jog.

The narrow sidewalk in front of the hotel was cluttered

with tall cans and huge plastic bags of last night's garbage. The curb and the middle of the street were sprinkled with Seventh Avenue titans and fashion buyers waiting for hard-to-find taxis to take them to the Porte de Versailles, looking in both directions, waving their arms when a cab passed at bisecting east-west streets.

As he came closer to the entrance, MacGlendon saw the drooping figure of Big Red standing sentinel at the door. In a concentrated rush of energy MacGlendon accelerated his pace into a run, barreling through the clusters of people on the curb, ignoring the attempts to attract his attention. He pushed Big Red in front of him and went into the lobby.

Inside, in the center rotunda, bathed in the same sunlight that twenty hours ago had bathed the mashed remains of the Chinese silk merchant, Marie Antoinette and Louis XVI were handing a ribboned parchment scroll to Joe Brooks, president of Lord and Taylor. MacGlendon waited while flash bulbs and strobes exploded. The bizarre anachronism of the scene was no more unreal than the unreality of his life since he had come to Paris, and no less garish. Why shouldn't Joe Brooks pose with Louis XVI?

MacGlendon, pushing Big Red ahead of him, walked toward the elevator. Joe Brooks waved to MacGlendon, shouted over the noise of the crowd. "Got to talk to you, Gus. When?" MacGlendon smiled, did not break his stride, did not try to answer.

Big Red was already at the elevator, jamming the call button repeatedly. "You okay, Boss?"

MacGlendon nodded, spoke through heavy, out-of-breath breathing. "What about you? What did the doctor say?"

"Surface wound. They cleaned all the splinters out. I'm okay."

The elevator door opened. A *Women's Wear* reporter, whom he knew slightly, smiled at him as she walked out, stood up on tiptoes, kissed his cheek. "The rumors are flying, Gus. Do you want to make a statement?" He was in the elevator cab, the door was closing before she finished her sentence. He looked sideways to Big Red. "What is going on around here?"

Big Red shrugged his shoulders, winced with the pain. "Beats the shit out of me."

The New Man, his arm in a sling, his face drawn and ashen, stood outside the door to MacGlendon's suite. He smiled to signal the relief of his concern for MacGlendon and to reassure MacGlendon of his own well-being. Mac-Glendon touched the clean white sling. "You okay?" The bodyguard nodded.

Both men followed MacGlendon into the suite. Everything was the way he left it: the bed unmade, objects knocked off the nightstand still lying there, and the crumbled silk sample twisted on the living room floor. The New Man pulled a sheaf of telephone messages from the cache of his sling. "This gadget comes in handy," he said. "It holds more than a pocket does." He pulled out his gun. "Great advantage for fast draw."

While he rifled through the pink message slips, MacGlendon asked, "What did the doctor say?" He hesitated at a message written in English. *Telephone your mother in New York. Urgent.*

"No problem," the New Man said. "The bullet didn't hit anything vital, just flesh and muscle. He said that I'll be good as new."

MacGlendon crumbled the message from his mother in his fist, faced his two security executives. "I'm not good at this," he began, "but I want you guys to know how sorry I am and how grateful I am." With his foot, he hooked the silk sample over his foot, raised his leg, caught the end of the cloth, and began folding it into a small square. "I know that everything that is happening doesn't make any sense to you. But it's not just a series of dumb, freak accidents. I don't believe that anymore." He inclined his head toward the wounded men. "We've all been lucky this far; we're still alive. But I can't give you any guarantees for what is going to happen. If you guys don't want to bust your balls or break your ass, I don't blame you. What I mean is that if you want to split, I understand. No hard feelings." He turned away from them. "What do you say?"

Big Red was hearing halftime, locker-room echoes in his mind. Because he did not know the words to say, he took a step forward, looked back at the hesitating New Man. The New Man said: "It's a job. We get paid. We knew what we were in for." He stepped forward, stood abreast of Big Red.

MacGlendon muttered his gratitude in indistinguishable sounds, told them to expect Ben Brayden, went into the bedroom, closed the door, stripped off his clothes, sat on the bed, and looked at the telephone for almost five minutes before he picked it up to call his mother in New York.

"Angus, darling. I'm so glad you caught me. Would you believe that I'm still awake. It's an ungodly hour. What time is it in Paris?"

"Almost eight in the morning."

"I've been trying to reach you all day and evening."

"What's wrong?"

"Wrong? There's nothing wrong. Why should there be anything wrong?"

"Your message said *urgent.*"

"Well, it was urgent. It still is urgent. I mean I'm leaving early in the morning. That's why I'm awake now. I'm packing. At the last minute, I've decided to enter the bridge tournament in Monte Carlo. You know how I am. I leave everything until the eleventh hour. I really had no intention of going. But the weather has turned frightful here, and I guess that I'm bored. Freddie stopped here on his way from

California . . . he and Paula are such dears and they . . ."

"Who's Freddie?"

"Sheinwold, darling. You must read his bridge column." She hesitated, then laughed. "But then why would you? It isn't on the financial page, is it?"

"How are Grandma and Grandpa?" He steadied himself for the answer.

"Fine, darling. Why shouldn't they be fine? I spoke to them in Florida the day before yesterday. Maybe it was the day before that. It doesn't matter, does it? They sounded happy and were excited about going to a Liberace concert at the Doral."

"What's so urgent?"

"I told you. Freddie and Paula talked me into going to Monte Carlo with them. What time did you say it was in Paris?"

"Eight o'clock."

"In the morning?"

"Yes."

"That means that it's tomorrow there, doesn't it? I'm so helpless with time zones. I'll never understand them."

"Are you going to stop in Paris?"

"No, not really. How's the weather there?"

"Okay. It's a little cold but sunny."

"It's dreadful here. The sky is all gray and it's turned bitterly cold. It's so early for bitter weather."

"Why don't you stop in Paris for a day?"

"I'd love to, darling, I really would, but the tournament starts the day after tomorrow, whenever tomorrow is in Monaco. There just won't be time. I'd love to see you. It's been ages. But I know that you must be busy there." She caught her breath, went on talking. "Did you know that *Women's Wear* carried a front-page story on you this morning?" She didn't wait for an answer. "It was something like . . . Hardware Tycoon Wrenches Fashion Industry. There was a big picture of you taken with a woman. *Women's Wear* didn't identify her."

"Blonde?"

"I couldn't tell, really. I imagine it was a terrible picture of a pretty girl." She hesitated. "To be honest with you, darling, I don't really think that. She seemed so cheap-looking. For a man whose taste and judgment is so impeccable in everything else, your taste in women is so—"

"Don't start that again, Mother."

"You've made one impulsive mistake, Angus. I wouldn't want you to . . ."

"It wasn't a mistake. Debbie was a marvelous girl. I couldn't handle marriage when I was that age. *I* was the mistake, not Debbie."

"Then it isn't serious?"

"What isn't serious?"

"The girl in *Women's Wear.*"

"I don't even remember who it was."

"Well, thank God for that. It was a lovely article. I still get goose bumps when I read about you in the papers. I just can't believe that they're writing about my little boy."

"Did it say anything about the price of the stock?"

"I don't think so. But it's not the kind of thing I would remember, is it? They just wrote about the high-fashion stores that you're gobbling up. Don't buy Bergdorf's, darling. Please don't buy Bergdorf's. It's the only store left for old ladies like me."

"Mother, you said it was urgent. My buying Bergdorf's isn't urgent."

There was a pause and then she said: "Well, some rather surprising family matter has come up. It's not bad news. In a way, I suppose it's very good news."

"Are you getting married again?"

"God forbid. It's nothing to do with me. Not directly, anyway."

"What is it? What's happened?"

"I'd rather not talk about it on the phone. It's not really the kind of thing one talks about on the telephone. That's why I said that it was urgent. My plane to Nice stops in Paris for two hours. I wondered if you could arrange your schedule so that you could meet me at the airport. I know how busy you must be, but I can't be late for the tournament, and I wondered if . . ."

"What time does your plane land here?"

"I don't know exactly, darling. You know how mixed up I get with the change in time. The flight leaves New York at nine in the morning."

"Air France?"

"Yes. The Concorde."

"I'll be there."

"Angus?"

"Yes?"

"It's not to worry," she said.

"I'm not worried. What makes you think that I'm worried?"

"I know how you are, darling. I know how you think. But it's good news, really."

"Do you want to give me a clue?"

"It's something we ought to talk about face to face. It's rather important to me. But it's not to worry. Promise me."

"What?"

"That you won't worry."

He heaved a deep breath of all his concern. "Okay, I won't worry."

"Do you have any idea what the weather is like in Monte Carlo? Everything is out of my closet, but I have no idea what kind of clothes to pack."

"Does it matter? You spend all your time in smoke-filled rooms playing bridge anyway. You'll probably never get out of the hotel."

"Don't be resentful, darling. A woman my age has earned the right to waste her life doing frivolous things. I do my good deeds. I work for charities. Not everyone has to be an overachiever. I've earned the right . . ." She did not finish the sentence.

"I'll be waiting at De Gaulle."

"Where, darling?"

"The airport. In Paris."

"Of course, darling. I'll see you then."

MacGlendon hung up, sat inert for several minutes, tried to guess at the reason for this meeting with his mother, rejected the concept that it was part of the pattern of destruction descending on him, prepared himself to stifle the anger he would feel when his mother confronted him with another of her inane projects. Probably, he decided, his mother was going to endow another shelter for abandoned cats. He wondered how this kind of mentality had attracted men like his father and men like Blair Brewster. For a moment he saw a quick flash of light into his own sexuality. He wondered at the power of the mechanism that was making him horny in spite of the intense pressure of exhaustion and confusion.

He leafed through the other telephone messages in his hand, urgent calls from urgent people all over the world. One by one, he crumbled them in his hand, tossed them into the wastebasket.

He dialed Miami. There was no answer.

There was a knock on the door, the New Man's voice calling out. "Ben Brayden is here."

Novelist at the Ritz

In the harsh reality of the morning light the deep wrinkles of Geoffrey Plantagenet's face were still creased from sleep, and his thin hair was matted in clumps exposing pallid bald spots. Denuded of grooming, he appeared to MacGlendon as an old, wasted man incapable of self-defense on any level. MacGlendon curbed his fury, sat quietly across the room-service table from the author and watched as Plantagenet tried to steady a teacup to his lips.

The Paris edition of the *International Herald Tribune* was folded open to an inside page showing a four-column photograph of the author seated at this same room-service table, wearing the same flamboyant silk robe.

HARD SELL MAKES BEST SELL,
AUTHOR PLANTAGENET CLAIMS:
CONDEMNS LITERARY CRITICS

Plantagenet turned the newspaper toward MacGlendon. "Read that! They've misinterpreted everything I said. But why should the Paris press be different? The media pans me all the time."

MacGlendon speed-read the interview. "The story says

that you're on your way to China to research your new novel."

"Possibly."

"What do you mean—possibly? Are you going or aren't you?"

"I go to a clinic in Yugoslavia twice a year: take youth injections. Extractions from sheep. Blood and semen." He ran his hands over his craggy face. "It's so damned painful. But the world today sees no wisdom in age. *Youth.* Everyone reveres the vitality of youth." He turned the newspaper around, studied his own picture and squinted to read the story. "In a sense, what the *Herald Tribune* says is true. I am a creation of the media. I flourish because I hit every damned talk show in every damn city. Plug, plug, plug. TV viewers don't want to look at old, wise men. They want youth and vitality."

"What about China? Are you going?"

"I may. It depends."

"On what?"

"I can't very well say to the press that I'm going to a clinic in Yugoslavia to be rejuvenated. So I told them that I'm going to China to research a novel. It's very *in*—writing novels about China. I may write the book anyway."

"With my mother as the heroine?"

Plantagenet did not answer: turned his head to look out the window, study the column in the center of the Place Vendôme. "But it wouldn't end like that—not with the heroine becoming a silly old woman, playing bridge and backgammon and making a fuss over stray animals."

MacGlendon said, "If you weren't old and pitiful, I'd beat the truth out of you."

"You're so much like your father. As violent as he could be, he always had a gentleness toward the very young and the very old. A compassion for innocence—a veneration for aged wisdom."

"You're reading me wrong, Plantagenet. My compassion and veneration have run out. I want straight answers and I want them now." MacGlendon stood up, his hulk casting a shadow on the novelist. "Who is my next contact?"

"I don't know that yet. They didn't expect Chou to be murdered."

"Who is *they?*"

"The people in China."

"Who are the people in China?"

"The new power structure," Plantagenet said. "I don't know names. I don't know faces. I didn't even know Chou on sight." He pulled his robe tighter around his body. "I'm a very unimportant pawn in the Chinese scheme of things. I do what they tell me. I know only what they want me to know."

"You're a Red Chinese agent?" The novelist nodded. "Why?" MacGlendon asked.

"My name used to be Irving Plaut. I was an overweight, underpaid writer for a Detroit newspaper. For my whole life I was everybody's whipping boy. Beginning with my own father, I was everybody's whipping boy. The *schlepp-along.* Even in the old days when I knew your mother and father—there was so much excitement then, so many new ideas and concepts—but I was always the boy they sent out for coffee. I mailed the letters and burned the contents of wastebaskets. No one ever asked me what I thought or what I was thinking about." He put his hand on the *Herald Tribune.* "The people in China bought a publisher, paid the media expenses—I sold out so that I could become Geoffrey Plantagenet, the notorious novelist." He thought for a moment. "If the same circumstances existed today, I'd do the same thing. Irving Plaut was a nothing. There are hours, sometimes, when even I forget that I was ever that man."

"What does Paula de Plyssy have to do with this? Is she one of you?"

Plantagenet shrugged his shoulders. "The people in China still treat me as Irving Plaut. They tell me no more than they think I need to know. She was the means to link you to me; and I, in turn, would link you to the next person in the chain of command. But they killed Chou, and the whole timetable fell apart."

"Who killed Chou?"

Plantagenet shrugged. "The Russians, I suppose. They're paranoid about the Chinese. Always have been."

"What about the consortium?"

"I can only guess."

"What's your guess?"

Plantagenet seemed energized suddenly. He stood up, walked to the tall French doors overlooking the street, opened them, and stepped out on to the tiny balcony, leaned over the rail and then turned back to MacGlendon. "The ultimate victory," he began, "would be if I wrote a novel about all of this: how the Chinese nurtured us through all these years, with their timing of the inevitable, preparing for their day of infamy. I could write that book, and I wouldn't need the hype of the media to make it a bestseller. An old man named Irving Plaut could write that book, and it would be great on its own merit, sell on its own. The truth would be shocking. The world would awake —all of this because Irving Plaut wrote the truth and wrote it with skill and dignity." Then the underlying chill of the Paris morning penetrated his body. Plantagenet stepped back into the room, closed the glass doors behind him, and sat opposite MacGlendon again. His head was lowered and his voice barely audible. "Irving Plaut was always a dreamer," he said. "He was a sniveling daydreamer, reaching for crumbs, snapping at scraps. *Run out for coffee, Irving. Empty the ashtrays, Irving. Open the window. Close the door.*

Fetch. Fetch, boy." He looked up at MacGlendon. "Irving Plaut lived in fleabags and YMCAs. He never stayed in the best suite at the Ritz." Plantagenet stood up, walked to the bedroom door. "As an old friend of your mother and father, I want to warn you that nothing that has happened has happened without design. Sooner or later one of them will contact me, arrange to meet with you."

"Meanwhile, innocent people are getting killed and mutilated."

"The world is like that, isn't it?"

"Not my world," MacGlendon said. "Maybe it's dog eat dog in the business world. Maybe, it's a lot of things. But it isn't physically violent." He stood over Plantagenet. "Normally, I'm not physically violent. But I'm being driven to it. Do you understand?" MacGlendon stood glaring at Plantagenet. "What has Ridge Bentley got to do with this?"

"Ridge?" The novelist laughed. "Why would Ridge have anything to do with this?"

"Last night at La Serre was no accident. He was there for a purpose." He leaned over, his hulk threatening. "How is Bentley tied into this?"

Plantagenet backed up his chair, crumbled a corner of the newspaper in his frightened grasp. "He has nothing to do with us. I swear it. Nothing."

"Where do I find him?"

"Here," Plantagenet said. "He's staying at the Ritz. On the Cambon side."

"If you're lying to me about Bentley, I'll find out."

"What a novel this would make," the author said. "But no one would believe it. No one."

Confrontation

Big Red preceded him and the New Man walked two steps behind as MacGlendon strode through the almost empty shopping concourse connecting the Place Vendôme and Rue Cambon sides of the Ritz Hotel. Glittery baubles sparkled in glass showcases crowding both sides of the arcade. Three quarters of the way down the narrow *allée,* walking three abreast, were the top executives of a giant women's sportswear manufacturer. MacGlendon was trapped in the tunnel, with no way to avoid face-to-face contact with them.

The big, apish-looking man, the one in the middle, confronted him directly, pushing Big Red aside. "What is going on, Gus?"

"What are you talking about, Morry?"

"Don't turn the big, innocent blue eyes on me, Gus. I got the information straight from the horse's mouth." He shifted the cigar to the other side of his face. "I was on the horn to our people in Hong Kong not more than ten minutes ago. The rumor is all over the Far East. My man there confirmed it. It wasn't more than ten minutes ago." He turned to the man on his right. "Isn't that right, Ralph?" Ralph nodded. "Don't shit me, Gus. Give it to me straight. It'll be all over the Prêt within a half hour. There are no secrets in this business. You're going to learn that."

MacGlendon shrugged his shoulders. "I still don't know what you're talking about, Morry."

The New Man had closed in, standing at MacGlendon's side. Big Red rooted himself on the other side, partially shielding MacGlendon. The six of them stepped aside as two blue-haired American ladies window-shopped near them, chattering to each other in lazy, southern accents.

"Give it to me straight," the American tycoon said. "What are you going to do?"

"I don't even know what the rumor is, Morry."

"It's not a rumor, Gus. It's the *emes*. I told you that I talked to Hong Kong not more than ten minutes ago. Wait until this hits Wall Street." The man started to reach for the lapel of MacGlendon's jacket but backed off when Big Red raised his hand. "We can make a fast deal, Gus. I've got great banking connections. I've made deals in stranger places than this."

"Morry, how many times do I have to tell you that I have no idea what you're talking about."

"All right, Gus, play it dumb, play it cute. But with the Hong Kong Shanghai Bank out of the picture, you're in a lot of trouble. You'll never make the merger. I got connections, Gus. I can get the dough. I want a piece of the action. I'm asking you like a gentleman, Gus. I don't have to, you know. I could let you drown and pick up the pieces for peanuts. But I'm asking you like a gentleman."

MacGlendon said: "There are no problems with the merger, Morry. All that you're hearing are rumors. The deal is wrapped up, nailed down."

"You don't know the rag business like I do, Gus. Nothing is ever nailed down. Your great international coup is coming apart. I got it straight."

Suddenly, from both sides of the hotel, groups of Japanese tourists converged into the concourse. Hordes of camera-clicking bodies swarmed around, filling the tunnel with squealing voices.

A glass display case shattered under the impact of the pushing crowd, and a burglar alarm screeched. A shot was fired. Then another. More glass broke. The lights went out.

In the directionless stampeding of bodies MacGlendon was slammed against a wall, then shoved forward. He felt the cold steel of gun barrels pressing against his back and his chest. An accented voice whispered in his ear. "Keep moving." MacGlendon tried to sidestep out of the vise of the two guns but doubled up with pain as a blow hit him in the groin. Momentarily he lost equilibrium: the hysteria in the concourse had no top or bottom—it was a dizzying circle of screaming voices and twisting bodies. He held his hands against the fiery pain, allowing himself to be steamrollered forward. There was another blow to the back of the neck, and he lost consciousness, regaining it when he was jammed into a tiny elevator cab ascending slowly, four unknown men holding him upright. The elevator jolted to a stop. The men pushed him into the hotel corridor. He fell facedown, sprawled on the carpet. The men in the elevator disappeared behind the closing door.

Using his arms as levers, MacGlendon tried to raise himself upright, but the pain in his groin shot through his body and he collapsed again. Brushing his cheeks against the dusty carpet, he looked both ways down the corridor: empty. All the doors were closed, and bleak lights reflected on the endless, tortuous pattern of the floor.

Time had no dimensions as MacGlendon writhed in pain. It could have been minutes and it could have been hours, but finally a door ahead of him opened, spotlighting him with daylight. Able to raise his head, he squinted into the sudden brightness. He closed his eyes, opened them again, but still saw the same apparition.

The Eurasian woman stood in the opened doorway, her breasts bare; a peach-colored bath towel was wrapped sarong-style around her body and a linen towel turbaned her hair.

In the hazy zone between the conscious and the unconscious, MacGlendon could not separate mirage from reality. The tattooed Garuda took slow flight on the woman's bobbing breast as she walked toward him, and the taut, pink nipple brushed his face as she leaned over him, and there was the heavy musk of perfumed oil on her hands as she rubbed his forehead.

The bulk of two men appeared. Details of their faces and bodies indistinguishable, they blocked the daylight coming through the opened door. Straining, they raised MacGlendon to a near-standing position and, supporting him from each side, dragged him into the suite, through a blurred room, and into the bedroom. No longer able to support his weight, they threw him facedown on the bed.

For an instant MacGlendon was aware of the cool caress of the satin bed-covering and the enveloping warmth of the cushioned mattress. Then he blacked out again.

Before he was aware of the pain, he felt the opposite sensations of fiery hot and icy cold. Consciousness came slowly, a zigzag line finally straightening out in a direct current toward reality. Plastic bags of crushed ice were encircling his head, packed against the bottoms of his bare feet, and jammed under his armpits. The Eurasian woman was pouring hot oil down the length of his torso, kneading it into his flesh. She worked his body with strong fingers controlled to a tenderness.

MacGlendon lay motionless, abandoning himself to the conflicting sensations restoring his consciousness. He fought back his impulse to break away, using the time, like a wounded animal, to regain his strength, relive the attack, and assess the dangers that remained.

The voice from the other end of the room came through to MacGlendon like an echo in a hollow cave, out of proportion to the original sound. "You're enjoying it too much," the man said. "Let me at him."

The caressing fingers stopped. Hard hands replaced them and began chopping at him, a staccato run up and down his legs, up his abdomen and across his chest. Then thumbs pressed against the base of the neck choking the jugular. Still the wounded fox, MacGlendon continued to lie motionless, feeling the rate of his breathing accelerate toward normal.

More hot oil seared his body. The ice packs were pressed harder against his feet. A new bag of ice was thrust between his legs, worked upward, then smashed against his scrotum. In an uncontrolled reflex, MacGlendon bolted upright, thrashed against the arms and hands hammering at his body. The sudden action dizzied him, but he held firm, bringing the room and the face of the man into focus.

Ridge Bentley said: "You're tough, MacGlendon. Tougher than I suspected. You're hard to put away, and you're hard to bring back."

MacGlendon grabbed the silky sheets to cover his nakedness, studied the immaculate figure of Bentley dressed in a silk robe with an ascot tied at the neck. Only his hands seemed menacing, gleaming with the residue of hot oil. *Weirdo. Genius. Hippie terrorist.* None of it fit the man he was looking at. This was a gentleman out of another era—a man who drove Packard automobiles and wore Arrow shirts and played polo in South America. He was a character in a Noel Coward play listening to Cole Porter singing naughty songs at the piano.

Bentley sat on the edge of the bed, wiped his hands on

the bedspread. "Being tough is good. Intelligence and toughness is a rare combination. Use it well, MacGlendon. Use it well." Then he lay down on the bed, kicking off his velvet slippers. Looking at the ceiling, he said, "Are you convinced now that we can destroy you?"

MacGlendon was afraid to speak, unsure of how his voice would sound. He fought back the seduction of unconsciousness, of falling into a coma and awakening to find that this was only another of his convoluted dreams.

"You've been beaten and subdued, MacGlendon. In spite of your own bodyguards and the CIA watchdogs, we've managed to capture you. A man of your intelligence must recognize a superior force." He turned his head. "Would you like a cold drink or a cup of tea?" MacGlendon managed to shake his head. "You've seen your ladylove ravaged by a black savage, and when you read the newspaper, you'll find that there are rumors that your financial empire is tottering. I would guess that there will be a panic of selling of your stock on Wall Street when the exchange opens in New York. My guess is that the stock will drop eight or nine points before the trading on it is suspended." Bentley sat up on the edge of the bed, carefully placed his feet back into the slippers, using his index finger to ease his heels into place. "And we're not through," Bentley said, smiling at MacGlendon before he walked across the room and looked out the windows into the gardens of the Ritz. "There's your mother. I'm not quite sure of your real feelings about her. But there's a lot of muck to be raked up about her—all the scandal when McCarthy was investigating Blair Brewster. The real truth never came out. It may not be page one anymore, but that kind of press certainly will do a man in your position no good." He reached to the desk, tore a piece of paper off a pad, crumbled it, and threw it into the wastebasket. "On the sentimental side," Bentley continued, "there are your grandparents, the Blumbergs.

They're in Florida now, aren't they? Old people can be so careless crossing streets. It happens all the time—run down by speeding, doped-up kids in souped-up jalopies."

Finally, MacGlendon managed to utter the word, "Why?"

"Simple," Bentley said. "These little exercises should convince you that our power is greater, more deadly than yours."

"But why?"

"An intelligent man, faced with a superior power source, follows the simple maxim, If you can't fight 'em, join 'em." Bentley went back, sat on the edge of the bed again, facing MacGlendon directly. "I know how you think, MacGlendon. I've made a long, careful analysis of you from your history. You have had situations like this before—not of this magnitude, but similar in concept. You've been a pragmatic man. When it appears that you can't fight 'em, you have joined 'em. Temporarily, I grant you. You play the other man's game only long enough to gain the power to destroy him." He reached across, put his hand on MacGlendon's knee. "Use those tactics with me. Realize at the moment that you can't beat me—so join me. I know you'll be lying back waiting your chance to beat me at my own game." Bentley smiled. "When you gave your acceptance speech for the Horatio Alger Award, you quoted your grandfather Blumberg. It was a very touching moment. You even imitated the old man's Jewish accent. *If you got a lemon, make lemonade.*"

"I'm not sure of your game," MacGlendon said. "But what if I say *yes*. What if I say that I'll play your game until I can beat you at it. If you know my history so well, you know that in the end I always win."

"I have my own history, MacGlendon. Not unlike yours in many ways. I'll take my chances with you. I had a grandfather, too. He spoke with an accent—a very cultured, Charleston accent. He told me—The bigger they are, the harder they fall. That will be a little side effect, a little personal pleasure that I can indulge in—watching you fall."

"What's the game?" MacGlendon stood up, felt his legs wobble for an instant but stood firm. His clothes were heaped on a chair near the closet. He walked over slowly, steadied himself against the wall, and began to dress.

"I had a brother like you," Bentley said. "Built like a bull —hung like a horse. He killed himself." A softness passed over the rigorous control of Bentley's face. "Everyone always thought *he* was the tough one and *I* the weak one. But I survived and he didn't."

"I've already accepted your power play, Bentley. Getting maudlin only weakens your position." MacGlendon could not steady his hands to work the buttons on his shirt. He sat down, his back to Bentley, left his shirt open, and put his socks on. "Read me the facts," he said, "as they exist right at this minute."

"Nothing—no facts—exist *only* as of this minute. There's always an umbilical to the past: all world history, all personal history influence what is happening at this moment."

"We're making a deal, Bentley. Don't give me that mumbo jumbo historical shit. Put it on the table."

"The consortium," Bentley began, then waited for a reaction. MacGlendon stood up, turned around, buttoned his shirt quickly, and tucked it into his jeans. "Simple geopolitics," Bentley continued. "China versus Russia. You can't ignore the long Sino-Russian history. The consortium is just another segment of it. China needs it. Russia has to stop it. It's that simple."

"Where do I fit in?"

"You're the Trojan horse, MacGlendon. You're the big, shining wonder-boy with the all-American glaze. You're going to penetrate the consortium and destroy it when Moscow pushes the button."

"What's in it for me?"

Bentley laughed. "I read you exactly right. I did my homework on you, MacGlendon, and I figured you'd come back with that *what's in it for me?*"

MacGlendon narrowed his eyes, straightened his shoulders, walked around the bed and stood at the closed bedroom door. "All right, genius—what *is* in it for me?"

"Negatives," Bentley said. "No positives. We call off the dogs. No more assaults. No more murders. No panic on Wall Street."

"What about my deal with the Chinese?"

"Build all the factories you want in China. Wars aren't won with ladies' shirts and cable-knit sweaters. We're gunning for the steelmakers and the oil producers. You're small potatoes in the consortium, MacGlendon. You're way down at the bottom of the pecking order."

MacGlendon opened the door. Bentley called across to him. "You have twenty-four hours, MacGlendon."

"For what?"

"A simple *yes* or a simple *no.*"

"What if I just blow the whistle now?"

"Meaning?"

"Go to the French police. Go to the American embassy. Call the FBI. Tell the CIA."

"At that point your destruction is irreversible." Bentley walked toward him. "You're too smart for that. You're going to play for time. Until you know who the other members of the consortium are and when the meeting is going to take place and *where* it's going to take place— you're going to stall for time. That's how your mind works, isn't it? But you only have twenty-four hours. In twenty-four hours and five minutes an accident could happen to two old people in Florida. Not killed. Painfully injured." He touched MacGlendon's arm. "Think of how proud your daddy would be if he was alive. By helping Russia, you'd be carrying on his work. Your father died for Communism. He's kind of an underground cult hero to all the secret Marxists in the world: he's right in there with Che Guevara, Lenin, and Trotsky. Think of how proud your daddy would be."

Cruising on the Seine

They were waiting on the embankment, under the shadow of the Pont Neuf, watching the commercial river traffic cut through the thick, murky waters of the Seine. Pug O'Connor stood near a weathered wood post, his arms folded over his chest, his eyes watching the river in both directions. Occasionally he would divert his attention, look over at MacGlendon.

MacGlendon sat on a concrete abutment behind him, feeling the pain still racking his body and, following a practiced discipline, analyzing the confusion in his mind. The lingering scent of the Eurasian woman's perfumed oil clung to his body, the heady vapor confounding pleasure with pain, muddling his ability to think clearly.

O'Connor looked at his watch again, shook his wrist and held the watch to his ear, and then walked back, sat beside MacGlendon, wrinkled his nose and sniffed. "You smell like a girl I used to know in Saigon," he said. "That was a long time ago, when Saigon was Saigon and women . . ." He looked toward the water's edge.

"What the hell are we waiting for?"

"A boat," O'Connor answered. "Maybe it'll come and maybe it won't."

"I'm going back to my hotel and take a shower." He started to stand. O'Connor pulled him back.

"You're not going anywhere, MacGlendon: nowhere without me. Whither thou goest—disaster follows. You're like a damn hydrogen bomb. You leave a wake of destruction. How you've survived this long, I'll never know."

"I have a schedule," MacGlendon said. "In spite of all this, I *am* in Paris on business. I have appointments, and my mother is flying in from New York. I promised to meet her at the airport while she's changing planes to Nice."

"The Concorde doesn't arrive until five thirty. You have plenty of time."

MacGlendon stood up, winced at the pain. "You have no authority to hold me, O'Connor."

"I have authority in my two hands, which is even more impressive considering your weakened condition. It would give me great pleasure to beat the shit out of you, MacGlendon. You haven't exactly made my life easy. I trusted you once. Remember? I put you on the honor system. You blew it. Now sit down before you fall on your ass."

Watching a tug tow a row of empty barges, MacGlendon walked to the edge of the river. In his head he computed the time change, figuring the hour when the New York Stock Exchange would open. It was still only eight in the morning Eastern time. Rumors would be rampant by now, transmitted in low-key voices at the high-level breakfast meetings in the private dining rooms of the investment houses. He knew the pattern, had been an insider watching the whisper-machine work in his favor against other companies. Now the breakfast tables would be turned against him. Ridge had given him twenty-four hours. There was a lot to be accomplished in those twenty-four hours, and precious minutes were being dissipated in this pointless vigil on the Seine. *Lemonade from lemons.* MacGlendon mentally time-slotted his actions, marshaling them in sequence so that when he went into counteraction, he could move swiftly and deftly. All his instincts were sensitized to another personal fortune to be made.

A small cabin cruiser followed the wake of the last barge, hugging the shoreline, bobbing in the following choppiness. One of the crew threw bumpers over the side as the cruiser cut engines and drifted under the cover of the bridge when the engines started again, but reversed speed against the current and maintained a steady position.

Using long strides, O'Connor was alongside the boat quickly, jumped on board, looked back and signaled to MacGlendon, then disappeared below deck. The deckhand stretched out his arm, tossed MacGlendon a rope, shouting something to him in French. MacGlendon pulled, holding the cruiser close to the embankment and considered the option of dropping the rope and making a run for it, but decided against it and giant-stepped aboard, following O'Connor through the open hatch, down the ladder and into the cabin of the cruiser.

The man sitting cross-legged on the bench was Oriental, proportioned on the scale of a Japanese wrestler, his face fixed in the benign smile of a bronze Buddha. He was wearing thick, metal-framed glasses that pressed against the fat of his face. Cascading folds of flesh, descending from his chest and bellying against his crossed legs, were accentuated by the Yale T-shirt he wore, the seal of the university stretched out of focus and shape. His thick legs were stuffed into denim jeans, and his feet were bare, surprisingly pink against the yellowish tint of the rest of his body. He extended his hand to MacGlendon, the wrist clamped by a tight gold bracelet watch. MacGlendon shook the hand, felt the strength under the flab and then sat down opposite the man. Pug O'Connor was at the forward end of the cabin, fumbling through an ice chest, examining beer labels.

The boat had started forward and was navigating through

the traffic to the center lanes, moving at a slow, labored speed. The engines were noisy, and there was a strong smell of gasoline.

"By way of introduction," the man began, speaking with a British-school accent, "my name is unimportant. As a matter of fact, I have many names, but none of them is my own. It's been so many years since I've used my real name that it has no sense of identity to me anymore." He refused the beer can being offered by O'Connor who, in turn, held it out to MacGlendon who shook it off. "My credentials," the man said, "will become self-evident."

"What do you want with me?"

"My job is to enlist your aid as a patriot."

MacGlendon asked, "Which country?"

"In spite of my physical and racial characteristics," the Oriental man said, "I am a citizen of the United States and a sworn agent of the United States government. Does that surprise you?"

"After two days in Paris nothing surprises me, nor do I believe what anyone tells me. How do I know that you're who you say you are?" He looked at O'Connor. "How do I know that any of you are who you say you are?"

"In my position," the Oriental man said, "one can scarcely run the risk of passing out engraved business cards identifying oneself as an agent of the CIA. We do have, and have had for some time, agents within the Red Chinese government. The CIA is not all bungles and blood the way the press makes us out. There are some very good and effective in-place agents within China." He recrossed his legs in the opposite position. "You have seen Mr. O'Connor's credentials, have you not? He carries official State Department identification. And he keeps saving your life. On his performance alone you must trust him by now."

"How do I know that his identification isn't forged?"

The Oriental man increased the width of his benevolent

smile. "Your reluctance—your inherent caution—these traits are understandable in light of what has happened to you. However, at one point in his life, a man must take a stand, based on nothing more solid than gut reaction, instinctive faith, and the ability to distinguish right from wrong."

O'Connor interrupted, speaking to the Oriental man. "Appealing to MacGlendon's finer instincts will get you nowhere," he said. "Make a deal with him. Talk the only language he understands. Offer him a proposition where he thinks he'll be able to fuck you in the end. He'll snap at that bait. Don't waste your breath trying to arouse any decent reactions from him. He doesn't have any."

"Unfortunately, Mr. MacGlendon, I can offer you no financial gains for what I'm about to ask you to do. Conversely, the indications are that a moral course of action on your part at this time will probably involve a personal financial setback. In the long run the righteous course always prospers, but in the short haul, being a patriot will probably nullify any financial coups you have come to Paris to accomplish."

MacGlendon turned to O'Connor. "I'll take one of those beers." O'Connor, glowering, did not move. "Please," MacGlendon added. When O'Connor handed him the icy can, he tore off the tab, took a swallow and wiped the foam from his mouth with the back of his hand. "You're dead right about me, O'Connor. You understand me perfectly." He turned to the Oriental man. "If you're going to talk business to me, you have to talk deals."

O'Connor moved forward, stood between the other two men. "What do you want, MacGlendon, for acting like a decent citizen?"

"Protection," MacGlendon said. "I want a guarantee of physical protection."

"That's funny. I've been trying to save your ass ever since

this hoopla started. You won't cooperate. I can't give you protection unless you play ball and stop acting like you're a one-man Marine Corps."

"I'm not talking about *my* ass. I need protection for other people."

"For example?"

"My grandparents in Florida."

"Easy," O'Connor replied. "The boys down there are so sick of playing cops and robbers with those crazy Cubans that they'll jump at the chance of baby-sitting with a couple of senior citizens."

"My mother," MacGlendon said.

"Not so easy. You told me that she's on her way to Monte Carlo, didn't you? Monte Carlo is an international zoo. It's going to take some doing to get the local authorities to cooperate without tipping our whole hand. We'll do our best. Who else?"

"Paula de Plyssy."

"That's like trying to track a hummingbird. She's flaky, MacGlendon. She's a kook. You don't know what the hell direction she's going to take. I understand about how beautiful her eyes are—but I'm not even sure whose side she's on. She has all the earmarks of a beautiful booby trap."

"Regardless. That's one of my conditions."

The Oriental man waved off O'Connor. "You have your reasons, Mr. MacGlendon. I assume that you have received direct threats against these people."

MacGlendon hesitated and then said, "I am being blackmailed with their lives and safety."

"Who? The Chinese? The Russians? The Taiwanese? Who?"

"Ridge Bentley," MacGlendon answered. "I.e., the Russians."

Another voice spoke now. A shadowy figure stood in the darkness at the forward end of the cabin framed in a door opened to a stateroom. "It's always the Russians, isn't it?" he said. "Every damn step we take in any direction is affected directly or indirectly by the Russians."

The voice was familiar, and when the man stepped forward into the light, the face, the silver hair and the military bearing were immediately and irrefutably recognizable. The Oriental man uncrossed his legs and stood up deferentially, his body rigid in a military kind of stance. O'Connor cowered and backed off.

The man said: "I am convinced of Mr. MacGlendon's innate loyalty. You people are demeaning his integrity by these petty questions." He narrowed his eyes, took off his glasses. "We've met before, haven't we?"

"Yes, sir. In 1977. There was a dinner for the YPO in the White House. We were seated at the same table."

"I'm one of those responsible for our current love affair with China." He sat down wearily, rubbed his hand over his mouth. "You know why I did it? I have no love for the Chinese. The Russians. Every step of history since World War Two is influenced by fear of the Russians. It's no different now." He gestured with his hand. "I'd like to talk to Mr. MacGlendon alone," he said, waiting until O'Connor and the Oriental man climbed up the ladder, then closed the hatch.

When they were alone, the man said: "I am very much misunderstood. If this China thing explodes the wrong way, history will lay part of the blame on me. Keep remembering Russia. China is our greatest weapon against Russia. But never forget that they're two of a kind. Both Marxists. China, at the moment, is the lesser evil. There is a delicate balance that must be kept between them, a stalemate of power that will keep both of them immobilized against the West." He sat down, ramrod straight. "That is why the consortium must be destroyed before it begins. If the consortium succeeds, China becomes too powerful—too soon.

That's the key phrase—*too soon.* And it cannot be destroyed without giving China a face-saving option. Face is important to the Chinese." He swung his legs across to the edge of the opposite bench. "You're in a unique position, Mr. Mac-Glendon. You are our only link to the consortium."

"What exactly is the consortium?"

"Our direct information is only fragmentary. Much of it unsubstantiated guesswork. But being a student of history, the pattern is age-old with the Chinese. Their basic problem is to feed nine hundred million people. Their Cultural Revolution didn't work. Marxism is not much better than the dynasties and warlords. To become self-sufficient, to again have the luxury of closing its doors against the barbarians of the West, China must temporarily play the capitalist game, play it long enough to develop its natural resources, industrialize quickly to be able to compete in the world markets. That's the function of the consortium, a power-house group from the Western world with the know-how to catapult China to a major power position within five years. The Chinese must go to the outside for technology and expertise, but they have their own natural resources, and they have the one commodity that is disappearing in every other major country: cheap, controlled labor. Granted that they now have to make certain capitalist concessions to labor to increase productivity—personal perks in conflict with Marxist principles—it is my opinion that these concessions are temporary. When China becomes self-sufficient, when they export more than they import, the jaws of the dragon will snap shut again." He kicked off his shoes and rubbed his eyes. "Oil," he continued. "Foreign money has been poured into China to determine their potential oil resources. They're sitting on a mind-boggling supply, both on-shore and off-shore. Why, then, have they suddenly thrown out the foreigners—stopped the oil explorations?" He pointed his finger at the ceiling, shaking it vigorously. "Because they are going to develop it themselves. But they need expertise and technology. They won't go to Texas for that. They'll go to the Middle East. In the long range of history, the days of Arab oil supremacy are numbered. If I were forming the conspiracy . . ." He turned to MacGlendon. "You notice that I call it a conspiracy rather than a consortium. Make no mistake. It is a conspiracy against the rest of the world and most of all against the Russians. It's always the Russians." He turned back, continued addressing the world. "One of the most important members of the group would be an oil expert from the Arab world."

"Any idea of who?"

"Even to this day our intelligence capabilities in that area are very weak. That is one of the pieces of information we are depending on you to supply us."

"Automobiles," MacGlendon said. "Automation."

"Exactly right. Look at the state of the automotive industry all over the world. Disaster. Except Japan. But with technology and expertise again, fortified with cheap labor, the Chinese could dominate the world market. I'd go to Italy for my man to handle the automotive industry. Perhaps France." He shook his head. "No. I'd save France for the aircraft industry. I'd go to someone like Agnelli for the automotive."

"Why not the United States?"

He shook his head. "A problem in ideology. Detroit will never admit that its days are numbered. The leadership of the industry is too fragmented. There is no strong figure. And the industry is too intertwined with the general economy. No, I'd go to Italy. Their labor market is out of control." He thought for a moment, smiled to himself, and then continued.

"For steel, I'd go to Japan. They have performed a miracle in capturing the world steel market. Think what their competitive position would be if they had been able to keep their labor cheap." He sat up quickly, faced MacGlendon. "Look at Japan and you'll get a glimpse of China. What was Japan? Cheap novelty goods—crappy knock-offs of American technology. Made in Japan meant poor quality. That was only ten or fifteen years ago. But look at what they've done in a short time. Now Made in Japan means the highest degree of technology, the finest quality. Think of how powerful they would be if they had their own natural resources, didn't have to depend on imports, and think of their prices if they had been able to control their labor market.

"China," he said, "can succeed across the board, even in the areas where Japan is limited."

"Where do I come in?" MacGlendon asked.

"You're the low man in the consortium, but in many ways the key man because they have some provenance for soft goods and textiles. You can expand an existing source, bring desperately needed currency into China to develop hard industries. And, your industry is labor-intensive. You're going to keep millions of fingers busy at sewing machines and textile mills. First there's oil. Then steel. Then the automotive industries. Then aircraft. Then agriculture. Finally, the soft goods. China is courting the world now with soft goods, beginning the love affair with baubles, pretty sweaters, straw baskets, and glittery artifacts. It's a ruse to condition the world for the big push of hard goods. You will eventually become expendable to the consortium." He looked over at MacGlendon again. "But not before you have become one of the richest men in the world. That's what you want, isn't it? Isn't that the ultimate Horatio Alger: the richest man in the world?"

"There are personal standards of conduct involved," MacGlendon said. "Horatio Alger became rich but stayed moral."

"Morality," the man said, "has shifting definitions. Moral

standards adjust to given sets of circumstances. At one point you're going to say to yourself, if I don't play ball with the Chinese, someone else will. I pointed out to you that China is a Communist country temporarily playing a capitalist game to accomplish Marxist goals. You'll convince yourself that you're a moral man, temporarily playing an immoral game, to accomplish moral purposes."

MacGlendon didn't say anything.

"You must take a position, Mr. MacGlendon. Continuing with the Chinese, taking an active part in the formation of the consortium is, in my opinion, part of which is based on a top-secret military memorandum, an act of treason. Withdrawing from it, in spite of personal financial loss, would be an act of honor."

"And what if I do what the CIA wants me to do—play spy?"

"We need the names of the members of the consortium," the man answered. "You could get them. It will be extremely dangerous, and an act of heroism."

MacGlendon did not discuss the fourth alternative: the Russian option.

Le Pigeon

Soaking in the bathtub, subliminally thinking about love, MacGlendon reexamined his priorities, reassessed his strengths and weaknesses vis-à-vis the nightmare of the day in Paris. First, there was the Russian intervention spearheaded by Ridge Bentley, and then there was the eerie, unreal quality of the cruise on the Seine giving the dimension of high-level governmental interference in what heretofore had been private business dealings with the Chinese. The battle lines were clearly drawn now. The opposing forces were identifiable.

He analyzed his options coldly, stripping away the patriotic and geopolitical aspects.

No matter how MacGlendon figured, he could not refute the arithmetic of the manufacturing capabilities he needed in China to support his takeover of the fashion industry. Unless he had those factories in China producing merchandise, his expansion plan was doomed to failure, the whole MacGlendon conglomerate collapsing with it.

He touched the thin gold chain around his neck, fingering the incising on the jade disk. *A friend is nearby.* The Chinese silk merchant had warned him to trust only Paula de Plyssy as the next link to the meeting of the consortium. He saw the scars and burns on her ravaged body, felt again the chill of trauma that had been in her cold flesh as he engulfed her in his arms.

Plantagenet seemed to be a dead end, an abandoned way station. The key to everything was the contact by the Chinese to inform MacGlendon of the time and place of the meeting of the consortium. For this contact to be made, they had all finally agreed, MacGlendon needed to be exposed on all flanks with nothing to inhibit access to him. Even Pug O'Connor was convinced now that MacGlendon had to go it alone, unprotected by the vigilance of CIA operatives. "You'll be a sitting duck," O'Connor had warned him. "A real pigeon."

"But that's the point, isn't it?" the Oriental man in the Yale T-shirt had asked. "A sitting duck is exactly what we need."

"I'll call off my dogs," O'Connor said, "but it would look funny if you were suddenly without your own bodyguards. At least keep them around. They're not pros, but they're better than nothing."

Out of the tub, MacGlendon dried himself gently over the bruises of his body, went into the bedroom and called the Paris office of a New York brokerage firm, using an assumed name, and asked for some current market quotations including that of his own corporation. The stock had dropped two points: nothing dramatic yet. He checked his watch. It was still early in New York. There would be time after he met his mother at the airport.

Lemonade out of lemons. It was the most useful piece of advice he had ever received. He saw the picture of the wizened little old man, the bright Florida sun. But then a careening black sedan leaped over a curb, plowed through pedestrians on the curb and then sped off.

MacGlendon closed his eyes to the continuing real and unreal nightmares.

In Transit: De Gaulle

The loudspeaker was announcing the arrival of the Concorde from New York. The aircraft was on the ground but, because of heavy traffic conditions, would not be at the gate for another twelve minutes. Other than Air France personnel MacGlendon was alone in this area. A special pass, dangling from an oversize clip on the lapel of his jacket, had cleared him through security and immigration.

His mind raced back to the other times in his life when he had waited for his mother at airports. He felt now the same anxieties he had always felt in anticipation of seeing her after a long absence. He was remembering the other times when she was scheduled on a flight but, for one reason or another, never arrived. These were the times when a sense of relief buffered the bitter disappointment, masking an ambivalent mixture of emotions.

The jetway was in place against the door of the Concorde. After a few minutes the outer doors opened into the terminal. Most of the disembarking passengers were men, affluent-looking, carrying expensive leather attaché cases and shoulder bags. They walked with the confident calm of the rich.

MacGlendon turned his head away as he recognized two

bankers from Boston, allowed enough time and then turned back to watch for his mother.

When he had not seen her for a long time, he was always startled by her appearance. Now, as she stopped at the doorway looking around in confusion, blocking the exit, she was a younger person, very pretty, chicly dressed, a tiny person discreetly carrying the authority of wealth and beauty. He stood up, crossed diagonally toward her. They met halfway, in the center of the lounge. He bent down, kissed her cheek, and took the Vuitton cosmetic case from her in one gesture.

"Darling, you're always such a shock to me. I never remember you being as big as you are. I suppose mothers are like that. Little boys never grow up in our eyes."

He took her arm, led her toward the far corner of the lounge. "How was the flight?"

"Divine. Absolutely divine. Three hours and thirty-six minutes. Can you believe that? New York to Paris in three hours and thirty-six minutes. It's the only way to go. When I think of the old days on the Boeing Stratocruiser . . . seventeen hours or so and that dreadful stop in Gander or Goose Bay. I simply adore progress. Don't you?"

"You look marvelous," he said.

"Do I? God knows I try." She laughed. "It takes longer and longer now to pull myself together."

He looked down into the fire of her red hair. "Not a bit of gray yet."

"My hairdresser knows for sure, darling, and I tip him enough so that he'll never tell." Partially obscured by a huge supporting column, they sat beside each other in the far corner. "Darling, you must absolutely say hello to Paula and Freddie." He looked puzzled. "The Sheinwolds," she explained. "He writes that syndicated bridge column. They're the reason I'm going to Monte Carlo." She squinted toward the group waiting in the lounge. "Every cent I lose to him at bridge, I make up with interest at backgammon. Such a love."

"Did you talk to Grandma and Grandpa before you left?"

"For a minute. You can imagine what a rush I was in." She studied him, saw his concern. "They're fine, darling. You worry so. If they weren't fine, do you think I would have left?"

He shook his head, smiled at her.

"Are you having a nice time in Paris? It's so exciting reading about you in the newspaper. All my friends are up in arms about Bonwit Teller. What are you going to do with those stores?"

"Turn them around, show them how to sell high fashion at low prices. I'll use some of the present stores as a nucleus for international expansion. I have some ideas about merchandising those kinds of stores without depending on sales help."

"When my salesgirl at Bergdorf's retired, I was distraught. I can't believe the kind of help you get in the stores today. Even the best ones. They don't care. They simply couldn't care less . . . or know less. The irresponsibility is destroying me. Are you going to do something about that?"

He shook his head. "Your era is over, Mother. It'll never come back."

"More's the pity."

"You'll survive."

"Will I be able to buy Bill Blass wholesale?"

"I think that that can be arranged."

"I just don't believe the prices."

There was an awkward silence between them. Then his mother said, "I sound like a silly old lady rattling on about Bill Blass, don't I, when there are important things to talk about?" She squinted at the face of her diamond-bezeled watch. "I wish I weren't so vain and would wear glasses all the time. I've tried contacts, but they make my eyes tear." She lowered her wrist. "What time is it, darling?"

"Five forty-five, Paris time."

"Well, we have almost an hour before the flight to Nice."

"What is it, Mother? What's the urgency?"

She thought for a moment. "It's not urgency really." She stopped again. "Well, perhaps it is. It's not urgent to you, but it's urgent to me." She lowered her head. "We've never talked much about your father or his family. When you were very young, you asked questions, but I avoided them. Frankly, darling, it hurt me too much then. I'm not sure that it doesn't hurt too much now." She opened her purse and fumbled for a monogrammed handkerchief, held it ready in her hand. "We should have talked about this before. It's my fault. I'm to blame, but it was painful. Your father and I were very much in love. I suppose we were even silly about loving each other. Blindly. Madly. No other thought but loving each other. I don't suppose love is like that anymore." She looked up at him. "I wish you had your father's capacity to love like that." She touched the crumbled handkerchief to her dry eyes. "Is there anyone in your life now?"

He shook his head.

"I knew it wasn't right for you when you married . . . isn't that silly, I can never remember her name."

"Debbie."

"Yes. Of course it was. I can never remember her name. It must be psychological, don't you think? But I knew that you two were not right for each other."

"It was a long time ago, Mother."

"You must know that your father's family never approved of me. It wasn't that they didn't approve of *me*, really. I never met any of them. But they disinherited your father because he was a radical. Your father's family was very rich. They were very rich when everyone else was poor and got richer while everyone else was getting poorer. Your father thought that was immoral. He thought that his father was taking advantage of other people's misfortune."

"I know the background," MacGlendon said. "Start with what's happening now."

"It was ironic. When I called you and asked you to meet me, your first thought was that something had happened to Grandma or Grandpa. Actually, I learned yesterday, or maybe it was the day before, that Jennie MacGlendon had died six months ago. A lawyer called me. God knows how he traced me or found me. He was handling your grandmother's estate. Your Grandfather MacGlendon died fifteen years ago, left everything to her. I imagine it was quite a bit. But when Jennie MacGlendon died, they found a document in the safety deposit box of one of the banks. You must understand, Angus, that your father never spoke against his parents. What I did learn about them I had to coax out of him. He tried to give the impression that they no longer existed for him just as he no longer existed for them. The Scots are proud people . . . stubborn people." She dabbed her dry eyes. "When the lawyer finally found me and we met in New York, I learned that although they never talked about your father, they kept mementos of him in this vault. Pictures. His high school diploma. Newspaper clippings." This time when she touched the handkerchief to her eyes, there were tears to dry. "I have all those things now," she said. "You can have them if you want them." She looked up. "Do you want them?"

"If you don't."

"I don't know. That part of my life is so far behind me. Yet it was the best part." She put her handkerchief back into her purse. "There's quite a bit of money, Angus. Quite a bit."

"Mine?"

She nodded. "It was to be given to your father when he was thirty. He was only twenty-three when he died." She stuffed the handkerchief into her purse. "The instructions were that if your father did not live to be thirty, then the money was to be held in perpetuity until any child of his reached the age of thirty. I don't understand why the document was not found when your grandfather died. The lawyer for the estate didn't understand it, either. He thought that perhaps your grandmother had hidden it. Who knows?" She shrugged her shoulders. "We'll never find out now, will we?"

"How much is involved?"

"Well, the lawyer wasn't sure. I mean the trust fund hasn't been audited to the penny." She looked up at her son. "In 1963, it was worth almost seven million dollars. The lawyer guessed that the amount has probably doubled since then. It was well invested."

The expression did not change on MacGlendon's face. He was analyzing the accumulation of what appeared to be coincidental happenings.

"Are you so jaded, Angus? Doesn't that amount of money impress you?"

"I was thinking what that amount of money would have done for me ten years ago. Everything would have happened sooner." He took her hand, felt the tremor in it, pressed it quiet. "The money isn't mine, Mom. It really belongs to you."

"But the point is, Angus, that I don't really need it, either. Brewster left me very rich, and all the stock in your corporations has made me even richer. It's funny to be able to say that, when I think of those early years with your father. Never a penny. But it's nonetheless true: I have more money than I'll ever be able to spend. I would think you have, too. Time does strange things. We were what we were because we were very poor. Now that we're very rich

. . . Well, it's terribly confusing. One never really forgets being poor."

She seemed so fragile to him, so vulnerable and so defenseless. He was considering the ways to protect her from being sucked into the storm of events. Ridge Bentley had threatened to reactivate old scandals about her, rehash old history and serve it up with a new sensationalism. MacGlendon wondered if this frail woman could stand up to that now, survive the ugly revival of her past.

MacGlendon knew that the sudden appearance of a secreted trust fund was not a coincidence. It was a deliberate element in this chain of elements intended to destroy him. The devices of destruction were still undefined, obscured by the mass and the maze of half-known evidence, secrets yet to be learned, keys still to be found. But priority number one was to protect the innocent. The picture of the scarred Paula de Plyssy was in his mind. He pressed his mother's hand.

"You have a plan," he said. "You have an idea. What is it?"

"Well, it's probably very impractical. You know how scatterbrained I am about money or how to use it." She smiled. "From a wild-eyed poor girl, I've become a silly, spendthrift, sentimental old lady."

He knew the words he should be saying, but he said nothing.

"All the way over on the plane . . . have you ever flown the Concorde?" He nodded. "I adore it. Simply adore it. It's the only way to fly. Everyone said that it's so small, but I was terribly comfortable. Of course, for a man your size, it could be a little narrow." She looked up at him, waited for his comment. His expression was indulgent, reflecting the patience used for young children and senior citizens. "There isn't time, is there," she asked, "to talk about the Concorde?"

"Obviously, you have an idea of something you want me to do with the money." He was thinking of the loan in Omaha, or how far the money would go if the Hong Kong and Shanghai Banking Corporation deal fell through.

"Well, it's not what I want you to do with the money, darling. You know how I don't understand money or how to invest it. I just don't have the head for that." She hesitated. "I was thinking more of what your father would have done with that money had he lived to be thirty. Flying over, I was thinking of how unjust the world can be. If your father had inherited the money when he was alive . . . or when he needed it most, how different all of our lives would be now."

Across the lounge the sound of activity increased. Small groups of connecting passengers were flocking together, shepherded to other gates.

Slowly, as though he were translating from one language to another, MacGlendon said, "What would my father have done with the money?"

"He would have given it away. All of it. He wouldn't have kept a penny of it." She smiled. "Oh, he might have held out enough to take me out to have a marvelous dinner. Candlelight and wine." She was remembering a long-ago time like that. "Your father had a wild, romantic streak in him. Other people didn't see that. They knew he was a gentle man, but only I knew his tenderness."

"He would have given the money to Trotsky," MacGlendon said.

She nodded. "Yes. He would have given it to Trotsky."

"Those times are over, Mother. That kind of Marxism is gone. It was a syndrome of the Depression years. There isn't the same climate now that there was in the thirties and early forties. Needs are different."

"Are you sure, Angus?"

"It's down to a hard-nosed game of Russia versus China. It's a game of bad guy against bad guy."

"There must be good guys out there somewhere. Your father would have found them. He would have helped them."

Anger burst through his modulated patience. "I'm not my father. I never was. No one is going to make me be my father." He lowered his voice, controlled his outburst. "All my life you've avoided talking to me about my father. Whenever I asked questions, you either said yes or no, never explained anything. You never told me that he was a tender man before."

She reached for her handkerchief again, balled into her tiny hand. "I was wrong, Angus. I know that now. I hid your father from you. I was selfish. I had so little time with him. Everything went so quickly. I didn't have enough memories of your father to share them. I thought that if I talked about him to anyone, everything would be dissipated. There would be nothing of him left."

"I'm left," MacGlendon said.

She touched the tips of her fingers to his cheek. "Of course you are, darling. Everything is perpetuated in you."

"But I'm not my father." His voice was loud enough so that some of the nearby people turned to stare at them. "Can't you understand that I don't want to be like my father? I'm who I am. Nobody else. Nobody." He lowered his head, felt undefined pains aching through his body. When he spoke again, his voice was controlled, the constraint he was using lowering the sound of it to a gruff whisper. "Except," he said, "I don't really know who the fuck I am."

"Watch your language, Angus. You're not talking to one of your common friends."

"Did you know that when I was sixteen years old, I wanted to change my name? Did you know that? I pleaded with Grandma and Grandpa to legally adopt me. I wanted their name. I thought that if my name was Blumberg, I would know who I really was."

"Those were difficult years for you. I know that now. I think I even knew it at the time. You were on my mind constantly when I was in China. China was so remote in those days. There wasn't much that I could do about it. But I knew how much a child needs a mother."

"I didn't need you, Mother. I needed someone to explain to me who I really was."

"Well, it's all water under the bridge, isn't it, darling? All's well," she said, "that ends well."

"Nothing has ended. Nothing is well."

"You've made a name for yourself. Everyone knows now who Angus MacGlendon is."

"Except me." He repeated his own words. "Except me."

His head was down, his eyes staring at the airport floor. She touched her fingers to his cheek. "I hate to see you so distraught. I don't understand why. Everything is going so well for you, darling." She touched his chin, raising his head so that he was facing her. "I hate to see you in this state. You look so strained, darling, so tense. Are you taking care of yourself?"

He nodded.

"You're burning the candle at both ends. I read about you on the financial page and see your picture in *Women's Wear.* Maybe it's too much."

His face had become tender at her concern. She seemed so defenseless and naïve to him: innocent.

"That girl . . . the one you were in that photograph with . . . the picture in *Women's Wear*—do you see her often?"

"I told you over the phone that I never even saw the picture. I have no idea who the girl was."

She took a carefully folded clipping from her purse, unfolded it slowly, smoothed it flat on the bench beside her, and handed it to her son.

MacGlendon looked at it quickly, crumbled it in his hand, and shoved the evidence into his pocket. "No," he said, "I don't see her often."

"What's her name?"

"Carol Anderson."

"I suppose you'll never marry her as long as your grandparents are alive, will you?"

"What's that got to do with it?"

"I know how you think. You think that it would destroy them if you married a gentile." She patted his hand. "They're more resilient than that. They survived my marrying your father."

"You didn't have the religious training that I did. A man is a Jew if his mother is a Jew. That's the law."

"But it worked out so badly the last time. The marriage was so short. I'm afraid I've even forgotten her name again."

"Deborah," he mumbled.

"Today is different, darling. This is *now*. It's not *Fiddler on the Roof* anymore. I'd like to see you marry again. Most of my friends have almost-grown grandchildren. I get a little jealous sometimes."

"You have your stray dogs and cats to fuss over."

"It's not quite the same thing, is it?"

"Let's talk about the money."

"There's nothing to talk about. You've stated your position quite clearly. Legally the money is yours to do with what you want. I only thought that since you have so much of your own, it would be appropriate to help others the way your father would have done. There must be some of the same kinds of causes your father fought for. There must be groups still fighting for the masses."

He laughed without apparent motivation.

"I don't see what's so funny, Angus."

"I thought you were going to ask me to give it all to your stray animals . . . establish a foundation or something."

"I'm not quite that shallow: not that impractical." She paused for a moment, then smiled. Her smile was flirtatious. Her touch against his face was sensual. "I certainly wasn't going to ask you for *all* of the money. Several hundred thousand would do nicely."

"You've got it."

"Thank you, darling."

"When do I get the money?"

"The lawyer didn't say exactly. He wants to talk to you. I told him that you'd be in contact with him as soon as you came back from your trip. Are you going on to the Orient?"

"I don't know yet. What's the lawyer's name?"

"I don't remember. I may have brought his card with me. I left in such a rush. I may have forgotten it." She made a tedious search through her passport case. MacGlendon restrained himself from grabbing it out of her hands, looking for it himself. "Here it is, darling. At least, I think it is." She squinted to read the print. MacGlendon snatched it. "Is that it?"

He nodded.

"Don't rush into anything, Angus, promise me that. Think about what your father would have done with the money. Think about that and then make your decision."

"Our criteria would be different."

"Of course, darling. I understand that, but still . . ." Her voice trailed off, and she was silent for a moment; then she said, "You could give the money away anonymously."

"You don't understand the world, Mother. Marxism was one thing in your day. It's completely another thing today."

"Is it? I wonder about that."

"I'm not financing my own destruction."

"We used to think it was the other way. We thought capitalism was destroying the world."

"You were all naïve," he said.

"I suppose we were," she said. "But just promise me to think about it. Consider the alternatives before you decide. It is your inheritance to do what you want with." She thought about that. "Of course it is. It's more than an inheritance of money. It's the MacGlendon legacy. It's exactly what your grandfather wanted. He disinherited your father and hoped that there would be someone like you someday. You'd be the kind of son he wanted, the kind of man to carry on the family name. I see that now. Without ever having known him, you've inherited all his qualities. It's a chain reaction, isn't it? I suppose it has to do with love and hate. They're the same thing, really: the same amount of emotional involvement. Your father reacted against his father, fought him viciously and became the man he became. Whether you're aware of it or not, you've done the same thing with your father—you've fought against the concept of him, reacted diametrically against what your father represented. In the process you became a political replica of your MacGlendon grandfather. It's exactly what the MacGlendons would have wanted." Then she added. "Skip a generation."

"No part of me is MacGlendon," MacGlendon said. "I have no control over what I am biologically. That part of me is unalterable. But everything I represent as a man and a human being, I've inherited from your father, from the Blumberg side. All the success I've had is directly attributable to Grandpa Blumberg."

"You've inherited nothing from him. *Nothing.* He's a sweet, darling, compassionate old man who wouldn't hurt a fly. He's my father and I love him dearly. But I love him for what he actually is—not what I wish he was. You mistake his Yiddish homilies for wisdom. You mistake his nebbishness for humility. You rationalize your own aggressiveness by attributing it to him. You think he was a hero to have escaped the oven at Dachau." She shook her head. "It was an accident of timing, not an aggressive act of heroism. You mask your own wisdom by reducing it to repetitions of my father's Yiddish parables. How many times do you start a sentence, 'As my grandfather always says . . .'?" MacGlendon turned his head away. She put her gloved hands against his face, made him continue to look at her as she spoke. "The real test of maturity, darling, is being able to look at your own parents, recognize their faults and weaknesses, and love them nonetheless. In the dynamics of history, my father is a nonentity. You're not, Angus. You have the intellectual power and the energy to become a great man . . . the man your father would have become if he had lived. Greater even. You're not burdened with your father's romanticism. Accept your greatness, darling. Don't feel guilty about it. Make the most out of your life. You can make the world ever so much better for so many more people." She released her hold on his face. His eyes stayed focused on her. "That's your real destiny, darling. That's your real inheritance. Don't shirk it."

There was an instant of icy terror as MacGlendon saw the truth of his mother, a steel trap camouflaged by soft, pinkish skin and glowing red hair. He saw for that instant the heroine of the novel Geoffrey Plantagenet would never write.

But then she took out a mirror and lipstick, brushed the color on her lips, and dabbed at the perfection of her hair. Reality receded: the apparition came back into focus. "I've been thinking about having plastic surgery," she said as she studied her face in the mirror. "So many of my friends are doing it. There's a fantastic doctor in Buenos Aires . . . maybe it's Rio. I'm so hopeless on geography. But this doctor is supposed to be an absolute marvel." She touched the lines around her eyes. "He makes all kinds of tucks without leaving a scar."

He smiled at her, relieved that the giddy image had returned. "You're flirting, Mother. You're fishing for a compliment. You want me to tell you that you're still beautiful, still young-looking." He held both her hands. "You *are* still beautiful, still young-looking. You don't need plastic surgery. You're still the same heartbreaker you always were."

She lowered her eyes as she smiled. "A lady needs reassurances once in a while."

"Why haven't you ever married again? I've always wondered about that. I mean, after Brewster died . . . well, you must have had lots of chances. Didn't you ever fall in love again?"

"There's so much we don't know about each other, isn't there? Perhaps it's just as well. We've been strangers for too long to suddenly become involved in each other's lives."

"Meaning that there is another man?"

"*Was,*" she said, lowering her head. "He died." Then she added, "Quite recently."

"Why didn't you ever tell me? Maybe I could have helped."

"You have a destiny, darling. You have your father's destiny to accomplish. Your life can't be cluttered or distracted by a silly old lady's problems." Her jaw was firm as she looked up at him. "Do what you have to do and do it in your own way. Don't think about me. I'm a survivor, darling. Always remember that about me. I'm a survivor."

He got up to leave, took a few steps away. She seemed so frail to him as he turned back for a last look: a tiny figure, backgrounded by the macro-proportioned De Gaulle terminal, waving a good-bye handkerchief.

MacGlendon stepped on the moving conveyor to the main terminal. He ducked his head as the conveyor dipped into a deep descent into a tunnel under the airfield, then he looked at the plastic-bubble advertising signs without seeing them, concentrating on the deluge of coincidences that were not coincidences but events in a planned strategy. The possibility of his mother's complicity gnawed at his preconceived concept of her. He considered the inheritance, wondered if his mother had been tricked. It seemed unlikely that that much money could have lay hidden and fallow in Erie, Pennsylvania, for so many years. Why hadn't it surfaced when his MacGlendon grandfather died? More likely, he reasoned, the inheritance was a disguise for money being offered to him by the Russians or the Chinese. Each would have a reason for bribing him: tempting him with a payoff. It could even be a bait dangled by the Taiwanese. He took the engraved card of the New York law firm, studied the raised letters. *Anyone could have a business card engraved.* His thumb rubbed over the digits of the telephone number, memorized it as though he was reading braille.

The telephone call to New York would clarify the motive. He had no doubt that sum of money was there. The question was, what price would he have to pay for it?

As the moving walkway began ascending, the plastic signs becoming eye-level, a small screaming child ran wildly past MacGlendon. A man, chasing the child at full speed, sideswiped MacGlendon with the impact of an offensive tackle exactly at that point in the tunnel where there was the least head room, jarring MacGlendon forward and up. MacGlendon's head was slammed against the arched ceiling. Knocked unconscious, he crumbled to the moving tread. A woman leaned over him for an instant, fumbled with an object, and then ran forward, burrowing her way through the confusion of screaming travelers.

MacGlendon's necktie, caught in the continuing mechanism of the conveyor, became a noose around his neck. His face turned red as the air was cut off from his brain.

A guard, hearing the screams, activated the emergency cutoff switch. The alarm bell clanged, reverberating through the tunnel.

A nattily dressed Italian man strolled away from the scene of the accident, joined a Chinese man, and they left the airport together.

Betsy Brewster had heard the alarm bell as she was talking on the telephone, paid no attention at first. Then she dropped the phone, leaving the receiver dangle from the curled cord, and ran toward the sound. The loudspeaker system was blaring out the final boarding call for the flight to Nice.

The flight left on schedule. Betsy Brewster was in the background of the crowd watching medical attendants lift her unconscious son onto a stretcher.

Aftermath

MacGlendon began to regain consciousness. He was aware first of the feeling of a noose choking him, cutting off the function of his breathing. He reached to his throat: felt nothing there. Then he thrashed violently trying to free himself from an invisible restraint. A doctor and a nurse called in Big Red and the New Man to help shackle Mac-Glendon's sporadic violence as he emerged from unconsciousness. Two ambulance attendants, who had brought MacGlendon to the airport emergency first-aid station, leaned their stretcher in the waiting station, went into the medical room, helped the two bodyguards hold down Mac-Glendon as the nurse prepared a hypodermic syringe with morphine. The New Man held back the doctor's arm as he began to inject the drug under MacGlendon's skin. "Don't do that! He's allergic." The doctor turned. The New Man said, *"Il est allergique."*

The doctor held the syringe, the needle quivering in his hand. *"C'est morphine,"* he explained. *"Est-il allergique à morphine?"*

"Attendez cinq minutes." MacGlendon was calming down, the violence subsiding as the New Man talked to the doctor. *"Regardez. Il sera bien. Regardez."*

Big Red had heard the conversation, was surprised to

hear the New Man speaking French, didn't understand what was happening or why the New Man had stopped the doctor from injecting the sedative into the boss.

Breathing heavily, his body and face wet with sweat, MacGlendon opened his eyes, looked around at the blur of figures hovering over him, touched his forehead, felt the bandage over the gash, tried to sit up but was held back by Big Red and the ambulance attendants. This time he submitted, lay back on the examining table.

Big Red leaned over, his face a foot away from MacGlendon's face. "You all right, Boss?"

"I guess so." This time he gently touched his own throat, his fingers skimming the chafed circle where his necktie had choked him and then running over the smooth, fresh bandage on his forehead. "Anything broken?"

Big Red turned to the doctor. "Anything broken?" The doctor didn't understand.

The New Man moved forward, approached the doctor. *"Les os, ils ne sont pas cassés, non?"*

"Une radiographie sera nécessaire." He nodded toward the two ambulance attendants. *"Ils le prendront à l'hôpital. Il faut faire les examens et le garder pour l'observation."*

"Pour combien de temps?"

The airport doctor shrugged his shoulders. *"Je ne sais pas. Peut-être trois jours. Peut-être plus. C'est difficile à prédire maintenant."*

The New Man turned to MacGlendon. "The doc doesn't think anything is broken. He says that you have to go to the hospital for a couple of days: take tests and stay under observation."

The grim set of his jaw and the ferocity of the anger in his eyes held off the attendants as MacGlendon sat up on the examining table, steadied himself with his hands by grasping each edge of the table. MacGlendon took a deep breath until the spiraling dizziness stopped; then he switched the pivotal support of his hands and swung his legs over the edge of the table. He rested there for a moment.

At a signal from the doctor the two attendants started toward MacGlendon, were blocked by Big Red and the New Man.

"Doesn't feel like anything is broken," MacGlendon said. He swung his legs back and forth, then lifted one arm at a time straight up and over his head. He smiled at Big Red. "This is how a football player must feel after a tough game." He released his support, flexed the fingers of both hands. "So far," he said, "everything seems to be working." He slid forward on the table so that his feet touched the floor.

"Wait a minute," the New Man said. "Give yourself a little time before you try standing up. Let the blood get flowing again."

"Are you a doctor, too? You're full of surprises, full of hidden talents. How come you never told us you can speak French?"

"I learned it in college," he said. "I never tried speaking it before. You forget that I was a high school gym teacher. They make you learn all kinds of shit which you never need to know in your job. I used to be pretty good at calculus, but it never helped my kids win a basketball game."

"Maybe you guys better give me a hand when I stand up." He smiled as they moved to flank him. "The bigger they are, the harder they fall." He submitted to their support as he slowly stood up, first felt a dizziness and a weakness in his knees, then seemed in control of his own body and pushed the men holding him away. "Not too bad." He straightened up. "I may survive," he said.

Using the examining table behind him as support, Mac-Glendon bent one knee, raised it, put it down again, and then raised the other. When he released his grasp, stood straight, he wavered only slightly. He started his first step, motioned off his own two men. The others watched silently as MacGlendon took two steps forward, hesitated, and then backed up successfully and leaned against the table. "If there is enough aspirin in Paris, I may live." He touched the bandage on his head. "I feel sorry for drunks," he said. "They must feel like this every morning."

Big Red asked, "Anything hurt besides your head?"

"Everything hurts," MacGlendon said. "Nothing hurts *bad* except my head."

"You could have internal injuries."

MacGlendon shook his head. "Like I said, I just feel like I've played in a football game. I guess I ache more than I hurt." He stood up and walked all the way to the door, turned around, rested against the door for a moment, and then walked at a faster pace back to the table. "Anybody know what happened to me?"

The bodyguards looked at each other. Big Red deferred to the authority of his partner, who now had greater stature because he spoke French. "Not for sure," the New Man said. "The first thing anybody knew, you were an unconscious heap stuck at the top of the moving ramp. There's goddamn little clearance near the top of that tunnel for a tall guy. The fucking architects didn't provide for anyone as tall as you."

"How come I hit the back of my head, not the front?"

Both men shrugged.

"There was a kid. I remember that now. He was racing up the ramp. Little kid." MacGlendon held his hand off the floor to indicate size. "He was screaming. I must have turned around. The guy chasing him . . . it must have been his father . . . well, he sideswiped me. He must have jolted me up just at the low point of the tunnel." He reached to the back of his head then moved his hand to the red line around his neck. "What's this from?"

The New Man shrugged again. "The only way we can

figure is that your necktie got caught in the mechanism. By the time we got to you, all the witnesses must have scattered. We couldn't get through passport control when we heard the screams and the confusion."

"Yah," Big Red interjected. "Them damn Frogs wouldn't let us through. We figured that someone could be taking potshots at you, and those fucking Frogs wouldn't let us through."

Details of the accident fell into sequence as MacGlendon walked across the first-aid station toward the bench where his clothes had been piled.

The doctor screamed rapid, angry words. *"Je ne prendrai pas la responsabilité pour cette situation. Cet homme fou doit être à l'hôpital. Je ne prendrai aucune responsabilité."* He screamed louder at the nurse. *"Trouvez la forme. Il doit signer la forme de dégagement. Je téléphonerai aux agents de police s'il ne signera pas cette forme."* The frightened nurse half ran through the side door and into a glass-walled office overlooking the examining room. The doctor blocked MacGlendon before MacGlendon reached the bench. His voice became less threatening when he pitted himself against the bulk of Mac-Glendon. *"Je ne prendrai aucune responsabilité si rien vous passe après que vous sortiez. Vous me comprenez? Rien de la responsabilité."* He stressed his words with a scissors motion of his arms. *"C'est la loi. Nulle responsabilité. Ni légale ni médicale."* Knowing that MacGlendon did not understand his words, he turned back to the New Man. *"Est-ce qu'il le comprend? Rend-il compte de la risque qu'il prenne?"*

MacGlendon broke through the torrent of words. "What's he saying?"

"Basically, he thinks you ought to go to the hospital in the ambulance. He says that he'll take no legal or medical responsibility unless you do. He sent his nurse for a release form. It's a waiver against claims."

The doctor drew back as MacGlendon raised his arm. But

MacGlendon touched the doctor gently on the shoulder. *"Merci,"* he said. "Do you understand that? *Merci."* He turned back to the New Man. "Tell him that I understand. Tell him that I'll sign the waiver. Explain how grateful I am for all his help. Do you have any French money on you?"

"Some." The New Man turned to Big Red who reached in his pocket, took out a wad of wrinkled francs.

"Give the nurse ... a hundred bucks will do it. And take care of the ambulance guys." Pointing his head back to the New Man, he said, "Tell the doctor what I said."

The doctor held up his hands in desperation, expressed one final word before his shoulders slumped in capitulation.

"What about the doc? What do you want to lay on him?"

"You don't tip doctors, do you?"

"This one is French."

MacGlendon sidestepped around the doctor, continued toward the bench, reached in the pocket of his pants, took out two one-thousand-franc notes, held them in his teeth while he pulled on his pants, zipped them and buttoned the waistband, then turned back to the doctor and slipped the notes into the pocket of his white medical coat. *"Merci,"* MacGlendon said. *"Merci."*

When he was completely dressed, MacGlendon reached for his necktie, saw that it had been cleanly severed at the broadest point. He studied the severed tie. There was no frayed end. The silk threads had been cut with a very sharp instrument by a skilled hand. He stuffed the evidence into the pocket of his jacket.

Traffic from De Gaulle to Paris was light at this hour. Settled back in the hired limo, flanked by a security guard on either side of him, MacGlendon said, "I don't know what to say to you guys except thank you again."

Both men mumbled reassuring words. Big Red started to speak. "Boss," he began, then hesitated, then started again.

"Boss, I think we ought to get the fuck out of town. I mean all of this is none of my business and . . . well, it really is my business. I mean, my job is to protect you. So far we've been very lucky. We've been batted around pretty good. I mean we've all gotten our lumps. But so far, we're still alive. I don't know how long our luck is going to hold out. Nothing can be important enough to warrant getting killed. I mean the New Man and I are getting paid to do a job. We knew that this kind of job could be dangerous." He leaned forward, looked across to the other bodyguard. "Isn't that right?" The New Man nodded. "If the odds were anywhere close to even, I wouldn't say nothing at all." He jerked forward, looked across to MacGlendon again, spoke to the other guard. "Isn't that right? Isn't that the way you feel about it?"

"Each time we survive, the odds get lower. It's like Russian roulette. There are only so many empty chambers."

MacGlendon hardly listened to the two men, heard only a word now and then. He had already decided to send them back home. The risks to the innocents were not justified.

MacGlendon leaned forward, spoke directly into the chauffeur's ear. *"Soixante-sept rue des Cinq Fleurs.* You understand?"

The driver did not seem to understand. He turned around and looked at the New Man. *"Qu'est-ce qu'il dit?"*

"Soixante-sept rue des Cinq Fleurs. Vous connaissez où il est?"

"Quel arrondissement?"

Big Red said, "Oh, shit. Not again."

"Tell him that it's near Square Charles Dickens," Mac-Glendon said.

The driver seemed satisfied with that explanation.

"Listen to me. Both of you. Listen carefully. There's no argument to what I'm going to tell you. Drop me at Rue des Cinq Fleurs, then have the driver take you both to the hotel, and then have him turn around and come back to the

Rue des Cinq Fleurs to wait for me. Tell him that no matter how long it takes, he has to wait. Is that clear?"

"I don't like leaving you alone in that house, Boss."

"I said no arguments, Red. Follow my instructions exactly. Is that understood?" Both men made vague nods of concession. "Don't give him any money. Explain that I'll pay him when I'm through using him."

"What are we supposed to do?"

"I'm coming to that. You two get back to the hotel, pack up, and get your asses to the airport. You've got your return tickets, haven't you?"

"What about Singapore and Hong Kong?" the New Man asked. "Aren't we going to go there?"

"I'm not leaving you, Boss," Big Red interjected. "I got a job to do and I'm going to do it."

"I said that there would be no arguments, Red."

"I've got a responsibility to the corporation. You told me yourself when you hired me that a lot of people depended on you, that that's why you need a bod—" He corrected himself: "Security officers. You told me that all those stockholders depended on you and that you depended on me."

"It's different now. I said all those things when there didn't seem to be any possibility of danger. It's different now."

"The New Man can do what he wants," Big Red said as he crossed his arms over his chest. "Maybe he didn't know what he was getting into, but I did, and I'm staying."

"You're fired, Red." MacGlendon made a gesture with his thumb. "Out."

"Okay, so I'm off salary. I'm sticking around as a friend. In a lot of ways, Gus, I'm your best friend. You know that."

"I'm staying, too," the New Man said.

MacGlendon spread his arms, hugged both of them to him. "Look, you guys, I know what you're doing and I love you for it. I really do. But you have to trust me on this one.

I promise you that I'll be all right. I know it looks crazy to you. I know it doesn't make any sense, but you have to trust me. They won't harm me. They need me alive."

Big Red turned his head away, contorted his face to hold back tears. The New Man said nothing.

"I'm being protected. It's you guys that I'm worried about. You're expendable. Do you understand that? They need to keep me alive. They'll eliminate you guys without a thought. They're those kinds of people."

"Who are they?" The New Man had a cold steel authority when he asked the question, a new dimension of confident cool. "Terrorists?"

"A kind of terrorist."

"Kidnap threats?"

"No. It's not like that."

"What if we appeared to get lost?" the New Man asked. "Say we book the flight back to Chicago. Maybe we get as far as the airport. We can tell if we're being tailed. If there's a tail on us, we may have to get on the plane, ditch it when it stops in Montreal and then hightail back here, stay underground but keep our eyes open. How about that?"

MacGlendon studied the New Man, saw him in a new light. "You were more than just a high school gym teacher, weren't you?"

"I've knocked around a lot since Vietnam, done this and that." He smiled at MacGlendon.

"I told you in the beginning that I wouldn't listen to any arguments about my instructions. Go back to Chicago, sit on your asses at the office until you hear from me. If I holler, you can be back here in twelve hours. That's final," he said.

Neither man answered him, and they rode in silence the remainder of the way back to Paris.

Old Acquaintance

The duplex apartment over the art gallery had been remodeled by a German couturiere in 1930 from top floors of a narrow eighteenth-century town house who kept shop on the ground floor, lived above. In 1952, posing as an American heiress, but actually funded by the Red Chinese, Phyllis Goldberg opened an art gallery in the salon and moved into the apartment as it was, retaining the *moderne* theme.

Now, from the tall French doors on the second floor she looked down on the street, watching the snail-paced automotive traffic and the rushing pedestrians. Without turning around she called back: "She should have been here by now. She sounded so distraught when she called from the airport. I hope nothing has happened to her."

"Rush hour," Geoffrey Plantagenet said. "It's crippling the world, immobilizing us all into obsolescent bipeds."

"Save that shit for your interviews. I'm really worried about Betsy. It's not like her to behave this erratic, this frantic. In the first place, she should never have left New York. The instructions were for her to sit tight: wait it out. Those orders were straight from Peking. I know that as a fact. It's all because of that damn Chinaman—the one who called himself Mr. Chou. His death destroyed all her discipline. Did you know that they had a thing going on for all these years?" She turned back into the room, paced over to a chrome table with a cracked glass top, took a cigarette, and lighted it with an old-model Ronson table lighter. "Talk about truth being stranger than fiction. They met in Hong Kong in the late forties. He was the guy who assigned her to Blair Brewster while Brewster was still with the State Department attached to Chiang Kai-shek. Mao should have given her a medal for the information she got out of Brewster. She also should have gotten a medal for fucking that cold fish Brewster for all those years."

"Did Brewster ever know that Betsy was a spy?"

"I figured he finally found out—that's why he killed himself." She smoothed the ruff of ostrich feathers on the collar of her robe. "That Betsy is one hard-luck broad as far as men are concerned." She shrugged her shoulders. "Well, I suppose it's better to keep loving and losing than never to get fucked at all."

Plantagenet turned his hands over, looked at the moisture on his palms. "Would you believe that I'm nervous about seeing her again? It's been so many years."

"You always had the hots for her, didn't you?" She sat on the arm of Plantagenet's chair, smoothed the thin hair on top of his head. He recoiled from her touch. "We're all products of our times," she said. "If I had been born five years sooner or five years later, my whole life would have been different. I'd probably be living in White Plains with an overweight husband and a spare room for the grandchildren." She stood up, went to the window again. "I used to think about converting and becoming a nun. I would have made a hell of a good nun. A little rowdy, maybe, but full of compassion. How I got suckered into becoming an in-place agent in this lousy city, I'll never know."

"Money," Plantagenet said.

"Never enough."

He came forward, stood behind her. "Is there anyone

suspicious-looking out there? I may have been followed
from the hotel."

"You're paranoid, Geoffrey. None of us is important
enough to be followed anymore. No one takes us seriously.
Except Betsy. She's still important, maybe, but she only
kept her power because of the Chinaman. Like I always say,
a tight pussy is a girl's best friend."

A taxi stopped across the street. Betsy Brewster stepped
out, looked at the numbers on the wrong side of the street,
finally crossed over, and went through the ornate door next
to the art gallery.

Phyllis Goldberg drew the curtains over the windows,
crossed the room, and opened the front door, then waited
at the head of the stairs. "They're steep as hell," she called
down. "Take your time. We're not exactly girls anymore,
are we, love?" She walked down a short flight of stairs to
a landing, watched Betsy walking up. "You look absolutely
divine, darling. Look at that figure. After all those years,
would you believe that shape?"

The two women hugged; then Phyllis Goldberg put her
arm around Betsy Brewster's waist and guided her up the
last stairs. "You haven't said one thing about the way I
look."

"I'm too out of breath." She smiled. "You look marvelous. As outrageous as ever."

"Age cannot wither," the art dealer said, "nor custom
stale . . ." She smiled. "In my case there are a few dents here
and there but, all in all, it's still together."

"Is Plantagenet here yet?"

She motioned with her head. "He's inside. Excited about
seeing you." As Betsy started through the door, Phyllis
Goldberg held her back, spoke in a low voice. "You're
taking a terrible chance coming here, aren't you? I thought
you were supposed to wait it out in New York."

"I got emergency clearance to go to Monte Carlo—

there's a bridge tournament going on there. I convinced Peking that it would be a good cover. Angus met me at the airport between planes. We had a nice visit but right after he left me, someone tried to kill him. Right at the airport. Thank God, he wasn't badly hurt. I have to do something to help him. I can't let anything happen to him. I've got to stop him while there's still time."

"You knew the risk," the art dealer said. "You've been waiting for this moment for all these years. It's a hell of a time to start acting like a Jewish mother."

Still breathing heavily, Betsy went back, sat on a step. "I can't let anything happen to Angus. I just can't. I've paid too many prices for too long." Tears had started, staining her face and streaking her makeup: the wrinkled lines of her face cracked through the veneer. "I've just had a frightening experience." She looked toward the open door to the apartment. "Do you think that Geoffrey can hear us from here?"

"I was just fondling his transplanted hair. There's a hearing aid concealed under it somewhere. I would guess that we're out of range."

"At the airport, after the accident—as I was leaving—I saw a woman I haven't seen in thirty years. A Chinese woman. Her name was Chen Kang then. The notorious Comrade Kang. Have you ever heard of her?"

"I've been in Paris, love—out of touch with all the inner workings in China."

"She was a close friend of Chiang Ching. There was a lot of gossip about them, but then you know how the Chinese love to gossip." She opened her purse, took out a mirror, and began repairing her face. "She was with a man I used to know—a friend of Blair Brewster's. He's a very well known scientist. Nuclear. Had something to do with the atom bomb when he was a young graduate student. I think he worked with Fermi or maybe it was Oppenheimer. It doesn't matter. The dreadful thing is that they're in Paris together. It can't be just an accidental meeting. The timing is too perfect. It must have something to do with the consortium. If Comrade Kang is involved in the consortium, it's a very different consortium than we dreamed of years ago. Frightening. Dangerous."

"Nobody ever said that we're in a safe business."

"But Angus . . ."

"What about him?"

"I have to stop him. I can't let him go through with the consortium. It's not only his own safety anymore. If Comrade Kang is involved, it's everyone's life at stake."

"Maybe you're just overwrought, honey. You've had a dreadful time. Maybe you're just dramatizing things too much."

"Chou never told me," she said. "He must have known. He never told me that Comrade Kang was involved. He knew how I'd react."

Phyllis Goldberg sat beside her on the step, put her arm around Betsy Brewster's shoulder. "Chou is dead, but it doesn't change anything. You can't stop the consortium now. It's too late."

"I must stop Angus. I must save him."

"They won't let you. They'll kill you first. You know how they operate."

She stood up, smoothed the wrinkles from her traveling suit. "Geoffrey Plantagenet knew Comrade Kang in the old days. He was always threatening to write a novel about her." She looked toward the door, lowered her voice. "Poor Geoffrey," she said. "People are always using him for one purpose or another. He's really such a pitiful little man." She patted her hair in place. "I intend to use him one last time."

Geoffrey Plantagenet stood at the opened door. "What the hell are you girls doing out there for so long?"

"Girl talk," Phyllis Goldberg said.

Betsy Brewster smiled brightly, ran over to him, kissed him on the mouth and then stood back. "Geoffrey, darling, I would never have recognized you. You look simply marvelous—younger than when you were young. If you had looked like this when we first met, it would have been love at first sight." She kissed him again then reached behind her, taking Phyllis Goldberg's hand. She looked from one to the other. "It's like old times, isn't it?"

67 rue des Cinq Fleurs Revisited

She was sitting ramrod straight in the bed she had slept in as a child. Her hair was snarled and distended in a wild, wiry tangle. The thumbprint bruises at the base of her neck had spread into large blobs, blue-black inkspots standing out against the pallor of her skin. The lines of her face and the distortion of her mouth reflected the continuing terror. Her eyes were expressionless, the glassy stare fixed in a vacant direction, seeing nothing.

MacGlendon, gripping the posts at the foot of the bed, felt his legs weaken, the reserve strength drain from his body. He sank to his knees, interlocked his fingers, and let his head fall against the mattress.

He heard the words first as part of the torment of a dream, but then as the words were repeated, he raised his head and turned toward the actual sound.

A friend is nearby.

Without forethought, MacGlendon touched the jade medallion suspended from his throat. He focused his eyes on the man standing behind him and zoomed in on the identical jade disk hanging from the man's neck.

"I am Alixandre de Plyssy."

MacGlendon forced his body into a standing position,

found he could not stay upright and sat at the foot of the bed, his back to Paula, and faced the tall, lean, hawk-nosed, white-haired man.

"Are you all right?" he asked. MacGlendon nodded. "I've been waiting for you. I am to alert you that there has been a change of plans. Because of the Russian interference and the unexpected death of Mr. Chou, the timetable has been speeded up." The man spoke English without effort. "Our Chinese friends have had difficulty establishing contact with you because of the heavy American security ring around you. How much do the Americans know? How much have you told them?"

"Nothing," MacGlendon said.

"How much actual information do they have?"

"Guesswork mostly. No hard facts."

"The Chinese will be pleased with that. We don't know how the Russians got on to us so quickly. Mr. Chou was careless. Not like him. But there must be some other internal leak. They know too much about us too quickly." He walked past MacGlendon, sat at the head of the bed, and stroked Paula's hair to unsnarl the tangle. He kissed her cold cheek, ran his hand up and down in front of her eyes. There was no flicker of consciousness.

MacGlendon turned his head. "You deliberately let them use her," he said. "You knew the dangers that there could be."

"I had no choice." He kissed her cheek again. "Once the commitment was made, I could not renege." He straightened the pillows behind her head. "In any war there are noncombatant victims. Read Chinese history. Innocents are an expendable commodity to them. Less costly than ammunition. More plentiful."

"But your own daughter," MacGlendon began. The older man interrupted him.

216 / ECHO CHAMBERS

"My wife's daughter." He shook his head sadly. "But even if she were my own blood, it would not have made any difference. I did what I had to do. There is a long historical precedent for men who have sold their souls to the devil. The devil exacts his price without mercy." He looked over at MacGlendon. "You can justify your own behavior to yourself any way that you wish, Mr. MacGlendon. You can delude yourself by applying acceptable labels to your own actions. I've been through that exercise in my own mind. But it's an exercise in futility. We have, in actuality, sold our souls to the devil."

"I don't believe that," MacGlendon said. "My free will is still operating. I'll play ball with the Chinese only so far. This is a business venture for me. Like any deal that I go into, I leave myself options, escape routes. I can pull out any time I please."

"Americans are so naïve," the Frenchman said. "You're all the same: bloodthirsty as Huns with the scrubbed faces of choirboys. You fool no one. Certainly not the Chinese." He stood up, walked to the window, held back the heavy drapery, and looked into the darkness outside. "I, at least, face the truth about myself. I have no illusions about what I'm doing."

"Then why are you doing it?"

"The de Plyssys survive," he explained. "We have a long historical record of survival. We survived the kings and we survived the revolutionaries. Not one de Plyssy head felt the block of the guillotine. Not one de Plyssy capitulated to the Nazi barbarians. We survived." He stood in front of MacGlendon now, projecting a fiber-deep majesty. "I carry a tradition based upon the perspective of history. The power source of the world is shifting from West to East. It has shifted before. Power is no more stable than the sands of the desert. It moves with the winds of time. For France and the de Plyssys to survive, China must win its war with

Russia. I intend to survive those times. France and the de Plyssys: We will survive until our time comes again. I must prepare for that." He fingered the jade medallion. "I have a son and two grandsons," he said. "It is my obligation to them as it was my ancestors' obligation to me."

"But Paula is expendable?"

"Lovely," he said, "but expendable."

"You're not the nicest guy in the world, are you?"

"A man is what he has to be. As you are, Mr. MacGlendon. We are not unalike. The Chinese have made sure of that. The tradition of your forebears is as much a part of you as the de Plyssy history is part of me. We have the same destiny." He started out of the room, stopped beside the bed. "You're as responsible for this as I am," he said as he studied Paula. "They tell me that you're a financial wizard. You must understand the mathematics: for every gain there is an offsetting loss." He touched her face with the tips of his fingers. "Are you in love with her?"

MacGlendon began to answer, then changed his mind and said nothing.

"Tomorrow," de Plyssy said, "at twelve o'clock in the evening, you are to be at the cemetery Père Lachaise. There is a grave there of an American. A rock star. Jim Morrison. He died in Paris under mysterious circumstances some years ago. His grave has become a cult center for the times he lived in. It is not unusual to see Americans there at any hour." He leaned forward, kissed Paula's cheek again, and passed his hands in front of her eyes. "You are to come alone and you are to tell no one of your plans. The Chinese will have a way of knowing if you don't follow their instructions precisely."

"What happens then?"

De Plyssy shrugged his shoulders. "You will be informed of the time and the place of the first meeting of the consortium."

"Is the meeting tomorrow night?" De Plyssy shrugged his shoulders again. MacGlendon pressed him. "Will the meeting be in Paris?"

"I know no more than you," he answered. "The Chinese will tell neither of us any more than it is absolutely necessary for us to know."

"If you build aircraft factories in China, what happens here in France? What happens to the de Plyssy factories in France?"

"The power shift is inevitable."

"What happens to the thousands of people you employ? What happens to the French economy? The French air industry?"

"The inevitable is inevitable," he said. "The die was cast many years ago. First your revolution, then ours, then the Russians', and finally the Chinese. None of them, so far, has been a viable solution. Toughen up, Mr. MacGlendon. This is not a consortium of choirboys. I have already explained that innocents are an expendable commodity in the long range of history."

"Will you be at the cemetery?"

He shook his head. "My rendezvous is at a different time and a different place, but we will meet again."

Noiselessly, without looking back, the Count de Plyssy left the room.

Slowly, mulling over the ramifications of his conversation with de Plyssy, MacGlendon got to his feet, and then wobbled around the bed, kicked off his shoes and lay down, putting his arms around Paula and forcing her rigid body into a position interlocked with his, interlacing his warmth against her chill. Finally, he felt the responsive thaw and the beginning of movement in her body. She whispered to him. "You didn't answer Alixandre's question. He asked if you loved me."

"You heard everything?"

He felt her head nod and her hands clutching his back. "Do you love me?" she asked.

For the length of time that he kissed her, the torment and terror ejaculated from his body, and there was only the knowledge and sensation of two mouths probing each other. But when the kiss was over, all the realities returned.

The Bentley Spur

As MacGlendon walked out of the far gates at the end of the Count de Plyssy's driveway, the limousine, which appeared to be the same one that had driven him in from De Gaulle, pulled up from a shadowy position, blinked its headlights, and stopped at the curb. MacGlendon signaled for the driver to stay seated, opened the back door himself, and slid into the empty seat. When he saw the gun he hesitated, then sat down and identified the man holding the gun as Ridge Bentley.

The limo started forward instantly.

MacGlendon stared at the serene, smiling, patrician face, then closed his eyes, leaned his head back, felt the pain there, and stretched his legs forward. "You gave me twenty-four hours," he said. "I thought there was going to be a moratorium on violence." He touched the bandage on the side of his head.

"I gave you my word, MacGlendon. I'm a man of my word. I'm not responsible for that." He pointed to the wound. "What happened?"

"Another fucking freak accident, I suppose."

"Don't blame me. You're everybody's target. I wouldn't put it past the CIA. They've been known to harass their own. Not O'Connor; he still has the mentality of a cop on the beat. Probably one of his bosses. The CIA plays fancy footwork with the French Sûreté."

"What do you want now? You gave me twenty-four hours. My time isn't up."

"You intrigue me, MacGlendon. Somehow, you're different than I thought you'd be. I like you. I didn't think that I would, but I really like you."

"Do you want to be buddies? Is that it, Bentley? Or do you have something heavier in mind?"

Bentley laughed. "I told you that I've done a lot of homework on you. You're straight as an arrow."

"If you don't want to fuck, then what do you want to do?"

"Since our first meeting I've been doing a lot of thinking. It occurred to me that we should both be on the same side. In many ways we're two of a kind. Our objectives are alike. We both want the same thing." He put the gun in his lap, straightened his tie. "We are both power-oriented men. We shouldn't be adversaries. Adversaries tend to negate each other. In many ways the long cold war between Russia and the United States has diminished both powers, allowed the Orientals and the Arabs to emerge as a power source. Geopolitical chess is a slow game, full of stalemates. You and I are bred to run on a faster track than that."

"Bentley, you forget who I am. I'm the all-American boy. You and I have different values. Human life for one thing." MacGlendon tightened his closed eyes and clenched his fists harder. "I keep score, Bentley: a running tab in my head. I learned to do that betting on football games." He opened his eyes, looked across to Bentley. "You're going to pay for what you did to Paula de Plyssy. I haven't figured out how yet. But I promise you that you're going to get paid back in kind and in spades."

Bentley laughed again. "If you've got rape in mind for Sumara—she'd love it."

"I don't need rape to get her away from you."

"You're a romantic, MacGlendon. On the surface you don't appear to be. But deep down inside, you're a romantic. Your father had the same weakness."

MacGlendon concentrated on his pain, tried to will it to a level that would block out his consciousness.

"You can't help being a romantic. In some ways it's a plus. It gives you a boyish kind of charm—makes people trust you without question. It's a quality that I lack. You and me as partners is not unlike putting a conglomerate together. Our respective strengths and weaknesses complement each other. For example, I can kill. You cannot."

"I'm not sure about that anymore. Any man, I realize now, can be driven to kill."

Bentley handed MacGlendon the gun, put it in MacGlendon's lap when he would not reach for it. "I know you too well," he said. "You are constitutionally incapable of murder."

MacGlendon fondled the cold steel of the gun, wondering about himself. "Where are you taking me?"

"To your hotel. We're going in a roundabout way to give us time to talk."

"We've said everything there is to say. You stated the deal. I have until tomorrow."

"Has anyone tried to contact you? The Chinese? Do you know any more about the first meeting of the consortium?"

"I have to get to a telephone," MacGlendon said.

"I've checked New York. Your stock has dropped nine points. There was a rumor that they were going to suspend trading." Bentley looked at his watch. "Probably have by now."

"I have to get to a telephone."

"You don't have to verify it. I'm telling you the truth. I never lie, MacGlendon."

"Get me back to my hotel. Stick to the deal you made."

"It occurred to me that the deal wasn't good enough: not for either of us. I was being shortsighted when I stated the Russian terms. It wasn't like me not to think ahead. I wasn't really looking out for old number one. You have to understand, MacGlendon, that I have no special love for the Russians. Philosophically, we're miles apart. And I have nothing specifically against the Chinese. But the Russians have become a convenient tool for me. I use them for my own advantage. For one thing, they've made me rich. At the moment—stinking rich. I like it. You never get rich enough, do you?" He waited for an answer. MacGlendon said nothing. "I got to thinking that when this assignment is over and I've succeeded, through you, in busting the Chinese consortium—what then? Where do I go from there? Frankly, I'm having a little problem with the SEC in Singapore. There are some investigations going on of public companies I control. The SEC and the CIA are looking for Russian funding behind these corporations. They'll never find it. I've been much too careful for that. But the heat will be on for a while and I'll have to play it cool." He reached forward, pulled out the jump seat, put his feet up on it, jiggled his right foot so that the tassels on his loafers swung like synchronous pendulums. "I got to thinking about this consortium of yours—Russia versus China. It may be in Russia's best interest for the consortium to fail before it starts—but what about my interests? Your interests?"

"No matter what you think, I'm doing business under the United States free enterprise system."

"You're not that naïve, MacGlendon. You know that in the long run, if the Chinese consortium succeeds, it will be wholly destructive to the American economy." He added, "To the whole Western world, as a matter of fact."

"It would depend, wouldn't it, on motives? Good guys or bad guys running it?"

"On that level of finance there is no morality except money and power. The industrial giants of the world have always been above classification as good guys and bad guys. You watched too much television when you were growing up. The kind of potential power structure the Chinese consortium represents makes it impervious to moral judgments or classifications. The fair-play rules don't exist in that ball park; they never have. Witness the Ruhr industrialists, the Hong Kong moneylenders, and the Mideast oil interests."

"What kind of a deal are you trying to make, Bentley? Lay it on the table."

"You have the entrée into the consortium. Between us we could gain control of it. It's the ultimate power source in the coming world."

"I don't think I believe what I'm hearing. Lay it on me again."

"It's no longer in my personal best interests to side with the Russians against the Chinese consortium. The consortium offers the greatest opportunity for maximum power. I'm offering you a partnership, MacGlendon. You be the front man. I'll stay behind the scenes."

"That's what you did in the Chicago Seven trial, isn't it? You ran the show and let others front for you."

"There's been some published material which puts forth that thesis."

"You've got the wrong boy this time. I'm my own man."

"You can't do it alone, MacGlendon. You don't have the balls for it."

"Say I do go along with you . . . say that I do. What makes you think the Russians will let you get away with it?"

"I'm not worried about my own safety. I'm a pro at this. It's not my first time out. The Russians know that I have enough secret information hidden in safety deposit boxes to blow the KGB and most of their secret maneuvers sky high. I've protected myself. I have good life insurance against the Russians."

"What about me? What makes you think that the Russians won't pick me off first chance they get?"

"At the moment you're their only link to the consortium. They need to keep you alive until you've served their purpose."

"And after that? What happens to me after that?"

At first Bentley did not answer. Then he said: "There'll be a way. There's always a way. There always has been."

"I don't know what you smoke, Bentley, but if I were you, I'd think about tapering off."

On the way out of the limousine, before he entered the hotel, a man striding head down, collided with MacGlendon on the narrow sidewalk of the Rue des Beaux-Arts. MacGlendon felt practiced fingers insert something into the pocket of his jacket. The man mumbled, *"Pardon,"* and, never breaking his stride, walked on.

In the wood-paneled elevator MacGlendon dug into his pocket, took out the note that had been inserted there: read it.

TOMORROW MORNING. ELEVEN O'CLOCK.
FLEA MARKET. MARCHE PAUL BERT.
RUE DES ROSIERS. STAND #218.
                                                      CHOU

MacGlendon thought back. There had been two Chinese men in the lobby of the hotel: Chou and a man who looked like him. Was it possible that Chou was still alive? Perhaps, but it was more likely that this was a trap. Now he had two designated times for the contact to the Chinese consortium:

eleven o'clock at the flea market and midnight at Jim Morrison's grave at the cemetery Père Lachaise.

He stopped, looked over the railing, down the circular shaft to the intricate marble floor where the Chinese silk merchant had lain facedown, spread-eagled.

The Current Tycoon

Reading from the engraved business card, which had the lingering scent of his mother's perfume, MacGlendon direct-dialed the estate lawyer in New York. While the telephone computer registered the series of numbers, Mac-Glendon scanned the desk top. Someone had organized the confusion of newspapers, mail, and telephone messages into neat piles. There was a bottle of Dom Pérignon champagne in a silver bucket, the ice melted into tepid water. A card had been tied around the neck of the bottle with a blue ribbon. "Thank you—Ben Brayden" was scrawled in an unsteady hand.

The voice in New York answered, "Mr. Strapthorne's office."

"Is he there? This is Angus MacGlendon calling from Paris."

"Mr. Strapthorne is in a meeting. May I have him return the call?"

"Get a message to him. Tell him I'm on the line from Paris. Tell him it's urgent. I'll hold on."

After a few minutes there was a relay clicking sound and a man's voice was on the line. "Mr. MacGlendon, this is George Strapthorne. I'm delighted to hear from you. I understand from your mother that you would be out of the country for some time and that I wouldn't be able to be in contact with you."

"Tell me about the inheritance, Mr. Strapthorne."

"There really isn't much to tell. It was a little baffling at first. It wasn't until after your grandmother died and we were inventorying the contents of the family vaults that we discovered a small locked box with a combination padlock. Very old-fashioned, one might say. The box contained some mementos that pertained to your father; I have taken the liberty of forwarding those things to your mother. Is that all right?"

"Certainly. What else?"

"Well, there were these legal documents setting up an irrevocable trust in your father's name. The funds and securities were held in another bank in a numbered account. It took some maneuvering and detective work to trace them. The terms of the trust were that the interest was to be compounded and added to the principal, and that entire amount was to have been made available to your father on his thirtieth birthday. If, for any reason, your father did not survive until his thirtieth birthday, the trust was to continue until your father's oldest issue reached the age of thirty, and at that time the entire principal and accumulated interest would be made available to that person."

"And if my father had had no child?"

"The provision was that the entire amount then be given to establish a MacGlendon library at the University of Pennsylvania."

"Has the trust been audited? Do you know how much money is there?"

"I don't have the exact figure at my fingertips, but the sum is sizable: fifteen million three hundred thousand and some odd dollars."

"What's the tax problem?"

"None. It was set up in the old days."

"What's the legal red tape to get at the funds?"

"None, really. We've been through the exercise of why the existence of the trust was not known at the time of your grandfather's death or why it was not made available to you when you were thirty. Your grandmother was afflicted with a rather early senility. That seems the only logical explanation of why she didn't make the existence of the trust known."

"She knew that I existed?"

"There were some newer newspaper clippings in the strongbox. You were a Horatio Alger Award winner, weren't you?"

"Yes."

"There were two other clippings from *The New York Times* that referred to you. I don't remember the exact contents, but it does indicate that either one or both of your grandparents knew of your existence. I take it that there had been some family conflicts that made for bad blood between your father and his parents."

"What's the legal hassle to get the funds made available to me?"

"None, really. A check has to be drawn from the Chase Manhattan. You have to sign some legal documents, but they have already been prepared for some time."

"There are two or three flights out of New York this evening that arrive in Paris early tomorrow morning. Please make arrangements to have someone here with the check and the documents."

"I'm afraid that that is quite impossible, Mr. MacGlendon. I am now the official designate for the trust, and it is my responsibility to handle this personally."

"Then you come."

"That's quite impossible. My calendar is booked solid tomorrow. I don't quite understand the urgency. I know who you are, Mr. MacGlendon, and I know your financial standing. There certainly can't be any urgency about the funds. As a matter of fact, the interest keeps accumulating."

"Mr. Strapthorne, what fee did your law firm charge the MacGlendon estate?"

The lawyer in New York hesitated. "It's not the kind of information I have at my fingertips."

"Would you say that it was sizable?"

He hesitated again. "Yes. I suppose you could call it sizable. The estate was very complicated. There were many aspects of it that . . ."

"In my experience," MacGlendon said, "it's always awkward when an heir requests an investigation of fees and related expenses in the settling of an estate. Not that I think anything is out of line. But I know that it can get awkward."

He waited for a reaction from Strapthorne. There was none. "I'll expect you at my hotel in the morning, Mr. Strapthorne. It's called l'Hôtel on the Rue des Beaux-Arts. Left Bank. Any taxi driver will know where it is. You should make it in from the airport by nine o'clock or so. I'll have breakfast sent up. Do you drink coffee or tea."

"Tea."

"I'll see you tomorrow." MacGlendon hung up.

He was looking at the headlines in the *Herald Tribune* when the voice behind him said, "There's a certain poetic quality about a tycoon in action."

MacGlendon turned and saw Pug O'Connor, who was wearing MacGlendon's silk robe, the heavy gun weighing down the thin pocket.

"What are you doing here?"

"I'm always surprised to see you alive, MacGlendon. Your survival quotient is staggering." He pointed to the bandage and the bruises on his face. "You're bloodied, I see, but not bowed. How you do it amazes me."

"Get out of here, O'Connor. I have business to take care of."

"Don't let me stop you. Go right ahead. I can see what kind of pressure that you're under." He walked to the desk, put his big hand over the neat stack of telephone messages. "I took the liberty of tidying up for you a bit. This stack of messages had to do with your crumbling empire." He moved his hand. "This group includes dress designers who want you to come to parties for the Prêt and broads who want to get fucked." He nodded his head toward a stack of envelopes. "Those are all invitations to galas." He swayed his body in a dancing motion. "I threw out all the messages from the press—people wanting interviews. I figured you wouldn't be interested, and I don't want you to have any more exposure than you already have. Everybody seems to be after your ass, MacGlendon—one way or another."

MacGlendon picked up the phone. "This call is private," he said.

O'Connor shook his head. "You and me are on the buddy system again. You don't get out of my sight. Or sound," he added.

"There's a Bible next to the bed. Get it."

"We're going to have a little reading? It's not even Sunday."

"Get it."

While O'Connor went into the other room, MacGlendon dialed his own lawyer in Chicago. When the switchboard answered, he said, "Let me talk to Larry Silverman." O'Connor was back in the room. With his index finger MacGlendon motioned him forward and switched the Bible from O'Connor's right to left hand then placed O'Connor's right hand over his heart.

"Mr. Silverman's office."

"It's Gus. Let me talk to him."

"He's not here."

"Find him," MacGlendon said. "Take down this number." He rattled off the digits for direct dialing. "He's got five minutes or he loses his best client." He hung up and turned to O'Connor. "Say some words, O'Connor, that have meaning to you. Swear on your mother's grave or the pope's Polish sausage. Make a pledge that will bring down the wrath of heaven if you break it."

"Take the fucking gun out of my pocket. It's not holy to swear on your mother's grave with a gun in your pocket." MacGlendon removed the gun, put it on the desk. O'Connor said, "Now what kind of sacrilege do you want me to swear to?"

"Mumble something that will convince me that whatever you hear in this room will never be repeated to anyone for any reason at any time. On your mother's grave, O'Connor."

"I swear it," he said.

"Swear what?"

"What you said. On my mother's grave. I swear it. So help me God." He made the sign of the cross.

"That was too easy." He smiled at O'Connor. "Your mother isn't dead, is she?"

"She's flexible," O'Connor said, throwing the Bible at MacGlendon, who caught it left-handed in mid-air. "The concept of an Irishman's mother is part of his charm. You get to thinking of a white-haired old lady scrubbing floors and working her fingers to the bone so that her sons can grow up to be God-fearing men."

"What was your mother really like?"

"Maybe you'll meet her one day—in this world or the next. I would certainly like to meet yours. She must be quite a lady."

The telephone rang. MacGlendon put his hand on it but did not pick it up. He looked at O'Connor. Grudgingly, O'Connor crossed his heart and backed off to the other end of the room.

"Larry," MacGlendon said into the telephone, "it's Gus.

... No, everything is fine. Don't listen to rumors ... I know all that. There's no time to call them back. They'll just have to sit tight ... I told you that everything is fine. Don't pay any attention to rumors. Listen carefully, Larry. I have a question. First of all, have you been following the price of the stock? ... Down that much? Have they suspended trading? ... What's my legal position if I suddenly begin to buy my own stock? ... I don't want advice, Larry. I want a legal opinion. What happens if I begin buying heavy at the deflated price and the stock turns around and goes way up again? Would there be a question of inside information? Could I get nailed for that? ... No, I don't have any inside information. But I believe in my own corporation. I know we're solid as hell. . . . Those are rumors, Larry. Unsubstantiated. All I want to know is what my legal position is? ... Maybe as much as ten million dollars. Maybe more if I have to. . . . Don't worry about how I'm going to come up with that kind of cash. Answer the question to the best of your legal opinion."

MacGlendon listened for a long time without speaking.

"Then you think I have a shot at it? . . . No, I don't suggest that you start buying. It's still too risky. The worst that can happen to me is that I'm back at square one—broke. I don't have a wife and four kids to worry about. Sit tight, Larry. I may be able to pull this off, but there are no guarantees. Do your homework on this." MacGlendon laughed. "You'd better bone up on bankruptcy laws, too." He hung up.

O'Connor said, "As a dropout from a night school law course, I'd like to know the legal opinion."

"The government is tough as hell on insiders trading their own stock. Guys get nailed all the time: right into the slammer. But those cases are usually when there's inside information that the stock is going to drop and the insiders unload before the shit hits the fan. Silverman thinks that buying it on the down is a calculated risk. In his opinion it's legal or at least defensible. Even if the stock goes up again, it would be hard to prove inside information. A man is entitled to back his own judgment, have faith in his own corporation. Selling off would be a problem. Buying it up doesn't seem to be." MacGlendon began dialing again. "Silverman is already seeing the handwriting on the wall: thinks I'm throwing good money after bad."

"I've got a question for you, MacGlendon. You mean you could sit down this minute and write out a personal check for ten million dollars?"

"I'll be able to tomorrow morning," he said and then talked into the telephone. "Ira. It's Gus. What's happening? . . . Off that much. Wow!" He looked at his watch. "The exchange closes in another forty minutes, doesn't it? You think they'll suspend trading tomorrow? . . . Look, don't ask any questions. Buy as much as you can before closing. Some of the institutions must be dumping big blocks of stock. Then begin buying heavy tomorrow. Buy big. Start your buy order through the European markets. Funnel a lot through Switzerland . . . I know all the problems . . . I know about the bank loans. You're wasting time, Ira. Begin the blitz now. Ten millions dollars. There's a few more if you need it. . . . You've got strings, Ira. Pull them. Don't let them suspend trading. Buy big." MacGlendon put the receiver back into the cradle.

"You bastard," O'Connor said. "No wonder I had to cross my heart and hope to die. You *are* acting on inside information, aren't you? Who did you make a deal with?"

"This is business, Pug. Don't get involved."

"What do you mean, don't get involved? You're not only playing footsie with treason . . . cool as a cat you're committing grand larceny."

"This is business, Pug. It goes on like this every day. Forget it. It's just routine."

"You overestimate my stupidity, MacGlendon. What kind of a deal do you really have with the Chinese? Or maybe it's the Russians." He stood up, stood over Mac-Glendon threateningly. "That's it, isn't it? You're double-dealing with the Chinese and the Russians at the same time. You deliberately drive the price of your stock down and you. . . What about widows and orphans, MacGlendon? What about the poor schmucks who invest in you because they think you're Mr. America?"

"The big boys on Wall Street—they're the ones who are panicking. I didn't start this. I'm taking advantage of an existing condition. I didn't start the rumors that my corporation was coming apart at the seams. I believe that I'm going to pull it out—make the Chinese deal work. I'm putting my money where my mouth is." He stood up, walked away from O'Connor. "That's in the best American tradition, isn't it? Isn't that what Horatio Alger did? Put your money where your mouth is, Mr. Alger said."

"How much do you stand to make personally, MacGlendon? Give me a number."

"It depends, first of all, if I can pull this off."

"Say you do. How much? Give me a round figure. It doesn't have to be to the penny."

"A hundred million—give or take."

O'Connor let out a sound of audible disbelief.

"Ask me how much I can lose," MacGlendon said. O'Connor said nothing. "Every damn thing I own and more. Wiped out and in debt for the rest of my life. Everything I've built up—all those years: down the drain. I'm staking everything on this."

"What if one of your Chinese or Russian pals puts a bullet through you tonight?"

"I lose all the way around, don't I?"

MacGlendon went into the bedroom, undressed, and then took a long, hot shower that steamed up the bathroom.

When he stepped out of the stall, O'Connor was sitting on the toilet encompassed by the cloud of steam.

"I figured it out," O'Connor said. MacGlendon opened the bathroom door, let the steam escape and reached for a towel behind O'Connor. O'Connor passed it to him. "They've made the first contact, haven't they? You know the time and place of the meeting of the consortium, don't you?"

MacGlendon tied the towel around his waist, took another one, and began drying his hair as he walked out of the bathroom. O'Connor dogged him into the bedroom.

"It's decision time, MacGlendon. What hat are you going to wear to the first meeting of the consortium?"

"I don't wear hats."

"You've got a chance to be a patriot, MacGlendon. You've got a chance to be a real hero. It may cost you a hundred million bucks, but you can go in there and feed us back enough information so that we can break up the consortium—beat the chinks at their own game. What's a hundred million when you can save your country from economic disaster?"

The telephone rang. When he heard the voice on the other end of the line, MacGlendon's whole bearing softened, a smile cracking the grim set of his jaw. He sat on the edge of the bed as he listened. "Why did you go back to your apartment? You shouldn't be alone. You should have stayed in your mother's house. Stay where you are. Don't let anyone in. Don't even answer the phone. I'll be there in twenty minutes." He listened again. "Yes," he said. "I love you." He looked up at O'Connor, talked into the phone. "I love you very much."

Before he hung up, MacGlendon whispered into the mouthpiece, "We have all night to talk about that."

Afterglow

The place where MacGlendon had lain was still warm beside her. She rubbed her hand over the wrinkled sheet, then buried her face in the burrow his body had made, inhaling the strong male scent. They had made love gently, soothing each other's wounds. Pain had become a bittersweet sensation: an erotic experience.

MacGlendon came out of the bathroom still toweling himself and leaned over her prone body, kissed the center of the small of her back. She wriggled in response but did not turn over. He dressed quickly and was tying his tie in the long, oval standing mirror at the foot of the bed when she rolled over. "Why are you leaving? You said we had all night to talk. We haven't talked at all."

He smiled over to her. "We said a lot to each other even without speaking, didn't we?"

"I want to know about you, what you're doing, and why it's so dangerous. You can't take me into just part of your life—close me off from everything else."

MacGlendon sat on the edge of the bed and held her hand. "When this is over, when my business in Paris is completed, we'll have all the time in the world."

"How are you involved with my mother's husband?" She clutched MacGlendon's hand harder. "Ever since I was a little girl, he tried to make me call him father." She shook her head. "He was never a father to me. He was always my mother's husband." She looked up at MacGlendon. "Don't be involved with him. He's an ugly man. No matter what he told you, he and his family collaborated with the Nazis in the war. He was responsible for keeping military planes from being delivered to Israel—diverted them to the Arab terrorists."

"Don't worry about me, Paula. I've come across men like him before. I can take care of myself."

She lowered her head and spoke without looking at him. "What is the consortium?"

"I can't tell you that now."

"Why do you have to go to the Père Lachaise cemetery tomorrow at midnight?"

"I'm dealing with the Chinese," he explained. "I don't know what they're up to, but either you play their game or you don't play at all."

She looked up, withdrew her hand, unbuttoned the top buttons of his shirt, reached inside and touched the jade medallion suspended from his neck. "What does this mean? Why do both you and my mother's husband wear the same insignia?"

"The Chinese characters translate to mean *'A friend is nearby.'* "

"Let me wear it. Let me possess something that's important to you."

"I can't do that. I need this medallion for identification. It's not worth anything anyway." She had lowered her head. With his hand under her chin, he forced her to look at him. "Tell you what. Tomorrow, tomorrow afternoon, we'll go shopping. We'll buy the biggest diamond necklace in Paris."

"I don't want a diamond necklace. A diamond necklace doesn't mean anything to you. It's only a lot of money. I want your necklace." She tried to unfasten the tiny gold clasp. MacGlendon pulled away, stood up out of her reach, and buttoned his shirt again. "Is this what it's going to be like," she asked, "being in love with you? Am I just going to be isolated as an object of love, on call when you're in the mood and not too busy?"

"That isn't fair. These are unusual circumstances. My life isn't normally like this."

"What would have happened if this had all been real? What would have happened if Mr. Chou had been simply what he said he was—a silk merchant? And what if you had just come into Phyllis's gallery and fallen in love with my paintings and commissioned me to design fabrics for you? What would have happened to us then?"

At first MacGlendon did not answer, and then he said, "I deal in realities."

She got out of bed, walked across the room to the shelves of miniature flowers, held a single porcelain rose. "The reality is that I'm no painter. I'm not an artist. I've clung to a delusion for all these years—waiting for you, I guess. Waiting for you so that I wouldn't need delusions."

"You've had a tough time," MacGlendon said from across the room. "You shouldn't be making any decisions or judgments about yourself until there has been time for all of this to settle down. Your real life started yesterday," MacGlendon said. He went over to her, encompassed her naked body in his arms, and kissed her.

She yielded at first and then pushed him away. "My real father ruined all our lives by becoming involved with the wrong people. My mother's new husband is the wrong people, too. Alixandre is an evil man. I know more than I should. Stay away from him."

There was a hundred million dollars on MacGlendon's mind. "You don't understand," he said.

"It's the beginning, isn't it, of a lifetime of discussions

that you'll close me out of, tell me that I don't understand?"
She pulled the cover off the bed, wrapped herself in it.
"Tell me now, if that's what it's going to be like. Can't you
share anything except your body? Are you always going to
be remote from me?"

He walked to the door, put his hand on the knob but did
not open it. "Isn't it enough that I love you? I didn't think
I could ever fall in love." He looked back at her and smiled.
"It's a big step for me. Have patience. Give me time."

"Is there time? Or are you going to walk out there and
get gunned down?"

"I'm going to leave Big Red here to watch out for you.
Let him answer the phone and take care of the front door.
He'll take care of you for me. You can trust him."

"When will I see you again?"

"Tomorrow. Remember? We're going to buy you the
biggest diamond necklace in Paris."

Out in the living room of Paula de Plyssy's apartment,
seeing Big Red asleep on the gray velvet sofa and the New
Man reading a French art book, MacGlendon went directly
to the telephone, dialed the Ritz Hotel, asked for Ridge
Bentley, and waited until Bentley's sleepy voice answered
the phone.

"I'm on my way," MacGlendon said. "Clear it with the
concierge." He hung up without waiting for Bentley to
reply.

The Bentley Confrontation: Part Two

Crammed close to each other in the narrow back seat of the taxi, MacGlendon and the New Man rode in silence, each absorbed in his own thoughts. As they crossed the bridge, headed toward the lighted obelisk of the Place de la Concorde, MacGlendon broke the silence. "Do you know that I've forgotten your name? You've been busting your butt, risking your life for me, and I don't even remember your name."

"Knute Jergens," the New Man said. "Like Knute Rockne." He spelled out his first name. "The *K* is silent."

"The Silent K. That's a good name for you." He looked over. "That isn't your real name, is it?"

"At the moment it is. It's as real as anything that's been happening."

"How long have you been working for Pug O'Connor?"

"Not too long. It's a temporary assignment."

"I feel like a jerk," MacGlendon confided. "You CIA guys knew more about this and knew it sooner than I did."

"We've been on the Chinese case for a long time: ever since Nixon cracked the ice. There has always been a hard core of skeptics who believed that while the Chinese were smiling at us with their mouths, they were using their hands to sharpen their knives. You were a piece of luck, MacGlendon—the first actual no-shit lead man we had. Our stake-outs kept sending in reports of this man named Chou coming in and out of the country like twice a week: pretty heavy traveling for a silk merchant. We finally wised up, put a tail on him, and he led us to you."

"Anybody else? Who else was he in contact with?"

The New Man shrugged his shoulders. "In this business you never see the whole picture: you're limited to the restricted range of your assignment. I only know about you."

"What's your guess about the Chinaman—about Mr. Chou? Do you think he's really dead?" The New Man did not answer. "There were two Chinamen in the lobby of the hotel that morning: Chou and another guy. Both about the same build. Chinamen all kind of look alike."

"All of that happened during Big Red's shift. I tried to quiz him about some distinguishing characteristics between the two men, but his eye isn't really trained for this kind of work. Nothing against him, mind you. He's a good enough guy and he'd break his ass for you."

"I think, maybe, it was the other guy—not Chou."

"Possibly. The same thing occurred to Pug O'Connor, but he's gotten nowhere checking it out. It's easy enough to switch identities. The guys in Washington think that Chou was too high up in the hierarchy to risk his life on a routine assignment."

MacGlendon said: "Chou knew that there could be trouble. He played the whole thing close to his belt. He was too smart not to cover himself. He wasn't the kind of guy you can push over a railing that easy. The other Chinaman with him could have been the surrogate victim."

"You learn, in this business, to live with unanswered questions and unresolved problems."

The taxi swung past the gleaming gold Jeanne d'Arc mounted monument, turned down the Rue de la Paix, headed for the Place Vendôme and the Ritz Hotel.

"Tell the driver to go around to the Rue Cambon side."
After repeating the instructions in French, the New Man asked: "What do you want me to do? Go up with you?"

"You can wait in the lobby. I can handle Bentley. He's not so dangerous."

The New Man smiled for the first time. "Your continuing innocence amazes me. Ridge Bentley is one of the most dangerous men in the world. Why do you think the Russians pay him all that money?"

"I know all about that," MacGlendon answered, putting his hand on the New Man's knee. "But up close, on a one-to-one basis, he's a pussycat."

Before they got out of the taxi, MacGlendon said, "Do you have to report in to O'Connor?" The New Man nodded. "I don't want O'Connor to scare off Bentley. I need him. Tell O'Connor to lay off. Tell him I can handle this one alone. Okay?"

"I'll tell him," the New Man said. "It's not going to do any good, but I'll tell him."

Ridge Bentley sat on the ornate desk in front of tall French windows that were partly opened to the night air. Billowing curtains moved like banners behind him.

Sitting in a hard, straight-back chair across the room, MacGlendon said, "I've been warned that you are one of the most dangerous men in the world."

"Then why did you come here?"

"To make a deal," MacGlendon said. "I've been thinking about what you said to me earlier. Some of it makes some sense."

"What part of it?"

"I'm not going to lie to you, Bentley. You're everything I despise. Morally and politically, you and I couldn't be further apart."

"But you need me. I have the capacity for violence you lack."

"And you're smart. And I know where you're coming from, and you know where I'm coming from."

Bentley put his feet up on the coffee table, leaned back on the sofa. "Before they went to war, Hitler and Stalin signed a nonaggression pact. When Mao first took control, he made frequent trips to Moscow, smiled and shook hands. Then, when he was strong enough, the jaws of the Chinese dragon snapped shut."

"You understand me perfectly, Bentley. I intend to play your game only as long as you're useful to me. When you're no longer useful, I'll get rid of you. One way or another, I'll get rid of you."

"Like you said, MacGlendon, we're both coming from the same place. We have equal motives and equal incentives. In the long run only one of us can survive." He bent forward. "It's an interesting alliance: better, I think, than one founded on mutual trust or shared goodwill."

"If you tell the Russians that I've knuckled under, agreed to play ball, will they believe you?"

"The Russians are paranoid—so paranoid, actually, that they are easily deceived by the truth. I'll tell them the truth. I'll tell them that all our threats and actions have forced you into temporary submission and that you've agreed to be a Russian agent in the Chinese consortium. I'll also tell Moscow that I don't trust you. Not for one minute. I'll tell them that I'll be watching you like a hawk every step of the way. They'll believe that."

"And they'll call off the dogs, lay off the rumors about MacGlendon Industries, and let all the bank loans and mergers proceed?" Bentley nodded. "And the violence against my people will stop? Can you promise me that?"

"I could," Bentley said.

"But will you?"

"Under certain conditions."

"Like what?"

"How much money, MacGlendon?" he said as he bit at the cuticle of his thumb. "How much is involved?"

"It could be as much as a hundred million."

"Fifty-fifty?"

"That's what partnerships usually are," MacGlendon said.

Godspeed

During the few hours MacGlendon had slept, fear returned: first as fantasy in tormented dreams, then as cold-sweat reality in the harsh light of another dawn. His decision to inform Pug O'Connor of the secret meeting at the flea market was made while he was half-awake. The New Man had contacted O'Connor.

The three of them sat together now in MacGlendon's suite drinking the bitter breakfast coffee and nibbling at the flaking, buttery croissants.

"Anyone could have signed Chou's name to that note," O'Connor was saying. "I don't know why you destroyed it. We could have had the handwriting analyzed or had it dusted for fingerprints. It was the only piece of physical evidence we had." He brushed the crumbs from around his mouth. "Didn't Chou give you some code word or symbol for contact identification?"

MacGlendon touched the jade disk at the base of his throat, remembering the duplicate of it around the Count de Plyssy's neck. "Nothing," he said.

"Whoever wrote that note must have known that Chou is dead." He thought for a moment. "Or is he dead?"

The New Man interjected: "MacGlendon and I were talking about that before. There was another Chinese man with Chou. Did the French police give you positive identification?"

"The problem with the French police," O'Connor said, "is that they're French. They assume that anyone who is not French lacks the intelligence to understand anything and, consequently, they give out no information. They're sweeping the murder under the rug. They don't want bad publicity during the Prêt." He poured more coffee from the silver pot. "That note is the kind of trick the Russians would use to lead you into a trap. Or the Taiwanese. Everybody wants a piece of your ass, MacGlendon." He winced as he took a sip of the coffee. "For the lack of an alternative, we are forced to make the logical assumption that this meeting at the flea market is the next link to the consortium. Chou's name is probably just a code name for the contacting agent. It's dangerous as hell to make this kind of assumption, but I don't know any other way to play it." He scratched his head. "No choices. It's the only lead we have." He looked over at MacGlendon, spoke slowly. "It *is* the only lead we have, isn't it?"

There would be time later, MacGlendon decided, to tell O'Connor about the de Plyssy contact and the scheduled midnight rendezvous at the Père Lachaise cemetery. "I don't see any other choices," MacGlendon said.

"Something bothers me," O'Connor mumbled. "I keep asking myself why MacGlendon has had this overnight change of heart. How come he suddenly wants me around?" He looked at MacGlendon directly. "Up to now, you've been playing this like a one-man army: why the sudden cry for help? Does this mean that you're ready to play ball with us?"

"I'm making no commitments. I just thought you ought to know what was happening. I owe you that much."

"You owe me a lot more than that, MacGlendon, but it isn't time yet to tally the final score."

"It's a two-way street," MacGlendon said.

"I wish that I trusted you. I wish that I believed your motives were pure and simple. I'd like to believe that you're scared shitless. I could understand that—even in a great tycoon like you." He walked to the window, held back the curtain and looked down into the courtyard. "What did you and Ridge Bentley talk about last night?" He nodded in the direction of the New Man. "Knute here says that you weren't there for more than twenty minutes. You guys must have come to a quick agreement. What kind of a deal did you make with him?"

"It was a business discussion," MacGlendon explained. "It doesn't affect the meeting at the flea market this morning. I didn't mention that to him. We talked about some international financial matters."

"I don't understand the corporate mentality—that whole set of rules you guys play by. Your thinking is like another world to me. I'm a simple American. I stand up when they play 'The Star-Spangled Banner' and put my hand over my heart. When I was a kid, I—"

MacGlendon interrupted him. "I'm not interested in your boyhood, O'Connor, or the tragic tales of your humble origins. And don't start with that stuff about your sainted mother." He looked at his watch. "I'd better get going."

"You're taking a hell of a risk going alone. You know that, don't you?"

"There's no choice. If you put a tail on me, you'll scare off the meeting. I have to go alone. Nothing will happen to me: they need me alive."

"The Chinese do," O'Connor said, "but I'm not sure about the Russians or the Taiwanese. The way I read it, once you've led them to the next consortium contact, you're as good as dead."

"I have to take that chance."

O'Connor came forward, put his hands on MacGlendon's shoulders but was unable to look him directly in the eye. "I'm rough on you, MacGlendon, that's my job. That's what I'm trained to do. I'm suspicious of you but that's one of my job specifications—to be suspicious of everyone and everything." He laughed. "In this situation I'd even be suspicious of my sainted mother."

"I can handle myself. I'll be all right."

"We'll be doing what we can for you, giving you as much cover as possible without blowing the operation. It won't be much but we'll do what we can." He watched MacGlendon open the door and start to leave. "God bless," he called after him. "Godspeed."

On his way out of the hotel MacGlendon's way was blocked by an elderly man carrying a thin briefcase. "Mr. MacGlendon?" MacGlendon nodded. "They wouldn't ring up your room. I've been waiting down here for over an hour."

"What for?"

"I'm George Strapthorne."

"Who?"

"You have short memory for fifteen million dollars."

MacGlendon put his hand softly on the other man's arm. "I'm sorry. All hell has been breaking loose around here." He led the lawyer out of the main line of traffic, sat beside him in the chairs at the far side of the lobby where Mr. Chou and the other Chinese man had waited for him that first morning in Paris. "You brought papers for me to sign?"

In a slow, practiced ritual, Strapthorne took his eyeglasses from his breast pocket, put them on, and then reached into his pants pocket, brought out a tiny gold key on a leather strap, ceremoniously opened each lock on the leather case, and brought out a sheath of papers held together with an oversize paper clip. "There ought to be some formal identification," he said, "to make this legal. I do recognize you from your photograph in *Fortune,* but nonetheless it is my obligation to verify your identity."

MacGlendon reached into his jacket, took out his wallet, and fished out his driver's license. "I hope this is good enough."

The attorney looked from the plastic-encased card up at MacGlendon and back at the card again. "You've let your hair grow." He took a pen, opened it, and handed it to MacGlendon. Turning the papers toward him, he said, "You sign the first three copies." MacGlendon scribbled his name without reading the documents. "You are in a hurry, aren't you?"

"What else?"

Strapthorne fingered through the papers, took out a manila folder, and opened it. The check was clipped to another legal document. "You sign this one to verify receiving the check."

MacGlendon scribbled his name again, pulled the check from the clip, and put it in his inside pocket without looking at it.

"I've been an attorney for almost fifty years, Mr. Mac-Glendon, but this is a new experience for me. You haven't even looked at the check to see if the amount is correct. We're talking about over fifteen million dollars."

MacGlendon stood up. "I trust you, Mr. Strapthorne, and I owe you an apology and a lunch." He looked at his watch. "I only have time to apologize now and to thank you." As he was striding away, he called over his shoulder, "I'll buy you the lunch in New York."

Marché Paul Bert

The driver came off the Périphérique at the St.-Ouen exit, made a series of sharp turns, and drove down a wide boulevard jammed with traffic. The sidewalks were lined with racks of used clothing, tables piled high with shirts and shoes. In between the stalls Africans leaned against the buildings, their native artifacts spread out on blankets in front of them.

As they made a left turn into a narrow street, the merchandise changed abruptly from clothing to ornate furniture and glittering antiques and bric-a-brac. Shoppers and tourists cut back and forth across the brick-paved road without regard for the slow-moving vehicles.

Keeping one hand on the horn, the driver blasted his way forward. At the first cross-street, he turned into an even narrower road lined on both sides with stalls of furniture blocking the sidewalks. Halfway down this block he stopped at the wooden gateway of the Marché Paul Bert. MacGlendon paid him, walked through the arch, checked his watch, and decided there was time for coffee at the small café inside the entrance.

While he stood at the crowded counter, a body forced its way between MacGlendon and the black man standing next to him. MacGlendon turned, looked down at a perspiring

Geoffrey Plantagenet. "I thought that was you," Plantagenet said. "What in the world are you doing here? I can't believe that you're an antique collector. I thought young people nowadays had no reverence for anything old."

"I'm through playing games, Plantagenet. What's this about? Is Chou still alive?"

Plantagenet looked from side to side, then behind him. "We can't talk here. Let's go outside."

MacGlendon downed his coffee, then followed Plantagenet out to the broad concourse of the market that ran for two hundred yards and then forked into two narrower *allées*. Plantagenet stopped in front of a pair of tremendous iron gates propped up with makeshift wooden braces. His index finger ran over the intricate tracery of the design. "These gates are probably two hundred years old. Would you believe the craftsmanship? You couldn't replace that workmanship at any price today."

"Is Chou really dead?"

"There's been a message from China. The consortium is canceled. Temporarily, at least. Your instructions are to return to the United States and wait for a new contact."

"Who do you really work for, Plantagenet?"

"It doesn't matter anymore. It's over before it began."

"I don't believe you. I need proof."

"There is no proof. You have to trust me."

"I trust no one."

"The message came from Peking yesterday. Chou's death has thrown off all the timing. Go back to the United States. Wait there. You'll be contacted again at some future time."

"You're in this with Ridge Bentley, aren't you? You work for the Russians."

"Nothing is what it used to be," Plantagenet said. He moved a few paces down, examined the ironwork on the posts supporting the high gates. "There are no heroes and villains anymore. It was so easy in the old days. The battle lines were clearly defined. But now, everyone is a villain. Villains versus villains. The battle line is between degrees of villainy."

A flatbed truck was backing up into the market, a hoist lashed to the deck with heavy chains and the huge iron hook dangling in mid-air.

"Look at this," Plantagenet said, fingering an ornamental seal worked into the iron post. "This is the Biron crest, the family coat of arms. The Duke de Biron fought with Lafayette for American independence." He walked in front of the gates across to the other post. "The Bourbon coat of arms should be on this other side. Biron was married to a cousin of Louis the Sixteenth."

The teamsters were off the truck, shouting instructions to the driver, maneuvering the hoist into position.

MacGlendon saw it coming, the big hook on the crane writhing wildly, uncontrolled. He screamed at Plantagenet as he backed off to the other side of the concourse. Plantagenet turned around, puzzled and unaware of the danger. As he started cutting diagonally across to MacGlendon, the iron hook smashed at the top of the gates, tore them loose from the wooden braces; the hook wavered in the air and then rocked forward and crashed to the ground, the impact of the gates' tremendous weight imprisoning Plantagenet between the twisted wrought-iron bars and the Tarmac roadway. Parts of Plantagenet's body oozed through the intricate ornamental design.

In the confusion that followed—screaming people, barking dogs, hordes converging around the accident—MacGlendon froze not more than a foot from the pronged, barbed spires at the top of the arched gates. He felt someone pulling him from behind. His eyes were transfixed on Plantagenet's body but he let himself be pulled back through the crowd.

In the darkness of the inner recesses of the stall across the concourse, he finally turned around. Pug O'Connor said, "There but for the grace of God . . . We've got to get out of here." But MacGlendon seemed incapable of moving. Grabbing him by the shoulders, O'Connor shook him roughly and screamed, "We've got to get out of here."

MacGlendon finally spoke. "No "

"What do you mean, *no?* You almost got killed. That gate was supposed to fall on you. Do you realize that? They weren't after Plantagenet. They were after you. That should be *you* under the gate. Do you understand that?"

"It has to stop," MacGlendon said. "It has to stop." He let his head fall forward. "I can't take any more. It has to stop."

"There's only one way that it's going to stop," O'Connor said, "and that's when you get your ass out of Paris and go home where you belong."

"That's what Plantagenet told me to do. He told me to get out of Paris." MacGlendon picked up a glass vase from a display table, held it in his hand like an awarded trophy. "Plantagenet was lying, trying to scare me off." For no reason, he smashed the vase to the ground. His anger expunged, he bent over, fingered through the pieces of broken glass, found the fragment with the price tag adhered to it, counted out enough francs, and placed the money on the table. "I won't be scared off."

"I'm scared enough for both of us. I'm getting your ass out of here. You're going to be winging your way across the Atlantic by tonight."

"I thought you wanted to smash the consortium."

"Not at the price of your life. I've gotten into the habit of keeping you alive, MacGlendon." He smiled. "I don't break my bad habits very easy."

"You wanted me to work for you, O'Connor. You wanted me to get in there and identify all the members of the consortium so that you can smash it once and for all."

"There has to be another way."

"I'm your best way. You know that."

"I still can't figure you, MacGlendon. What about the hundred million bucks you're about to make on your own stock? What happens to that?"

"You keep saving my physical ass, O'Connor. You're getting good at that. Let me handle the financial end. I'm good at that part. I'm even going to cut you in on a piece of the action."

O'Connor shook his head. "You don't know what I'm about any more than I know where you're coming from."

There were screeching sirens in the market now, rotating yellow and red lights.

"The meeting in the flea market was to be in stand two-eighteen. Plantagenet intercepted me before I got there."

"Are you telling me that you want to go on with this?"

"It has to stop," MacGlendon said. "All this killing has to stop." He put his hand on O'Connor's chest, felt the gun in the holster. "We can do it together."

"Odds are that whoever was going to meet you has taken off by now."

"It's worth a try."

Past the crowd of gapers, the *allées* of the market were deserted. Identification numbers of the stalls were mounted above the awnings. O'Connor and MacGlendon moved quickly through the maze of little paths twisting through the market, made several wrong turns before they found the right stall.

A red awning, stenciled with a design of Chinese calligraphy and block-lettered Les Artes du Chine, identified stand 218. A padlocked, metal mesh screen had been drawn over the opening, and the furniture in front of the stand was hidden under a waterproof tarpaulin. O'Connor pushed a pile of furniture aside, peered into darkened space, and called back to MacGlendon, "No one around."

MacGlendon had backed off and was looking up to the second story, above the awning. There was a faint light behind a moon-shaped window, a quick flicker of shadow. "There's someone up there." He jogged over, stood beside O'Connor. "Let's just wait here."

In a few minutes a young Chinese man walked down the narrow, railingless stair, stopping halfway. *"Nous sommes fermés."*

"I had an appointment here at eleven o'clock. I was delayed. There was an accident at the other end of the market."

The Chinese man backed up the stairs and disappeared into the darkness there. O'Connor pulled away part of the tarp, uprighted an overturned black wood chair, and sat down. MacGlendon stayed in the shadows, close to him.

When the young Chinese man appeared again, he was outside the building, walking down the center of the *allée,* continually looking behind him. "Very tricky, these Chinese," O'Connor muttered. "These stands must all be connected on the second floor."

Continuing to look both ways and behind him, the Chinese man inserted a key into the padlock, studying both MacGlendon and O'Connor before he turned it. He pointed his finger at O'Connor. "You stay."

"No way. We're both going up there."

MacGlendon said: "It's all right. He works with me."

The young man hesitated, shrugged his narrow shoulders, and finally turned the key, releasing the padlock and rolling up the metal barrier high enough for MacGlendon and O'Connor to bend under. "Be careful," he warned them. "Don't break anything." He lowered the screen, relocked it, turned over the chair O'Connor had been sitting in and covered it and then ran off down the *allée.*

Gun drawn, O'Connor preceded MacGlendon up the stairs, stopped just before his head was about to emerge on the second floor, passed the gun back to MacGlendon, motioned him to wait, and then continued up.

The room on the second floor was low-ceilinged, dimly lighted from a dangling bare bulb. Tables and chairs were piled on each other. Stacks of black Chinese screens leaned against the walls. There was almost no floor space left to move through. O'Connor motioned for MacGlendon to come up, then looked around the small room. "There's another way in and out of here, but I sure don't see it."

Then, noiselessly, activated by a concealed electrical mechanism, two panels of one of the carved Chinese screens swung open into the room. The same young Chinese man motioned them forward, turned, and led them through a series of storerooms, carefully threading his way around the fragile objects. He stopped at a door, knocked lightly, and then cracked it open. A small sliver of bright daylight cut through the darkness. O'Connor kicked the door all the way open. He made an illuminated target in the flood of sunshine.

A woman's voice called out as his eyes were adjusting to the brightness. "The gun is not necessary," she said. "I would like to talk to my son alone."

Blinded by the shock of the truth, it took MacGlendon a moment before he realized that what he was seeing was a beautiful woman in an exotic setting. He looked at his mother as if he were looking at a stranger, feeling the radiance of ageless sexuality.

Slowly, with deliberate concentration, MacGlendon focused on the reality of the situation.

"It's true," his mother said. "All of it is true. I am what they say I am."

MacGlendon turned his back and started out of the room,

but he ran into O'Connor standing guard. Lowering his head so that he would not have to look at her, MacGlendon went back and stood in front of his mother.

"I've lived my life," she said, "trying to shield you from the truth. There isn't time now—and there are too many dangers—to go through the rationale of whether the decisions I made were right or wrong. Right or wrong, they are decisions I have made, and I am what I am and you are what you are because of those decisions." She looked up through the angled skylight to the sky beyond it. "Your life is in danger. Your life is the most important thing in the world to me at this moment. Do you hear me, Angus? Do you understand what I'm saying?"

MacGlendon made a vague, noncommital gesture with his head.

"God willing," she said, "there will be time later for us to talk—for you to ask the thousand and one questions that must be in your mind. But not now. There is no time now. I know these people, Angus. I know how dangerous they can be. I know because I am one of them."

Two moths fluttered in a beam of dust-specked light. MacGlendon concentrated on their directionless pattern of flight.

"I'll never ask for your forgiveness. Perhaps, when the danger is over and if we all survive, there will be no need to ask for forgiveness." She stood up, walked over to him. He turned his face away. She touched his cheek. With an angry, impulsive gesture, he pushed her arm down, shoved her away with such force that she fell backward, knocking over a table and lamp, crumpling to the floor.

Her face hardened as she looked up at him; her jaw stiffened and her eyes were wet with tears that she forcibly held back. "I don't deserve that," she hissed at him. "No matter what I am, what I've done—I'm your mother." Slowly, she brought herself up to a sitting position and awkwardly, gripping a heavy floor lamp, got to her feet, walked back and sat in the chair again. "Whatever I did, my motivation was love. I loved your father totally: every fiber of me loved him. Your father had a dream of a better world. His entire being was dedicated to that better world. His devotion to his Marxist dream superseded everything else in his life: his family and, finally, even me. He was revolutionary in the classic sense of the word. He was cast in the mold of the American revolutionary. He had that same dream—freedom for all men. It was all so clear to me that day you were born. Everything was black or white. There was no question of alternatives." She turned to him. "Why don't you sit down. You look so awkward standing there."

MacGlendon did not move.

"Everyone said that I gave you up to the custody of my parents because I didn't love you, because I didn't want to bother with you, because I was too interested in being a wild radical and saving the world." She shook her head. "I gave you up—gave up the joys of having a son and watching him grow up—because I loved you too much. I wonder if you'll ever be able to understand that—why I did what I did? It seemed so clear-cut at the time. I never questioned my decision." She opened her purse, took out a handkerchief and a compact, wiped the stains from around her eyes, and peering closely into the tiny mirror, coated her lips into a cupid's bow with bright red lipstick.

"Through Communist contacts in Chicago," she said, her voice controlled now, unwavering, "I established a liaison to Mao, went to China and became a spy under Mao's direction. I whored and lied and cheated to accomplish my objective of fulfilling your father's dream. There was no question of right or wrong—no second thoughts. I did what had to be done. I had a long-range plan in mind. You were never out of my thoughts. I was preparing the way for you to take over your father's mantle.

"The concept for the Chou Consortium was created thirty years ago. I was part of it because I saw it as an eventual power source for you, a way for you to fulfill the purpose of your father's life."

For the first time MacGlendon looked up, looking through the skylight into the same rays of sun spotlighting his mother. He moved a chair, straddled it, and folded his arms across the back of it. "You pulled all the strings, didn't you?"

"I did what I thought was right. You must believe that."

"I'm not a self-made man, am I? The Horatio Alger Award is a fraud. You and your Chinese friends funded everything—you made the wheels turn, didn't you?"

"You had to succeed. It was part of the master plan."

"All the bank loans that got me started . . . all the financial hurdles that seemed insurmountable—that was all Chinese money, wasn't it?"

"You did it on your own, Angus. It was your own brain that made it happen."

He shook his head. "It was your filthy, whoring, Communist money. It greased the way. It's still greasing the way." His head fell against his folded arms, his voice was close to tears. "What a damn fool I've been. Why didn't I see it? Why didn't I know? It all happened so easily. Too easily." He cried openly now. "What a fool I was not to see it. What a fool."

She went over to him, smoothed his hair, and fondled his ears. This time he relented to her touch—needed it. "*I* was the fool, Angus. I was wrong about China. The whole world is wrong about China. In the end, they will turn out to be no better than Russia. The Marxist dream is gone. Even Mao stopped dreaming it years before he died. China is playing a game of seduction now, opening up to the world and teasing like a reluctant virgin. *I* was fooled. The world is fooled. China is an ancient, historic whore." She thought for a moment and then said, "Like me—an ancient, historic whore."

Still sobbing, MacGlendon stood up, engulfed his mother in his arms. Momentarily, her body went limp against him; then she stiffened and drew away. "The Chou Consortium is what China is really like—greedy men with the know-how to run the world. But, in the end, not even they will be strong enough to fight the dragon. Once China has what they want from these men, the jaws of the dragon will snap shut—devour them. You included. Not even you will be strong enough to control them." She sat down again, opened her purse, and repeated the ritual of making up her face. "All my illusions are gone." With an eyebrow pencil, she made wild upswept lines over her eyebrows and under her eyes. She gashed the red lipstick over her mouth in straight, bloody lines without contour. Her voice was shrill when she screamed at him. "Look at me now, Angus. Look at me." MacGlendon didn't raise his head. "Damn it, look at me. See me for what I really am."

Slowly, he raised his head.

"Get out while there's still time. Get out before they destroy you like they've destroyed everything else. Get out! Get out!" Her screams became sobs and her body wracked with inner torment. MacGlendon went over to her, kneeled in front of her, held her hands in his own. "Don't let them kill you, Angus. Save yourself. I love you. You're the most important thing in the world to me. They've killed everything and everyone else that I've loved. Don't let them kill you. Please. Please."

MacGlendon stood up, leaned forward and put his lips against her distorted mouth. Then he backed off through the opened door into the darkness. He felt the firm grip of

Pug O'Connor's hand steadying him as he wavered. Blinded by tears, he crashed into a table of objects that shattered to the floor. O'Connor supported MacGlendon with his own body and led him through the maze of attics, bolstering him like a wounded football player being led off the field.

Turning Point

The traces of her lipstick were a red wound gashed across his mouth. MacGlendon ran the tip of his tongue over his upper lip tasting the fragrant, greasy residue of it. He lay on the bed of his hotel suite, limp with exhaustion, inexplicably drained of tension and thinking about love. The pictures in his mind were blurred images of his mother and Paula de Plyssy superimposed on one another.

Pug O'Connor came out of the bathroom, tossed Mac-Glendon a wet washcloth. "Wipe off your fucking face." He smiled. "You look like a creep."

MacGlendon rubbed the cold, rough cloth across his mouth, studied the red stain, then wadded it and placed it against his forehead. "You've seen it all now, haven't you, Pug? You've seen it all. Even a grown man cry."

"Irish guys cry a lot. I'm used to it."

"Funny," MacGlendon said.

"What's funny?"

"The way I feel."

"How do you feel?"

"Easier than I thought I'd be with you. Not humiliated."

"Why should you feel humiliated?"

"No one has ever seen me break down like this. Go to pieces. Nobody has ever seen that side of me. Not even

264 / ECHO CHAMBERS

when I was married. Even through that, I never lost my strength."

"You're human, MacGlendon. For a while there I thought you were a different species. Being human isn't all that bad, is it?"

"What time is it?"

"One o'clock."

"It seems like forever." He took the cloth off his head, dropped it on the floor beside the bed. "I can't believe it all happened. It's like a nightmare." He looked directly at O'Connor. "I'm grateful to you. I don't know how else to say it. Grateful isn't a big enough word."

"You said it all right. Considering the source, *grateful* is a big word."

"What's going to happen to her?"

"Your mother?" O'Connor shrugged his shoulders when MacGlendon nodded. "She's a survivor. Maybe she'll survive."

"You don't believe that. The Chinese will kill her, won't they?"

"She's a hell of a lady, MacGlendon. It took a lot of guts to do what she did—admit the truth about herself to save your life. That's one hell of a lady." He sat on the edge of the bed, started to look at MacGlendon, then turned his head. "You're booked out of here tonight. You're flying to Boston. Our people in Boston will look after you for a few days until all of this cools off."

"They'll kill her, won't they?"

O'Connor shrugged his shoulders again. "In the business she's in, you take your chances. I know from personal experience. Nothing comes free. There's always a price to pay."

"Isn't there any way you can give her protection?"

O'Connor stood up, walked across the room to the window, held back the drapery, and looked down into the courtyard. "I was a witness to a woman confessing treason.

I heard her admit that she was an agent for a foreign government. There are rules that cover that: there are federal laws, and there is my own fucking conscience."

"You could forget what you heard."

"I wish that I could."

"You could take her into custody."

"Then what?"

"I'll make a deal with the government."

O'Connor shook his head. "You'd put her through hell again, MacGlendon, raking up her whole history again. And you'd put yourself through hell. And for what? Treason is punishable by death."

"Forget what you heard. I'll make it worthwhile."

"Are you offering me money, MacGlendon?" His anger was quick, scathing. He stood over the bed now, his body threatening MacGlendon. "You dumb asshole, haven't you learned anything? With everything that's happened to you, haven't you learned a damn thing? Don't you realize what that lady was doing? She was signing her own death warrant so that you could live. She wants you alive. She doesn't care what happens to herself. Didn't any of that get through to you? Do you still believe that money buys everything, that money rights all wrongs?"

MacGlendon's voice was feeble. "I owe her a lot. I owe her everything."

"Then pay her back in what she wants. Get the hell out of Paris. Forget the Chinese. She told you what they're really like."

Propping himself up, supported by his elbow, MacGlendon said: "You've accused me of having only one dimension—a wheeler-dealer mentality. Okay. I'll make you a deal, O'Connor. Does this sound more like me? You've got something I want and I have something you want. So we negotiate."

"You don't understand me any more than I understand

you." He grinned suddenly, relaxing. "What I really want is a beer. Stress tends to dry out a man's mouth, and a man can't function from strength with a dry mouth."

"Call room service." He waited while O'Connor dialed and ordered two cans of beer. "I don't want a beer," he mumbled.

As he hung up, O'Connor said: "They're both for me. Each man handles stress in his own way. You wheel and deal under tension. I'm a simple man—I have a couple of beers to cool everything down. Life seems less complicated after a couple of beers."

"What about my deal? Don't you want to hear it?"

O'Connor shook his head. "You're going to Boston. Boston is out of my territory. Make your deals in Boston."

"You wanted a spy, didn't you? You wanted an insider in the Chou Consortium, didn't you?"

"No deal, MacGlendon."

"You can't let her die. You can't let them kill her."

O'Connor walked out of the room. MacGlendon sat up, swung his legs over the edge of the bed, felt a dizziness in his head, lost his equilibrium. The room spun around. He gripped the edge of the mattress, held tight until the whirling motion tapered off and finally came to a full stop. Tentatively, he stood up, braced himself against the table. This time the new spasm of dizziness abated quickly. He stumbled across the room and went into the bathroom, studied his face in the mirror. Unchanged. Unscathed. All the scars were inside.

After a punishingly cold shower he dried himself and tied the towel around his waist, then went into the living room of the suite.

O'Connor was slumped in the only comfortable chair, his legs stretched out in front of him. He was clutching a can of beer. The other can was on a silver tray on the desk. MacGlendon grabbed the ring, tore it open, took a swal-

low. "What happened to Big Red and the New Man?"
"Rest period," O'Connor answered. "I'm all the protection you need at the moment."

MacGlendon sat cross-legged on the floor, touched the jade medallion around his neck, and took another swallow of beer. "You never talk about your sainted father," he said to O'Connor.

"The bastard is still alive: shacked up with an old biddy in Florida who drinks him dry and never cleans the oven."

"Do you ever see him?"

"A couple of times a year. Under duress. He was never much good for anything. We get along well enough. He likes to fish. We both do."

"Maybe it's easier," MacGlendon said.

"What's easier?"

"Not living with a legend. Maybe if my father had lived, I'd see his frailties. He'd be in his mid-sixties now. Maybe he'd be too fat or fart uncontrollably."

"Your mother loved him very much."

"He was a Communist. A raving radical."

"So?"

"What kind of role model is that for a son?"

"Times were different then. Words and labels had different meanings. You can't second-guess what he'd be like today—how he would think or what he'd believe in."

"My destiny is supposed to be to accomplish his dream of a better world. I only exist in his image. I'm nothing by myself." MacGlendon laughed. "*Fortune* magazine says that I'm a self-made man—the legendary American success story." He laughed again. "Maybe they'll do a piece called 'MacGlendon Revisited'—tell the truth about me. The great American success story—funded by the Chinese Communists. It would make great reading, wouldn't it?"

"You need some time to sort things out: get back your perspective. As my sainted mother used to say, 'You can't make a silk purse out of a sow's ear.' You're a silk purse, MacGlendon. You would have made it anyway."

"I'll never know for sure, will I?"

"You'll find a way to prove it to yourself. Give yourself some time. It will all come back into focus."

"I'm not going to Boston. You know that, don't you?" O'Connor crushed the empty beer can in his hand: nodded.

"There's a contact tonight at midnight. It's the first meeting of the consortium. Père Lachaise cemetery. Jimmy Morrison's grave. Paula de Plyssy's father. The Count de Plyssy." He held the jade medallion between his thumb and index finger. "He wears one of these. This medallion identifies a member of the Chou Consortium."

O'Connor stood up, went to the phone.

"Wait a minute. Who are you calling?"

"Room service," he said. "You're drinking my other beer."

Love Manifest

With her fingertip Paula de Plyssy traced the line of pubic hair feathering up his abdomen to his navel. "Does that tickle?" MacGlendon shook his head, continued staring at the ceiling, distracted with his own thoughts. "You're different today," she said. "You've changed somehow."

"Better or worse?"

"Different."

"Does it make you love me more or less?"

She laughed. "I'm not sure that I love you at all. I'm not sure what love is. So much has happened and it's happened so quickly." She kneeled up on the bed, leaned over him, putting her face in front of his, blocking his line of stare. "You've been in love before. Is this what love is like?"

"I haven't been in love before."

"But your wife? You must have thought that you loved her."

"That was different. Times were different then. Words had different meanings. I thought love was one thing, and it turned out not to be love at all."

"What's happened, Gus? Why are you different today?"

Instead of answering, he put his arm around her, bringing her down on top of him, his mouth against her mouth.

She pulled away, sat up straight. "Why can't we talk? Why are you afraid to talk to me?"

"I'd rather make love to you. Is that so terrible?"

She put her arms around herself, hiding her nakedness and the scars of rape. "You make me feel much more like a woman but much less like a person. Can you understand that?"

"Which is more important?"

She waited a moment and then she said: "I don't want to be like my mother—not a person at all anymore. She only exists in direct relationship to a man wanting her. She lives and breathes for Alixandre. And he's so rotten to her."

"He's European, has the heritage of a double standard. Not I. I'm the all-American boy." Inexplicably, he began to cry, soundless tears streaming down his face. He twisted his mouth, bit his lips, but the tears would not stop.

She covered his face with kisses, pressed her mouth first against one eye and then the other. "Tell me what happened. Tell me."

He jumped up, went to the far end of the room, his back to her as he stood in front of the shelves fingering the fragile porcelain flowers.

"It's no good, is it, Gus?" Her voice lowered to a whisper. "It will never be good between us. We can't make love all the time. We'll have to face each other as person to person—not always as woman to man." She came up behind him, nestled her head between his shoulder blades and put her arms around his waist. "You can't handle that kind of relationship. I feel sorry for you. You have so much to give but something is blocking you. Is it fear, Gus? Is it fear?"

MacGlendon unlocked her hands gripping him and unwound her arms from his body. He went over to the chair, began to get dressed.

"I feel so guilty," she said. "I feel that I've stolen your

strength. You've given me strength, you know that, don't you? I was the one who was always afraid, and now I'm not afraid anymore. All the horrors of the things that have happened to me have, for some reason, made me stronger. I'm not afraid to meet other people head on. You've given me that by loving me. But you've paid a terrible price, haven't you?"

"A man I know—a friend of mine—told me this afternoon that nothing comes free. There's a price to be paid for everything. If you feel good about yourself now—it's worth the price." He looked down at the floor as he pulled on his socks. "I love you, Paula. I love you as much as I am capable of loving anyone or anything. The inadequacy is in me. I know that now. I have no dimension, no capacity for real feeling. I'm an automated replica of a dead man."

"You're not making sense."

"There is no sense to it. But it exists. The truth exists."

"You're leaving Paris, aren't you?"

MacGlendon nodded.

"Will you ever come back?"

"Will you be waiting?" he asked her.

She walked to the full-length mirror at the foot of her bed, wheeled it to the far side of the room, and turned it glass-side toward the wall. "No," she said, "I won't be waiting. I waited before I met you. Now that I've met you, I don't have to wait anymore."

"Will you stay here?"

"In Paris?" She shrugged her shoulders. "I don't know. I want to learn how to really paint—not just those seed-packet flowers in Phyllis Goldberg's gallery. I may go to China or Japan—learn to paint flowers there."

"When the time comes, wherever you are, I'll find you."

"I feel so sorry for you," she said.

Val de Carconne

Always, when he was here, Alixandre de Plyssy felt a strong sense of history, his own deep roots in the soil of France and the inevitability of family survival. The past was alive here and the future secure.

The new gravel road crunched under the impact of the tires of his Mercedes. Setting sunlight filtered through the trees of the dense forest, casting brilliant light on the turning leaves in some areas and creating ominous islands of shadows in others.

He drove slowly, gaining strength and confidence as he went deeper into his own land, farther back into the ancient de Plyssy glories.

In the eighteenth century this land had been deeded to the second Duke de Plyssy by Louis XV. The ruins of a minuscule twelfth-century village, devasted and depopulated by a plague, had been restored and converted into a hunting lodge, a secret trysting place for the duke's male friends in the Bourbon nobility. The cathedrallike church had been remodeled into the duke's private quarters. The choir loft, with its circular, leaded-glass window overlooking a twisting tributary of the Seine, had been made into a sumptuous bed chamber; an oversize goose-down bed, capable of sleeping three, was elevated on a platform and positioned to take advantage of the view. The main part of the church had been refurnished as a dining hall, the stone walls covered with tapestries to insulate against the dankness. The altar had been reconstructed into a stone fireplace high enough and wide enough to roast a whole buck venison with five-point antlers. The original, twelfth-century primitive wood-carved Christ figure still hung in the towering space over the opening.

Until a year ago the lodge was accessible only by barge from the river side. Now, with the new road, the original medieval wall had been restored, the drawbridge and guillotine-type spiked iron fence were repaired and motorized with a sophisticated computer-operated mechanism. The stone piers, supporting the gate, now housed two television security cameras, each making a ninety-degree lateral arc and each with a forty-five-degree vertical capability.

The drawbridge was up, the spike gate down, when Alixandre de Plyssy stopped in front of the lodge. He got out of the car, took deep breaths of the autumnal air, looked up through a clearing to the ruins of an ancient manor house that was once the castle overlooking the village, broken stone piers rising from the overgrown debris, spotlighted into grotesque shapes by the beginning sunset.

The drawbridge lowered noiselessly. An armed Chinese man waited behind the iron gate, peered at de Plyssy through his narrow eyes and thick glasses, signaled behind him, and the spiked ironwork rose vertically between the stone trestles. De Plyssy got back into the car, drove across the wooden planked bridge, under the guillotine gate and into the courtyard. Another armed Chinese man sat on the steps in front of the church, guarding the Gothic arched doors. There were other guards stationed along the string of stables, which the second Duke de Plyssy had had converted into bedrooms for his male guests and equipped with the softest beds, finest embroidered linens from Paris, and the choicest young girls from the south of France. They still functioned as guest rooms now.

He left his car, engine running, in the center of the court, jumped out and watched the gate behind him lower, the drawbridge rise.

An old, white-haired Frenchman, wearing a long, brown leather apron, walked slowly toward him, dragging his left foot in a slight limp. "He's been sleeping in your bed," the old man said. He made a vague gesture toward the Chinese men watching them. "They are everywhere. Your father is turning in his grave." He shook his head sadly.

"It's the times, Jean-Pierre," de Plyssy said, patting the man on the shoulder. "You've seen enough to know. You saw the Germans here. We survived."

"The Huns," he said, "were not like this. They laughed and they farted and they made heavy noise with their boots. Not like these men. So quiet it's like mice running over the floors."

"It's the times," de Plyssy said. "The times change, but we are always the same." He pointed to the trunk of the car. "Take my bag into one of the guest rooms, then park the car."

"I don't like that Chinese man sleeping in your bed. No one but a de Plyssy has ever slept in that bed."

De Plyssy laughed. "Except for girls, Jean-Pierre. You've seen enough of that." He patted the servant on the back again, walked toward the church, passed the guard without looking at him or acknowledging his presence. He used his key to unlock the door and went inside, standing for a moment in the dark apse, allowing time for his eyes to adjust to the light level. Then he looked down the long nave of the church, vertical shafts of light penetrating through the long, narrow, leaded windows, to the high-flaming fire blazing in the open hearth at the far end. He moved slowly, touching familiar objects as he passed them, sapping strength from their antiquity.

The exceptionally tall Chinese man was dwarfed by the scale of the stone shaft. He was facing the fire, his arms behind his back, his long, manicured fingers locked together. He turned when he heard de Plyssy approaching from behind him. His face was haggard, his eyes lined from sleeplessness: his mouth drooped and his skin sagged in a loss of vitality. He wore the rough cloth, the unornamented simplicity of the Mao uniform—no color and no shape. "We are grateful," he said to de Plyssy, "for your hospitality."

"You've been to China and back?"

He nodded. "It was not intended that I return to Paris. But there has been misdirection—needless deaths. Success is close. It cannot slip through our fingers because of ill-timed tempers or mistakes in judgment. Deng considered it best that I return here."

"My wife's daughter was brutalized," de Plyssy said, not knowing that he was going to say it.

The Chinese man nodded. "I know everything that has happened. I am unable to cope with the ravages of violence. I cannot remain aloof from it. A great man would be untouched by this; it is one of the qualities that make them great. The blinders they put on their emotions keep their course to success unencumbered by personal feelings." He bowed his head, then suddenly looked up at the decaying Christ figure over the fireplace. "Unfortunately, I am not a great man. I cannot restrict my vision so that I do not see the tragedies." He took a deep, exhausted breath, gasping for air. "I regret what happened to your daughter."

"It was the Russians," de Plyssy said.

"It is always the Russians," the Chinese man said. "But we provoke them as they provoke us."

"I've made the contact with young MacGlendon. Midnight tonight at the Père Lachaise cemetery. You have made the arrangements to bring him here?"

"We will all be assembled here by noon tomorrow."

"I'm concerned about MacGlendon," de Plyssy said. "I think that he has made a deal with the Russians."

"Americans," the Chinese man said, "are curious people. Opportunists. Opportunists for the immediate. But they have no sense of the long range. They do not prepare for that. But don't underestimate their ability to perform within the limits of their mentalities." He smiled, his face tightening in a kind of pride. "Young MacGlendon has gotten the best of the Russians. He beat them at their own game. I have just spoken to our people in New York." He smiled again. "Young MacGlendon is making what the Americans call a killing on the stock market today. His stock is making a brilliant recovery." He looked at his watch. "And the action has only begun. He will add many millions of dollars to his personal wealth by the end of the day in New York."

"How does that affect his usefulness to the consortium?"

"You know the American popcorn?" He laughed at his own memories. "It is like a narcotic. Addictive. The more one eats the more one wants. Like wealth," he said. "Like money."

"I think my wife's daughter and MacGlendon are in love with each other."

"Love," the Chinese man said, but then he did not say any more. The word hung in the hollow air of the empty church.

"The others? Are any of them here?"

He nodded. "Toshibito has arrived from Tokyo. Guggenheim from Israel will be here momentarily. He is being driven here from Belgium."

"Does the driver know the turnoff? It's hard to find."

"Our people are all well trained."

"When do we go to Peking?"

"It will be decided tomorrow at the meeting."

De Plyssy backed off from the heat of the fire, turned around, and looked through the round glass window over the choir loft. The top edge of the setting sun was still visible from this angle. He walked to the center of the nave, sat in a high-backed hard thronelike chair and rested his head, closed his eyes. The Chinese man followed him, sat in the opposite chair. "I ask the indulgence of your hospitality once more."

The count opened his eyes and leaned forward.

"There is a woman," the Chinese man said. "I have taken the liberty of inviting her here. She is one of us. Her life is endangered by what has happened."

"But you yourself warned us about security." He pulled the jade medallion from under his shirt. " 'A friend is nearby.' She must wear one of these."

"The lady," the Chinese man said, "invented the jade medallion. Without her, there would be nothing now."

"But you said that it was a personal matter. My understanding is—"

The Chinese man interrupted the count. "We are at a point that is beyond understanding. I am weary of the discipline of my mind. This matter is a matter of the heart." He closed his eyes, saw the familiar picture of Deng Xiao-ping haranguing him. "I have made another foolish and sentimental gesture."

"I don't understand."

"Nor do I. But a man does what he is destined to do."

Another man, dressed as a workman, but with immaculate hands betraying his disguise, had entered the church, calling down the aisle: "Chou. Chou." He ran then to where the men were sitting. He looked at de Plyssy without any sign of recognition. "I must talk to you alone," he said to the man called Chou.

The Chinese man remained calm, gestured with his hand. "Sit down, my friend. There is no longer any need for secrets between any of us. We will leave here either successful or destroyed. Either way, the secrets we have from each other will no longer be important."

"The Arab," he began, ". . . the oil man."

"Salod." Chou filled in the name.

"His plane from Baghdad landed at Orly. No problem. But as it was taxiing toward the private terminal . . . whoosh." He made an explosive gesture with his hands. "Dead," he said.

"Activate the alternate plan." Chou looked at his watch, calculated the time back to the Middle East. "The man in Kuwait is on a stand-by basis."

"The Russians?" de Plyssy asked.

"Possibly. I have learned that there is a Russian agent in Paris who is assigned to work against us," the Chinese man said. "He is an American named Ridge Bentley. He is an accomplished terrorist. He is capable of anything."

Drones Die in Mating

They were two insatiable animals going at each other with peak-season frenzy: climaxing, uncoupling, lying apart in deep-breathing exhaustion, and then going at each other again with revitalized vigor. There was no tenderness between them, no words of love. It was an equal matching of equal hungers. It was an encounter of sharp nails, biting teeth, soft and hard flesh, taking place in the scented aura of body secretions and orchestrated with shrieks of pain and murmurs of pleasure.

With his eyes closed in a moment of half sleep, MacGlendon was comparing the man he was here to the man he had been in Paula de Plyssy's bed. The difference was the ingredient of love.

Here, each towering climax was a fractional instant of blinding joy, but then everything turned hollow: his hunger was unsated, and there were no lingering feelings, no ascending pleasures. With Paula . . . He began remembering but stopped himself. This, this instant, was the man he really was. Sex was a body function—without love.

He closed his eyes and the pictures of Paula were vivid, lifelike.

Unable to endure the pain, he opened his eyes to the reality of the flesh beside him.

The Eurasian woman was propped up on one elbow, the tattooed Garuda on her breast momentarily flightless, the pink nipple distended but still gleaming wet with saliva. Her long legs were crossed at the ankles, and one hand lay demurely between them.

In the other hand she held a pearl-handled pistol steadily aimed at MacGlendon.

He looked over to the empty bed next to them, the impression of Ridge Bentley's body denting the pillow, wrinkling the satin comforter. "When will Bentley be back?"

"You will not kill him," she said. "I will stop you."

MacGlendon turned his head, looked down the line of his own body, the feather of pubic hair that Paula's finger had traced. Slowly, testing the words, he said: "Why should I want to kill Bentley? Bentley and I are in this together now." He hesitated. "Partners."

"They know that. They have found out that he made an arrangement with you. That is why they have taken him."

"Who?" he asked. "Who has taken him?"

"The men in black leather: his friends on the motorcycles."

"Russians?"

She shrugged her shoulders: the Garuda fluttered and, for an instant, the gun wavered but then steadied. "They speak Russian and they also speak French and German. Who knows what they are?"

"What did they tell you?"

"They told me that if you came here, I was to keep you here at any cost."

"Is that why you balled me?"

"You knew it would happen," she said. "From the first time we saw each other we knew that it would happen."

"Do you know about queen bees? Do they have bumble bees in the Orient?" She did not answer. "In a bee hive, the workers bring in all the pollen, the queen lays all the eggs, but only the drone fucks the queen." He smiled. "The drones," he said, "die in mating."

"I will not kill you. The men in the black leather warned me not to kill you. They need you alive to lead them to the Chinese consortium." She lowered the sight of the gun to his penis and then reaimed it between his eyes. "I can wound you, make you bleed, but I cannot kill you."

MacGlendon laughed. "You *are* a ball buster, aren't you?" He looked across the room to the gold clock on the marble mantel. The time before the midnight meeting was running out. He leaned back against the pillow, remembering too much. "In one way or another," he said, "you're all ball busters."

As they lay immobile, side by side in the silence, with her free hand, distractedly, she began fingering her clitoris without wavering the aim of the pistol between MacGlendon's eyes. As the pace of her circular motion quickened, MacGlendon raised his head, bent toward her with his mouth open and his tongue extended. Her left index finger continued the undulation. Her right index finger slid against the trigger.

The hard, butt end of the pistol dug cold inside MacGlendon's ear as he mouthed the Garuda-tattooed breast, made endless circles around the nipple with the tip of his tongue, began nipping at it with the edges of his teeth as the pace of her masturbation increased and the gun pressed deeper into the cavity of his ear.

At the exact moment of the apex of her orgasm, he bit full force into her breast and broke her gunned arm away from him. The pistol fired wildly, shattering the mirror over the fireplace.

He wrested the gun from her, threw it across the room. She lay back moaning, undulating this time with pain. The wounded Garuda sagged and bled.

Checking the clock to see how much time was left, Mac-Glendon dressed hurriedly and wondered about himself as he slipped into his shorts. He wondered why he still had a hard-on.

Outside the Ritz Hotel, looking both ways down the dark and lifeless Rue Cambon, MacGlendon heard the sound and then saw the black-and-chrome gleam of a motorcycle turning off the Faubourg St.-Honoré, sparking as it roared through the narrow lane between parked cars. Instinctively, he stepped back into the shadowy shelter of the hotel entrance.

The tires screeched as the rider braked to a sudden stop, balanced the machine with a booted foot against the brick pavement.

The helmeted rider in the pillion seat sagged against the driver. The driver unfastened a leather strap from around his waist and the rider slid off, the body collapsing in the middle of the street.

The motorcycle leaped up on the back wheel in a sudden surge of power, roared off, sputtering exhaust and showering sparks.

MacGlendon ran out to the prone, spread-eagled body, rolled it over, pulled up the goggles, and removed the metallic-speckled helmet.

Only Ridge Bentley's eyes were recognizable in the bruised and battered face. There was still life in them as he searched the night, finally focusing on MacGlendon's face. His voice was hardly audible. "Fifty-fifty," he whispered. "Fifty-fifty." His eyes closed, his head turned to the side.

MacGlendon battered on the locked door of the Ritz until the immaculate concierge, unhurried, went through the elaborate ritual of unlocking it. MacGlendon pointed to the street, the body lying on the pavements. "Call an ambulance," he shouted. "Call a fucking ambulance." Then he ran through the hotel, down the long corridor boarded up and plastered with Danger signs, through the series of lobbies to the other side of the Ritz and ran past a startled watchman into the serenity of the Place Vendôme, the huge bronze column casting a phallic shadow in the moonlight.

Gravesite, Graveside

He stood over Jim Morrison's grave: felt nothing. Mac-
Glendon was a living dead man here, a vertical corpse,
human agony at last laid to rest. Every feeling inside him
had died: there was no love or hate left. He was an automa-
ton, programmed by the man he had used to be, acting out
a course of events without blood and without tears or laugh-
ter. Without love.

The midnight was bright. The sky was cloudless. Mac-
Glendon was an exposed target here, undefended game for
predators. He stood straight in the night, his head high, not
looking around him nor listening for live, human sounds in
this landscape of dead objects.

The mound of the grave was strewn with dead flowers,
placed there singly or in bunches by individuals in a cult of
international mourners linked in an underground network
dedicated to keeping the memory of the rock star alive and,
thereby, keeping part of their own youth alive. The engraved marble marker was defaced with signatures and esoteric words in many languages. The edges of the tombstone
were ragged, pieces chipped off to be carried away as trea-
sured souvenirs.

After waiting ten minutes, MacGlendon heard sounds in

the distance, footsteps clacking against the cobblestone path, unhurried and maintaining a constant cadence. Then there was the noise of dead twigs and dried branches crunching underfoot against the hard ground as someone walked across the graves. He took his hands out of his pockets, held them up in the air to indicate that he carried no weapon.

The shape of the figure, when it appeared, was undefined except for the medium height. The body was wrapped in a belted, oversize trench coat, which hung long over high laced workman's boots. A wide-brimmed hat, turned down all the way around, hid the features of the face in shadows, and an oversize scarf, wound twice around the neck, obscured the lower face structure. Bright white workman's gloves hung out of the coat sleeves like the hands of a scarecrow, covering any identifying characteristics.

Using the tombstone as a body shield, the figure faced MacGlendon. MacGlendon put his hands down, stretched his fingers back and forth spider style. "A friend is nearby," he said.

Now there were sounds around him. Shadows moved through the low skyline of tombstones, figures appeared in the distance. MacGlendon knew that he was surrounded, all escape paths blocked.

With head down, the person in front of him was looking at the grave. The gloved hands began awkwardly to unwind the circles of the scarf, letting it fall to the ground, then both hands pulled the hat up, off the head.

Her long hair cascaded to her shoulders, the reddish tints fired by the moon and the light of the stars. Paula de Plyssy raised her head and faced MacGlendon directly. Her furrowed eyebrows warned him of danger. "They are everywhere," she whispered. "The Chinese guards are everywhere. You must be careful." She took a tissue-wrapped package from the pocket of her trench coat, removed the paper, and it crackled as she wadded it into a ball and threw it on the ground. The bunch of violets she held were wilted. She came around and kneeled at the graveside, her face directed toward the ground. One by one, she placed the violets on the mound of the grave. "The men waiting for you think that I have come here because I have a special message from the Count de Plyssy. They think that I am working with Alixandre. But I came to warn you—plead with you. You must escape. Please, please, don't go to the meeting."

MacGlendon knelt beside her, touched the limp flowers on the cold, damp ground. "Do you know where they're taking me? Do you know where the meeting is?"

She looked up, searched the area around them, and then looked down at the grave. "Val de Carconne," she whispered. "It is the de Plyssy ancestral hunting lodge. I don't know where it is. I've never been there. Neither has my mother. It is hidden in the forest somewhere east of Paris." She had placed the last violet. She touched MacGlendon's hand. "Don't let them take you there. Please. You will never be able to escape. It will be too late."

"How do I know that this isn't another trap?" He was not looking at her as he spoke. "Who are you working for? The Russians? Your stepfather? Who?"

The hurt inside her welled up as tears in her eyes. At first she said nothing, then, when she had bitten back the tears, she said, "How can you believe that?"

"What else am I supposed to believe? Why else would you have pretended to be in love with me?" Her head shook in denial, but she did not answer. "De Plyssy put you up to this, didn't he?"

Her voice was low-pitched. "I did love you." Then in a stronger voice, she said, "I do love you. Still."

"Then why?"

She thought before she spoke, then spoke cautiously. "You don't love me enough to let me be free." She looked at him, turned his face with her fingertips so that he was looking at her. "It's so hard to make you understand. Through you, I found my own identity. You brought me alive when so much of me was dead. You were tender."

"I was a fool." MacGlendon moved his head away from her touch.

"But then I felt that I was only another acquisition to you. You took me over like I was another corporation. I realized that I would only become another part of the MacGlendon conglomerate—not a separate being. Can you understand how I feel?"

"Whatever it is, it's too late now." He stood up, looked down at her crouched body, and wanted desperately to believe her. He wanted to hold her in his arms and bury his face in her hair and lose all track of time and place as he made love to her. But all his senses were signaling danger.

"If we had met sooner—" she began.

MacGlendon cut off her words. "It was all predestined. We are what other people meant us to be. You were a baited trap." He turned his back, faced the tombstone. "You're a whore for de Plyssy. You're no better than my mother. You've done your job. I'm here. I'll do what they want."

She stood up, huddled herself in her own arms against the chill of the night. "I love you so much," she said. "You must trust me. You can't go to Val de Carconne. In the end it will destroy you."

"I don't trust you. I won't. I've made the commitment. I'm going ahead with the consortium."

She threw herself into his arms, forced his arms around her, lifted her face in the position of a kiss. When their mouths were close together, she whispered: "On the way out of the cemetery, I will trip over a headstone and begin to cry and scream. Run then. Escape then. Do you understand?"

He kissed her without opening his mouth, then held her away.

Turning and thrusting her hands into the slash pockets of her trench coat, she began walking diagonally between the graves toward the cobblestone path. MacGlendon picked up his small, canvas overnight bag and followed her.

Shadows of men moved in a cordon around them, appearing momentarily and then disappearing behind a mausoleum or a monument. MacGlendon looked for the familiar hulk of Pug O'Connor, wondered if he was here masquerading as one of the de Plyssy men.

Ahead of him, Paula stumbled over a tomb, screamed and fell to the ground. When MacGlendon reached her, bent over her, she whispered: "Run. Run now. Please."

He picked her up, cradled her in his arms. "Find a man named Pug O'Connor. CIA. Find him. Tell him where I am."

Other men were around him before he could say any more. He motioned them aside and carried Paula down the path to the cemetery entrance. Outside the filigree gate, Paula said: "I think I'm all right. I was more frightened than hurt. Put me down. I think I can walk."

Tenderly, MacGlendon held her while she tried to stand. She tottered at first, tried a few steps as he supported her arm. "I'm all right."

There were two cars parked at the curb. Paula walked to the small Peugeot, got into the driver's seat, started the motor, and took off without looking back.

One of the dark-coated men was holding open the door of a black four-door Citroën sedan. Two large men were in the front seat. MacGlendon tossed his bag inside, looked once more for the shadow of O'Connor, and then got into the back seat.

Instantly, the automatic door locks clicked closed. The Citroën started slowly, proceeding at a funereal pace through the parkway leading out of the Père Lachaise cemetery.

Hunter's Quarry

MacGlendon was manipulating seven-figure sums in his head, calculating fixed costs and profits, computing compounded interest rates, mentally projecting sales figures, subtracting carried-forward tax credits and write-offs.

As the large black Citroën sped through the night to an unknown destination, he shuffled and reshuffled these numbers in the columns of his mind. He had the edge now, the wild card, of the personal windfall he had made in the manipulation of his own stock. But the profit was still on paper. Tenuous. He assumed Bentley was dead or close to dying and would be unable to start up the machinery again to financially destroy the MacGlendon industries. It would take time for the Russians to replace Bentley, regroup, and reactivate the plot against him.

He sat alone in the cushioned back seat, riding smoothly over the air-suspension system. The two men in the front seat, their faces shadowed by broad-brimmed hats, looked straight ahead, did not speak to MacGlendon nor to each other. They had treated him with deference when he had gotten into the car at the cemetery, giving MacGlendon the VIP treatment. But neither of them had answered MacGlendon's questions about the route they were taking or the name of the final destination. It appeared that they were traveling northeast from Paris on a main autoroute.

Each time MacGlendon juggled the totaled numbers in his head and rearranged assets and liabilities of his various corporations and subsidiaries, he was faced with the same missing quotient of production capabilities to make the numbers work. No matter how he computed, he still needed the factories in China.

Even with all that had happened, he was back to square one: factories in China.

The Citroën turned off the autoroute onto a secondary highway. The sign read: Montmirail 28 Km.

Eliminating the element of love, temporarily putting aside the legal and moral aspects of national loyalties, subtracting the traumas of murder and terrorism, and mentally cutting the umbilical ties of genetic heredity, MacGlendon was dealing with these problems using the same discipline he applied to any other business transaction. His underlings and the platoons of lawyers, the teams of accountants and tax experts all had the authority to negotiate and negotiate, but a deal was never a deal until MacGlendon himself approved the bottom line, affixed his signature to the document. *Fortune* magazine had called it "the MacGlendon style." *Forbes* had written about "MacGlendon's innate, last-minute instinct for the kill." *The Wall Street Journal* had called it "MacGlendon's infallible bottom-line mentality."

He started again, rearranging columns of figures in his head, using the same numbers in different patterns. But the solution to the problem was the same: his infallible bottom-line mentality said *factories in China.*

Closing his eyes to stop the dizzying display of numbers, MacGlendon succumbed to the interweaving pictures in his subconscious—Paula and his mother, the isolated cunt of the Eurasian woman, all fusing together in a giant, grotesque Picasso portrait with parts of the body reassembled in a maniacal order and the picture painted from an impossible perspective.

Beyond the Montmirail exit the Citroën turned off on a blacktopped country road without any identification signs. Darkened farmhouses dotted the landscape at spaced intervals. Occasionally the towering silhouette of an ancient château appeared in the distance, off to the side. On one stretch tall, ladylike poplar trees lined both sides of the road, a mile of conical shapes bending in ballet chorus to the force of the soft wind.

Taillights of another vehicle appeared in the distance, loomed larger and brighter as the Citroën raced toward them. At a fork in the road, where the vehicle was parked, the Citroën stopped, the driver turned off the lights. MacGlendon waited, tried to identify the automobile ahead. It was a Jeep wagon, high-suspension, four-wheel drive, equipped for cross-country driving.

The two men leaning against the fenders snapped to attention, bringing their submachine guns to shoulder-arms position, then approached MacGlendon's car in military cadence, stopping five paces away.

The driver of the Citroën remained seated. The other man got out, came around, and opened the rear door for MacGlendon, keeping his head down and in shadow. He took the small, canvas overnight bag that MacGlendon had carried, held it out to one of the at-attention figures behind him.

These two armed men were dressed in olive-drab fatigue coveralls without insignia and wore heavy, meticulously laced and polished combat boots. One of them released the tailgate and placed MacGlendon's bag inside. The other opened the door, pulled the front seat forward, stood stiffly as MacGlendon maneuvered through the narrow opening and finally settled in the back seat of the Jeep. The two guards climbed in beside the driver.

They waited for five minutes after the Citroën had taken the divergent fork in the road, then proceeded ahead at high speed, hitting the ruts in the dirt road hard. The foliage became denser, the land more wild. The driver cut off the road, drove across a rocky clearing, heading toward a forest to the right. MacGlendon bounced in the back seat, repeatedly hit his head against the head liner, as the Jeep tore across the rough terrain.

Mentally, he eliminated the rescue factor of Pug O'Connor. There was no way O'Connor or his men could have tailed them without being detected, and if they had, they would have been misled, following the Citroën down the wrong fork of the road.

A twisting clearing had been hacked through the trees— the trail only wide enough for the Jeep to go through. Branches scraped against the windows.

At one point there was a clearing, a treeless expanse where the light of the night reflected against the river in a picture-postcard serenity. Then they plunged back into the continuing forest.

The tributary of the Seine appeared again ten minutes later. The Jeep rumbled toward the river's edge. Because of the men in the front seat sitting three abreast, it was difficult for MacGlendon to see directly ahead, but he detected flickering lights, the red flames of torches buffeted by wind. The driver made a sharp left turn, parked broadside by a wooden dock with a small barge lashed fore and aft with iron chains wound around heavy posts. A half-circular, turreted structure acting as a bridge was at the stern end of the deck. MacGlendon counted three men huddled in this partially walled enclosure. Another man sat cross-legged at the blunt bow, holding a horn-shaped megaphone and staring straight ahead.

A tent had been erected in the center of the barge, a black canvas roof curving up to a circular top with a short flagpole flying an ensign of a coat of arms, rampant lions supporting a shield. The sides of the tent were made of a lighter-weight canvas, striped in black, purple, and red overprinted with a regular pattern of metallic-gold fleurs-de-lis. Iron poles supported the structure, each post topped with a blazing torch.

The three men in the front seat of the Jeep stayed in position until a man appeared from inside the tent, stepped up on the dock, approached the station wagon, then stood twenty paces away and nodded his head. Both side doors of the vehicle opened quickly, and the uniformed men jumped out. The driver stood guard on his side, one of the other men ran ahead with MacGlendon's canvas bag and put it on board the barge, and finally the third man held the front seat back for MacGlendon to get out.

Alixandre de Plyssy held out his hand. "Welcome to Val de Carconne, Mr. MacGlendon."

MacGlendon shook his hand briefly, looked around to measure distances and estimate eventual escape routes.

De Plyssy touched MacGlendon's elbow, led him toward the barge.

"Isn't there an easier way?" MacGlendon asked.

The Count smiled. "There are always easier ways than the traditional ways, I suppose. But you feel the land of France here. You feel our history. All my ancestors have met their guests at this dock. There is a ritual of our hospitality handed down from generation to generation." They stepped aboard the barge, a soft, rolling motion under their feet. "I always forget that Americans are in such a hurry. Young people," he added, "even in France now, are in a hurry." He preceded MacGlendon into the tent, turned and motioned him inside. "I take the time to savor what belongs to me. Nothing can be cherished in a hurry." He picked up a broad-bottomed ship's decanter of red wine from a center table, held it up in front of the candle burning in a single brass candlestick. "No color looks quite like this. Burgundy. Candlelight. This wine is from the same vineyards that the first Duke de Plyssy owned in the eighteenth century. When a man has a sense of history, particularly his own history, time no longer becomes that important. Survivors," he said, "survive." He motioned for MacGlendon to sit in one of the four tall straight-backed armchairs. He poured two glasses of wine, handed one to MacGlendon, raised his own glass in silent toast. MacGlendon cupped the goblet in his hand but did not drink.

Chains clattered in the night, twin motors revved up, and the man in the bow shouted instructions through his megaphone as the barge prepared to shove off.

De Plyssy took a gold-encrusted padded velvet blindfold from the table, walked around, and stood behind MacGlendon. "This, too, is part of the de Plyssy tradition. Not even Louis the Fourteenth objected to it." As he put the blindfold over MacGlendon's eyes, he said: "There have been many kings at Val de Carconne. When we get there, I will show you the guest book. Signatures and insignia of great men who have come here."

MacGlendon did not resist the blindfold. "Why the blindfold?"

"Val de Carconne is a secret retreat, hidden in the woods. There is a maze of little branches of the Seine that run through here: little blood vessels shooting off from a main artery. No one but the head of the de Plyssy family and his barge crew knows the exact route through these waters. A man can feel safe at Val de Carconne, know that he is free to indulge his secret pleasures without being unexpectedly discovered. Not even Louis the Fourteenth could find his way back to Carconne."

MacGlendon tasted the wine. The Burgundy had a seductive bouquet, a smooth, dry taste in his mouth, and became a warming glow in his stomach. "Is everyone here?" he asked, then added, "The members of the consortium?"

"By tomorrow morning."

"Who are they?"

"It is not my position to reveal the names. Don't be so impatient, Mr. MacGlendon. Everything will happen in its own time. Enjoy the wine. Savor it. Think of the land and water that you can't see. This is France. This is the real France. Feel it. Feel it in your blood."

"How do you justify it?"

"Justify what?"

"The Chinese consortium. It's going to take a big chunk out of the French economy, change all the balance of power." He waited. "It's going to destroy France as you know it. If you're such a great French patriot, how do you justify that?"

He heard the count's footsteps treading a circle on the wooden deck. "This land cannot be destroyed," de Plyssy said. "The consortium will happen with or without me. The change to the world is inevitable." He was silent while he refilled his wineglass. "Newspapers will call me a traitor," he said, "but history will describe me as a savior of France."

They made the rest of the trip in silence except that once, unexpectedly, MacGlendon blurted out, "I'm in love with Paula."

The count did not answer, either because he didn't care or because he had gone out on deck, leaving the shelter of the tent. Blindfolded, MacGlendon could not be certain of which.

There were voices on the shore in the distance. The motors were cut and the man in the bow was calling out landing instructions. The barge bumped against a dock, rolled slightly, settled down, and then came the sounds of the chains again securing the barge. MacGlendon waited, finally called out, "Are we there?" No one answered him. Still holding the wineglass, he untied the blindfold with his free hand, adjusted his eyes by focusing on the flickering candle. There was no one else in the tent. The decanter was gone from the table. De Plyssy's empty goblet was turned upside down, leaving a red ring on the purple cloth.

Without exactly knowing his motivation, MacGlendon set his wineglass on the deck, stood up, and then crushed the fragile crystal under the heel of his boot.

Chinese uniformed guards then took over, leading Mac- Glendon off the barge, up a path through some pine trees and into the courtyard of Val de Carconne. At the far end the dark cathedral was silhouetted against the bright night, the pale colors of the circular window glowing softly, lighted from inside the building. Guards stood at attention at twenty-yard intervals in front of the long line of con- verted stables.

Gravel crunched under their feet as they walked along the path. The men escorting MacGlendon turned at the fourth stable near the main building, then led him to the large, iron-hinged wooden gate. One of the men took a massive iron key, turned it in the lock, once to the right and then a double turn to the left. The door creaked open. But before MacGlendon stepped inside, he turned to the sound of running on the gravel. One of the men from the boat was bringing MacGlendon's canvas bag. Out of breath, he handed it to MacGlendon. This man was not Chinese.

Carrying the bag, MacGlendon went inside. The door behind him closed and was locked from the outside.

At the far end of the large room a modern window had been inserted into the ancient stone wall—one large sheet of fixed glass. The concealed landscape lighting outside illuminated huge tree trunks, highlighting the autumnal colors of dying leaves still clinging to the branches. Beyond the trees a section of the river was visible and the wooded shore beyond it. A long, heavy, rough-hewn table was in front of the window with multibranched, hand-wrought iron candelabra flanking it, the flames burning smokeless and straight up in the mechanically ventilated air. Decanters of wine and brandy, bottles of mineral water, and a silver bowl of fruit were carefully arranged on the mellow patina of the table surface. The bed was on a platform in an alcove. A draped, dark blue canopy over the bed and side curtains with the de Plyssy crest emblazoned appeared dusty and threadbare in this light.

The toilet was in a doorless recess of the room. Still holding his canvas bag, MacGlendon stood in front of it, urinating. When he heard a sound behind him, he turned his head.

An elderly, gray-haired manservant, dressed in a striped jacket and holding a single candle, stood in the background. He waited until MacGlendon had flushed the toilet, then stepped forward to pull a long tapestry bell cord that electrically lighted the bathroom. He blew out the candle he was holding, turned on the faucets in the lead sink and held a towel ready while MacGlendon washed his hands.

Not certain of the language, MacGlendon just smiled at the man, mumbled, *"Merci."*

"Would you like me to unpack for you, sir?" He spoke with a British accent.

MacGlendon looked down at the small bag on the stone floor. "Not much to unpack."

The servant took the bag, set it on a bench beside the bed, began turning back the bedspread. "You must be tired after your journey," he said.

"Did you just appear from nowhere?" MacGlendon looked around the room. "How did you get in here?"

He pointed to a dark corner of the room. "The staircase," he said. "I have quarters right below here. Call me if there is anything you need." He turned his head as he was propping up the pillows. "Day or night, sir. I am always there." He pointed to another bell cord, frayed and darkened from age, which hung next to the bed. "Call me at any hour. I am here to serve you."

MacGlendon walked to the darkened corner, looked down the narrow, circular stone stairs. There was a flicker of light below. "Do you have a way of getting in and out of there without going through this room?"

"There is a door to a tunnel that connects to the kitchen building." He added, "It is always well guarded by the count's security staff."

"The Chinese soldiers?" MacGlendon asked.

The servant nodded. "It wasn't always like this." He turned back the corner of the covers at a crisp angle, then spread out the fur comforter.

"I have to ask the obvious question," MacGlendon said. "What's a nice English gentleman's gentleman like you doing in a place like this?"

"It's a long story, sir, and I'm sure that we're much too sleepy tonight to listen to it."

"Maybe you are," MacGlendon said, "but I'm not. I'd like to hear it."

The servant took his candlestick, lighted it from one of the candelabra, padded softly toward his staircase. "Will there be anything else, sir?"

"What will I do about the candles? Let them burn out?"

"I will make certain that they keep burning through the night unless you prefer complete darkness."

MacGlendon went to the table, wet the tips of his fingers in his mouth, began snuffing out the flames. "I'm not afraid of the dark," he said. By the time he started on the second candelabrum, the servant was gone as noiselessly as he had appeared.

Still fully clothed, MacGlendon lay back on the soft bed, rubbing his hand against the thick wolf fur of the blanket, allowing himself to be off guard long enough to feel the pain and weariness of his body.

The lock on the stable door grated as a key was opening it from the outside and the hinges scraped as the door swung back. A tall figure and two armed guards were outlined against the still-bright night. Pulling the door closed behind him, the tall figure walked into the room, turned on the flashlight he was carrying, held it so that it revealed his face, then focused the beam on MacGlendon. "You don't seem surprised to see me," the man said.

MacGlendon stretched his arms over his head, felt the soft surface of the velvet hangings, saw the musty dust whirling in the flashlight beam. "I'm immune to surprises." He swung his legs over the edge of the bed and sat up. "I knew that you weren't dead. It was the only answer to a lot of things." He stood up. "Do you have a match?" He took the cigarette lighter the Chinese man held out to him, went back to the window, lighted one candle, and with the flame of it began lighting the others. "I figured it out—but not until today." He scratched his head. "Or is today yesterday? Maybe it's tomorrow. It doesn't matter anymore." The end of the room was bright again. MacGlendon handed back the gold lighter. "The other Chinese man—the one waiting in the lobby with you—he was a kamikaze, wasn't he? He came to Paris for the sole purpose of dying. I mean, he knew that he was going to die. You pushed him over the railing yourself. You wanted everyone to think that you were the one who had been murdered."

"The Russians still believe that I'm dead."

"But the other man—why would he allow himself . . . ?"

"Dying for one's country is an honorable death."

MacGlendon thought about it and then said, "Bullshit."

"Your mother . . ." Chou said, finding difficulty in knowing what to say after that. His voice trailed off.

"She's dead, isn't she?"

The Chinese man shook his head. "No," he said, "she's still alive."

"She's been hurt?"

He shook his head again. "No, I didn't mean that. She hasn't been physically hurt." He took a deep breath. "Orders have come from Peking—from Deng himself. She is to be eliminated."

"Why? Because she tried to scare me off the consortium?"

This time he nodded. "She has deviated from orders, endangering the operation and revealing her affiliations with the People's Republic. She is no longer useful to China. Expendable."

"She's here? Is she your prisoner?"

"I am protecting her. I love your mother," Chou said. "We love each other. We have for many years." He studied MacGlendon's face. "You never suspected?"

MacGlendon's face showed no emotion.

The Chinese man said: "Your mother would like to see you. She knows that you are here."

"I can't go through that again. There's nothing she can say to me that will change my mind about the consortium. I'm committed."

"Is there anything that I can say?" he asked. "What can I tell you that will make you change your mind?"

"Tell me how I can build factories in China without pledging myself to the treachery of the Chou Consortium."

"I am Chou," he said. "Tzao-Tzao. Mao always called me that. Tzao-Tzao." He cleared his throat. "It is the name by which your mother calls me."

"You haven't answered my question. You set me up for this. You arranged to get me on the hook for over one hundred million dollars. I made all the acquisitions based on your assurances that I could get the necessary production capabilities by building factories in China. You didn't tell me then that the real purpose of the consortium was to destroy the Western world."

"The Chou Consortium was not conceived to be evil. Evil men have made it evil. There is a quotation from your Bible—casting bread on the water. We were casting Chinese money to the West in the belief that it would return to us in harder currency manyfold. Our change from the Mao doctrines, the new concept of bilateralism, is a desperate move on China's part to quickly expand our economy, give work to our many people, and increase their standard of living." He clasped his hands together. "There are so many poor people in China. You have no concept. It is beyond a Westerner's comprehension. Don't you understand that we need your factories in China as much as you need to have them? The original concept for the consortium was that simple." Then he added, his voice sad, "It was that benign."

"What happened? What changed that?"

"Different men with different motives. Greedy men," he said, "with greedy motives." He looked directly at Mac-Glendon. "Like you," he said.

"What are you trying to tell me—that I should destroy everything I've built, play 'The Star-Spangled Banner,' and let my whole life go down the drain?"

"Unlike me, you are young. You can begin again." The Chinese man closed his eyes and remembered many things. "I am a stranger to you," he said, "but you are not a stranger to me. Through your mother's eyes, I have watched you grow up and develop into a man. I fantasized many times that you were my own son—a child I never had." He smiled. "Your mother used to tease me about it. She used a word I believe to be Yiddish. *Kvell.* It means to be very proud."

"I know what it means," MacGlendon said.

The Chinese man was smiling. "Every time something

important happened to you, every honor you received, every award—'You're *kvelling,*' she'd say to me." His face hardened, the lines around the jaw set in determination. "I'd like to be *kvelling* now," he said. "Your mother realized her own mistake—the life she led and what she believed in. To save you, she revealed herself. She loves you very much. You are the most important thing in the world to her. You must believe that."

"More important to her than you?"

He nodded his head slowly. "More important even than her own life."

"Is she going to die?"

"I cannot let that happen," he answered. "I cannot let her be killed."

"That will make you a traitor to your own country."

"Not to China. Not to the real China. I am only betraying the betrayers."

"They'll kill both of you."

"Eventually. But each day we live together we will cherish."

MacGlendon was silent for a while, wondering if he should expose himself, his true purpose, to the Chinese man. Chou obviously knew all the names of the members of the consortium, had documents in his possession that would be hard evidence against the members. That was the information that Pug O'Connor needed.

Would his mother's lover *kvell* if he knew MacGlendon's real purpose in being at Val de Carconne? Or was all of this another Chinese trick, another deception? Would the identity of this Chinese man change again? MacGlendon decided to play it close to the belt: reveal nothing.

"I must go," the Chinese man said. "Time is running out. Must I tell your mother that you will not see her?"

"Tell her that I understand—that I understand many things now. But it's too late. I am what I am."

"May I also tell her that you said that you loved her?" MacGlendon thought for a moment. "You may," he answered. His whole structure softened. He touched Chou's shoulder. "I do love her. God help me, I do love her."

Responding to a coded rap on the heavy oak door, the guard unlocked it from the outside, opened it into the courtyard. MacGlendon took a step forward to breathe the night air. As the Chinese man held out his hand to Mac-Glendon, they heard shouts coming from the cathedral. Both men turned.

A small figure in a flowing garment was running barefoot across the courtyard pursued by uniformed guards. Her long red hair was unbound and flew in the wind.

A single gunshot pierced the night, a single streak of fire. The sound reverberated in the enclosed area. The body crumbled to the ground.

MacGlendon outran Chou, reached his mother first, knelt beside her, felt the pulse in her neck. The faint, diminishing throb stopped completely as his finger pressed against the artery. The small spot of blood over her heart spread in a slow, expanding circle. MacGlendon turned around, looked up. The tall figure of Chou stood rigid: tears flowed uncontrolled from his eyes.

The Count de Plyssy came out of the shadows, walked toward them, rubbing the muzzle of his hunting rifle against the leg of his pants. "Your superiors in China," he said to Chou, "thought you might not have carried out their orders. They instructed me to do what you did not have the courage to do."

Chou lunged at de Plyssy, attacked him savagely, knocking him to the ground. They struggled, evenly matched, near Betsy Brewster's body. MacGlendon grabbed de Plyssy's rifle, which had fallen to the ground, and began to aim it but saw the guards' submachine guns sighted on him, and he backed off, standing aside as two of the guards pulled Chou off de Plyssy.

In Chinese, breathing hard and spitting out the words with venom, Chou gave instructions to the guards, pointing first to de Plyssy and then to MacGlendon. Two of the guards strong-armed de Plyssy, leading him into one of the stable rooms. A single guard took the rifle and tossed it to another man, then put the muzzle of the submachine gun into MacGlendon's back and pushed him across the court-yard, forcing him back into his room, and locked the door behind him.

The candles still burned.

MacGlendon threw himself, facedown, on the bed but not even the thick mattress, the goose-down pillows, or the heavy velvet curtains could muffle the sounds of his sob-bing.

He lost track of time: minutes were hours and it seemed that morning would never come. The candles had burned low in the holders, but it was still night outside the big window. MacGlendon stood there, staring out into the darkness, watching for the faint light of another day.

The sound behind him was barely audible; it lasted for only a second. MacGlendon stepped back into the dark corner of the room and strained to listen for the sound repeated.

A pencil-thin beam of light was moving in a circle up the stairs. MacGlendon held his breath, heard the drumbeat of his heart. The shape of the man was discernible now, but no distinguishing details were visible in this light. The man's head was lowered and his shoulders hunched to-gether. A rectangular object was tucked under one of his arms. The flashlight was directed toward the bed, making a circle of the empty pillow, then started a frantic pattern around the room.

"I'm here," MacGlendon said, and stepped forward into the flow of the candlelight.

The Chinese man had changed clothing, now wearing the drab, gray, high-collared Mao uniform. "There isn't much time," he said, "you must move quickly before daylight." He took the package from under his arm. It was a small flat box wrapped in waterproof oilskin. "It is all here. All the evidence is in this box: every name and every dossier of the members of the Tzao Consortium. There are official Chinese documents with signatures—irrefutable evidence of the conspiracy." He held out the box. "Tell the world before it's too late. That is your destiny."

MacGlendon took the box, gripped it tightly. "How did you know?" he asked. "How did you know my real motive was to break up the consortium?"

"You are your mother's son," Chou said. "And your father's son." A faint smile veiled the hardness of his face. "And, in many ways, you are my son."

The two men embraced each other. Then Chou pulled away. "You must hurry. You must take great care."

"How do I get out of here?"

"Follow me."

Together, in single file, they threaded down the stone stairs. At the bottom the British manservant sat in a straight-backed wooden chair beside the stub of a burning candle. His head was dropped to the side at an awkward angle, his eyes stared motionless in horror and the long slit across his throat gushed with blood.

An opened iron-barred door, beyond the dead man, the key still in the lock, led into a long tunnel with wall torches mounted near the vaulted ceiling, placed at intervals coinciding with the rooms above. Chou turned left, began talking Chinese to MacGlendon in a normal voice, and walked at a casual pace. But at the end of the tunnel, he hunched forward and began to run. MacGlendon kept pace with him. They climbed a wide staircase and came into a room that was dark except for a fire burning in a wood stove under a copper hood. The remainder of the kitchen was in darkness.

Chou slid back a big door that operated on a chain mechanism. Dark outlines of trucks were parked in the clearing outside the building. It was a five-foot drop to the ground. Chou said: "Hide in the woods until daylight. Wait until the sun comes up. Then follow the river, always moving with the sun on your left."

"How far?"

The Chinese man whispered, "Mao said that there is no distance too great or a bridge too far." He put his hand against MacGlendon's back, started him forward. MacGlendon jumped down, turned around as the door was sliding closed.

Daylight began as a thin slit of gray on the horizon, widening and becoming pinkish and then orange. MacGlendon was hidden in the cover of the crook of a multistemmed linden tree on the river edge. While he had waited, he had heard voices, sounds of men thrashing through the woods coming closer and closer to him. But a voice, which MacGlendon thought he recognized, redirected the searching party in the opposite direction to where he hid, the voice instructing the searching party to keep the rising sun on their right.

When the sun was visible, MacGlendon, carrying the box of documents like a football, moved forward along the river bank, pushing and kicking his way through thickets and underbrush. Birds were flying back and forth across the river, from forest to forest, in a senseless, undirected quest.

MacGlendon stopped: listened and then listened again.

The staccato hum of an outboard motor was approaching from the south. He took cover in the trees, flattened his body against the trunk of an oak. A small, flat-bottom boat appeared from around a bend in the river. One man was seated at the stern, his hand behind him on the rudder. Another man was sitting in the center, a submachine gun braced against the slat seat. A big man stood in the bow, his arms folded across his chest and his head turning in a constant arc as he searched both banks of the river.

MacGlendon broke his cover, ran out to the shore, secured the box under his arm, cupped his hands to his mouth and shouted, "I never thought I'd be glad to see your ugly, Irish face."

MacGlendon's Choice

"It's your last chance, MacGlendon. You can still do it my way." He leaned forward, looked across Paula de Plyssy, studied MacGlendon's reaction.

The three of them were sitting in the back seat of a limousine parked in front of the Capitol building. The Washington day was bright, the sun warm, in a last lingering fragment of Indian summer.

"I appreciate what you're trying to do for me," MacGlendon said, "but your way is no good. There's been too many secrets, too many deaths. If the CIA breaks up the Chou Consortium, the world will never know that it was threatened. People must be warned in case it ever happens again." He looked up to the steps of the building, all the way to the white dome against the blue sky. Then he looked at Paula. "I know that by giving the Foreign Relations Committee this evidence, I'm endangering everything— everything I worked so hard to build up. There will be scandals and panic. I know that. I might even go to jail. I have to face that." He squeezed Paula's hand, then released it and fingered the jade medallion she wore around her neck. "You understand, don't you, why I can't let the CIA handle this, why I have to do it my own way?"

She nodded, bit back tears.

MacGlendon opened the door, clutched the oilskin covered box, began walking up the steps without turning back.

Pug O'Connor kissed Paula de Plyssy's cheek, opened the door on his side of the limousine. "That son of a bitch may shape up yet," he said.